Arms of a Stranger

By

Anne-Marie Clark

Diva Dog Press
Madison, TN USA

Arms of a Stranger
Diva Dog Press
PO Box 288
Madison, TN 37115-0288

Copyright © 2011 by Anne-Marie Clark

All rights reserved. No parts of this book may be reproduced in any form or by any electronic means, including information storage and retrieval systems, without permission in writing from the Author, except by a reviewer who may quote brief passages in a review.

First Edition Published July, 2011

This book is a work of fiction. Names, characters, places, situations and incidents are either the product of the author's imagination or are used fictitiously. Any resemblance to actual persons, living or dead, or to actual events or locations is coincidental.

Diva Dog Press can bring authors to your live event. For more information or to book an event contact Diva Dog Press at the address above.

Manufactured in the United States of America

ISBN-13: 978-1-4636-9291-9

If you're reading this book and did not purchase it or it was not purchased for your use, please return to a bookstore of choice and purchase your own copy. Thank you for respecting the author's hard work.

ACKNOWLEDGMENTS

Thank you to my parents and stepparents for your encouragement and love. Thank you mom and dad for passing those creative genes on to me, and teaching me to follow my dreams.

Thank you to my mom Susan for your extraordinary proofing and editing. Your eagle eye for catching all my boo-boos is so greatly appreciated! I love you.

Thank you to my niece Heather Clark for the awesome cover art. I told you exactly what I wanted and you went above and beyond my expectations. Your talents never cease to amaze me!

Thank you to my best friend Kim for being there for me always. Your cards and care packages always arrive at the most opportune times. We are truly kindred spirits and I am so very fortunate and thankful that you have been a part of my life for so many years.

Thank you to my Facebook family. You are all very special to me and I can't imagine going through a day without your support, comments and friendship. Sometimes the people closest to you are one you rarely see, or perhaps have never even met in person.

And most importantly, thank you to my husband Russell for *everything* you do. For keeping me sane and supporting my crazy notions, for taking care of the dogs when I'm "in the zone", for making the perfect fried egg, and for unconditionally giving me the freedom to follow my dreams, I thank you and love you.

To Rusty –

For believing in me when I didn't always believe in myself.
I love you always.

Prologue

She walked hurriedly out of the insanely overpriced coffee shop, just like every other weekday morning, and pulled her black wool coat tighter around her body, ineffectively trying to shield herself from the bitterly cold wind as she walked quickly down the sidewalk. The hem of her coat flapped around her knees as she adjusted the perpetually sliding strap of her leather satchel, keeping perfect balance of the cup she held in her gloved hand. He knew exactly what she carried in that cup, and it wasn't coffee but tea, orange spice to be exact, with one packet of real sugar and a dash of soy milk.

She stared straight ahead and walked with purpose, seemingly oblivious to the other early morning commuters who were also making their way to work. He had watched her long enough to know most everything about her, which he enjoyed writing down in a notebook and analyzing in his spare time. People were a funny breed with all their many quirks. One could learn so much about people just from mere observation, but most are so wrapped up in their own lives that they don't take the time.

Everyone wants to think of themselves as unique, individual, anomalous even. But they aren't. They are all more or less the same, generation after generation, with none of us being so different than the people we pass every day on the sidewalk without a second thought. They all want the same things – love, security, sustenance, money, acceptance and today, shelter from the cold.

He inched along, as was always the case with traffic in New York City, and watched as she made her usual stop at the newsstand on the corner and bought several newspapers. Today must have been special because she added a couple of fashion magazines to her purchases, tucking them all into the large black satchel that was slung over her shoulder. She was an avid reader, and her daily purchases confirmed that fact. He also knew the satchel housed an iPhone, laptop computer, a pricey digital camera with two lenses, a shoe-mounted flash, and a notebook with a blue ink pen clipped onto the cover.

He turned his attention to the old guy manning the newsstand, who had greeted her with a gap-toothed grin, the buttons of his red and green plaid coat straining against his ample gut. He was obviously happy to see her, just as he was every other morning with every other customer. He chatted her up while she paid for her items, and then turned his attention to another customer, giving her a parting wave as she turned from the stand and made her way toward her office building, which was a block down the street. Her long, auburn hair whipped around her shoulders as she walked. She usually wore a red beret, but today, one of the coldest days they'd had all winter, the beret was missing. The wind was strong and the sky grey. It looked like it might snow again. She looked up at the sky too, probably thinking the same thing. Her satchel again slipped off her shoulder, but she kept walking as she hitched it back up, never missing a step or spilling a drop of tea from the flimsy paper cup.

Warm air from the car's heater blew directly onto his face and feet, but still he trembled as anticipation built while he watched her. He absently caressed his holstered gun, the metal cool against his fingertips. The waiting was killing him and he was ready to move this along. Far too much time had gone by and he still hadn't managed to get her alone. Soon, very soon, she would be right where he wanted her. The risk was very great and the ironic thing was that she probably didn't even know what she had. She was all wrapped up in her own little world, her own little unimportant life. He had worked too hard to let this opportunity pass him by, and when it had fallen into his lap he had thought long and hard about what he had to do. The rest was just a waiting game, and he hated waiting.

With that thought he felt anger building up in him. His hands started shaking so he clenched his fists tightly while he took a few deep breaths to calm himself. He then took a sip of coffee, but it had grown cold. His anger began to brew again over the coffee. Again, a few deep breaths, this time with his eyes closed for just a few seconds. Okay, that's better. Much better.

Inching along, he ignored the symphony of car horns behind him as he stopped just shy of the Manhattan newspaper office where she worked. It wasn't a major newspaper, but an up and coming operation housed high up in the building. He tapped his fingers irritably on the steering wheel, knowing she'd be invisible to him for the rest of the day. Leaning forward he garnered one last look before she disappeared inside.

He let out the breath he didn't realize he'd been holding. *Your life is about to change, Julianna Brennan*, he thought smugly as he blew warm breath against the cold of the window, then dragged his finger across the fog that had been produced. *My life is about to change, too*, he reminded himself. Both hands returned to the steering wheel and clutched it tightly in anticipation. He couldn't wait.

Chapter 1

Snowflakes were beginning to fall lightly around her as the sound of feet pounding on the sidewalk urged her forward, and the adrenalin rush of blind fear kicked in. She gasped for air as she felt herself slowing down while her pursuant homed in on her. Don't stop, she thought; keep running. Keep running, keep running, *keep running*. The phrase built like a mantra in her mind, willing her forward as her heart pounded in rhythm to the words in her head.

She ran down the street, through an alley, and past drunken men who were huddled in dark corners, their only refuge from the cold being the bottle of booze in their hands. Where was everyone? Wasn't there a restaurant or bar open? This was New York City for God's sake! And even though it was late, this was the city that never slept, right? But as far as she could see there was no one who could help her, and she had no idea where she was going because she had stupidly panicked, and was now completely turned around in the unfamiliar neighborhood. Guided by instinct and blind fear, she simply knew that she had to keep running.

Keep running, keep running, keep running!

Her lungs were burning so badly that she found she couldn't even make the required scream to summon help. *Oh, God, please help me. Someone please help me.* She wanted to scream the words, but the only sound that escaped her lips was pathetic wheezing. She was angry at herself for being so naïve, so stupid. Not to mention the shoes. Why had she worn boots with *heels*? She slid more than once, but by some miracle she managed to remain upright.

Celebrating a co-worker's birthday had been the highlight of Julianna's particularly mundane week. Only a short twenty minutes earlier she had been sitting in a restaurant, laughing with some friends from work, and enjoying an evening out of her small apartment and solitary life. Living alone with her cat Bella in a city as large as New York had been major culture shock for a girl from Tennessee, but in the past year and a half she had adjusted, and she counted on nights with friends to keep her sane.

The later it had gotten, the more deserted the restaurant had become. Her friends lived in the opposite direction and had walked together the short distance to their respective apartments. Julianna had been left alone, her friends having drunk too much to notice that the streets were deserted, with no cabs in sight. She told them she would be fine, that she'd just walk to the subway, and although she believed it she still had an uneasy feeling about being alone in the streets of a city that was still largely unfamiliar to her. *Idiot*, she inwardly chided herself, *why didn't I call a cab from the restaurant? How stupid could I be?*

She had gotten about a block down the street when a cab came whizzing down past her, "Hey!" she yelled after the cab. She started running while wildly waving her arm. "Taxi! Stop!", but the cabbie obviously didn't see her. Or didn't want to stop. Probably the latter. She saw his tail lights as he turned right, and he was out of sight. "Great," she moaned aloud, sighing.

She reached into her coat pocket for her cell phone, but it wasn't there. "No," she wailed in frustration. "How much worse is this night going to get?" She decided to head back to the restaurant and call a cab from there. She didn't even see a subway station in this neighborhood. *No more apple martinis for you ever, dumbass. This is what happens when you lose your rationalization skills.* She turned back toward the restaurant, and continuing to silently berate herself, she saw a man a few feet away walking toward her.

"Julianna," the man's friendly voice called. "Were you looking for a cab?"

Julianna had stopped walking and her heart froze. She remembered this guy from the restaurant. He and a woman had been sitting at the bar all evening while she and her friends had sat across from them at a nearby table. He had glanced her way several times during the evening, but she and her friends had gotten a little loud as the evening wore on, and most of the restaurant had cleared out so they were a fairly obvious spectacle of typical women.

"What do you want?" she dubiously asked the stranger.

He stood there smiling at her. "I thought you wanted a cab."

"I..." she shook her head slowly. "No, I was actually headed back to the restaurant. I think I left my phone there."

Walking toward her he held up a smartphone and turned it backward so she could see the red protective case with the little owl drawing on it. It was unmistakably hers. "You mean this phone?" he sneered, the friendly smile gone.

She looked frantically around her. Which direction to go? "Somebody help me!" she screamed. "Help!"

"This is the middle of the night in New York City, baby! No one's going to help you!" he laughed at her. She heard a car horn somewhere in the distance, but otherwise the streets around them were quiet. It was as if they were the only two people in the city.

"Do you want money? I have money!" she asked him frantically. It was then that she saw the gun in his right hand.

"I don't want your money, but let's make this fun. What I *do* want is for you to run." He grinned at her once more, but his eyes were stone cold. "You have three seconds Julianna, and then I take what I want. One, two..."

Julianna hesitated for only a split-second, unsure of which direction to go, then started to run in the opposite direction from which he was standing. He lunged after her, grabbing at her coat, his hand catching her cross-body purse strap at the same time. As the purse strap snapped back across her chest she tumbled against him, forcing them both backward.

They simultaneously stumbled, but she regained her balance first, firmly planting her feet, and with her body shoving him backwards as hard as she could, as he once again reached for her. He didn't fall, but it was just enough to catch him off guard.

She ran down the darkened street, but nothing looked open. "Help! Someone help me! Call the Police!" she yelled, praying someone would hear her.

There were mostly retail shops down this particular street, with apartments above. She would never be able to get anyone to open their door, and by the time they did her attacker would be on top of her. Thinking maybe she could lose him or dart into the back of a building she ran down the first alley she came to, past garbage cans and drunks who were too passed out to notice or care. Keep running, keep running, *keep running*!

She knew she couldn't continue to run forever, but what could she do? She darted to the left, down a different alley. Big mistake. As she reached the end of the alley, she realized it was a dead end, complete with locked chain link fence. Icy terror gripped her heart and realization hit. *I'm going to die*, she thought, tears suddenly blurring her vision. She was trapped like a caged animal, and she had absolutely nowhere to go other than back the way she came, and that was not an option because *he* was hot on her heels.

Frantically, Julianna clawed at the gate of the fence, trying to force its padlocked entry open, or at least wide enough that she could slip through. Even with here gloves the metal prongs of the gate tore into her skin, but she was unaware of the pain as she frantically continued shaking the chain link fence. There was a green dumpster on the other side, and she could see the darkened doorway of what appeared to be the back of a restaurant. Maybe someone was still inside.

She finally found her voice again and screamed for someone, *anyone*, to help her. But the only sound she heard was the pounding of her own heart, her labored breathing, and footsteps, which were getting closer by the second.

Then she heard the footsteps stop, and as she turned around, her hands frantically pushing on the gate behind her, the man began to laugh.

"You didn't really think you were going to get away, did you, Julianna?" he sneered. His mouth turned upward in a menacing pseudo smile, but his black eyes were stone cold, and Julianna could see the very soul of pure evil reflected in them.

"Who are you? What do you want?" she demanded, glancing backward at him and trying unsuccessfully to control the sound of fear in her voice as she continued to push on the gate of the fence. If she could just get it open wide enough to slip through she might be okay. The guy wasn't huge, but he was definitely larger than she, so she reasoned that he probably wouldn't be able to follow her through it. At least not easily.

"You know exactly what I want, so quit playing dumb. I want the pictures," he demanded, no longer smiling.

"Pictures? What pictures? I don't know what you're talking about, I swear," she pleaded. Her voice was shaking, partly from the cold, but mostly from terror. She worked her hand up under the chain and pulled it partially loose. There was still just a small amount of slack, but it was more than before and if she could just get her head and shoulders through then maybe her body could squeeze in as well. Unfortunately, she knew that it would be a very tight fit and she didn't have the luxury of time in which to accomplish her feat.

"Julianna, give me the damn memory card!" he demanded once more, stepping closer to her, the gun raised in front of him and pointed right at her. "Take your hands off of the fence, turn around, face me, and give me the memory card," he ordered. His voice was low as he tried to maintain control of his anger, but his furrowed brow and narrowed eyes showcased his rage.

Julianna turned around, but slowly stepped sideways, trying to figure out a way past him. She glanced around for something to use as a weapon, but she didn't dare take her eyes off of him completely. When she looked back at him their eyes locked together and Julianna knew that he could see the fear in hers, and on that fact alone he had the upper hand. She raised her chin in defiance and pursed her trembling lips. She wasn't going to give up easily and wanted him to know that.

"I do not have any memory card. What is it you want? I take pictures every day. Tell me what you're looking for and I will get whatever it is, but I don't have any memory cards with me. I swear to you that I don't."

He suddenly grabbed her by the collar of her coat and shoved her into the fence, which rattled loudly as her body hit it with the sudden force. Julianna screamed as she struggled, trying desperately to kick him, but his body was pinned tightly against hers, the fence pressing into the back of her head as he held her there

"I don't want to kill you, but I will," he threatened, his voice low, his breath hot on her face as he leaned in close. She felt something hard and solid against the side of her head and closed her eyes as she realized it was the cold barrel of his gun.

"He said you have the card. It's in your bag, in the camera."

"He? He who? I don't. I don't have my camera. It left it at work because I didn't want to carry it. It's not in there, I swear! Take my purse and see," she pleaded. "Take it!"

He eased his hold on her while she pulled the purse over her head. He roughly grabbed it from her, but kept the gun pointed at her as he moved away by a couple of feet and into the lone light that was more effective at casting ghostly shadows around the alley rather than actually illuminating it. Dumping the contents onto the ground he threatened, "Do not even think about moving or the contents of your head *and* this bag will be all over this ground."

She nodded her head, her eyes wide, while she frantically racked her brain. What pictures did he want, and who was this *he* to whom he referred?

"Where is it? Damn it, you stupid bitch!" he spit as he threw the empty purse onto the ground.

"I told you it wasn't there. My camera and memory cards are at the office, and depending on when the pictures were taken they would have already been uploaded and stored on the computer."

"No! Not this one. This one is with you."

"It's not! I told you, I don't even have a camera with me except on my phone, which you already have."

Angrily he stomped around as he contemplated the situation. Clearly, he wasn't expecting her to not have whatever it was he was looking for. He threw his hands in the air and let out an angry growl.

"If you tell me the date the pictures were taken I can find them for you."

"Shut up!" he growled through his teeth. "If you had been listening you would have heard me say that these pictures are with *you*, you stupid bitch! *You* have the card!"

Julianna shook her head slowly, "I don't have it. I don't."

He studied her for a few moments, then narrowed his eyes at her, and she could see something wild in them, something not quite human, as he walked back toward her. He grabbed her once more and shoved her face into the fence, pressing himself into her body. She could feel him, all of him, press against her and she widened her eyes. *This was not happening. He was going to rape her! No! No matter what she would not let that happen!* She struggled against him, trying desperately to turn out of his grasp, but he was strong, much stronger than she, and he also had a gun.

He pinned her legs together with his own legs on the outside. Her own body held her hands captive as his weight forced her into the fence.

"Now you've really pissed me off, *honey*," he whispered in her ear, his breath hot against her cheek. Julianna went still, knowing that whatever came next was not going to be good. "Let's see if I can refresh your memory."

Switching the gun to his left hand he reached around in front of her and fumbled with the opening on her jeans. She didn't care if he shot her; she was not going to let him rape her. She would rather die first. She once more began to struggle, trying to remember the points to hit from a self-defense class she had taken in college. She struggled to get one of her legs out from between his so that she could mule-kick him, preferably in a sensitive area of his anatomy.

"You have no idea who you're dealing with!" the man screamed at her, spittle spraying her cheek. "No idea!" he repeated, as his fingers dug into her scalp, grabbed a handful of her hair and jerked her head backwards as he spun her around. "You don't wanna piss me off!"

He shoved her back into the fence then once more locked her legs between his own so she couldn't kick him, as he held her hands above her head with one of his own, his other hand still clutching the gun. He suddenly tucked the gun in the back waistband of his jeans, then slapped her across the face. She continued struggling while he laughed, slapped her again, and laughed some more as she grew weaker. It felt like numerous hands were hitting her all at once, and as Julianna tasted her own blood, she thought that this must be what it was like to die. She saw flashes of white light and the world began to spin and turn dark.

No, Julianna! Her inner voice scolded her. *You are not going to die! You are not! Fight this bastard!*

She had struggled desperately to get her legs free, and to tuck her face down into the collar of her coat to protect herself from his blows, but it wasn't enough. Sh felt her body growing weaker and weaker. He held her against the fence as he continued to yell, his words meaningless and repetitive as they grew farther and farther from her consciousness. This man, this stranger, had won whatever battle he had set out to conquer and she just wanted it to be over.

She was exhausted, and her body was growing numb from both the cold and the pain. Her attacker must have sensed that she was no longer capable of holding herself up any more because he loosened his grip on her and she slid down the fence as darkness began to overcome her. She was dizzy, so very dizzy and so tired.

"This will be a little reminder for you," he said, leaning over her as he unzipped his pants. Because if you don't come up with that card, the next time we meet I won't be so gentle. That is, if you make it to a next time."

His breathing was heavy now, whether from their struggle, from his arousal, or both.

"Are you ready, *honey*?" he grinned down at her as he dropped to his knees.

She shook her head slowly as she felt herself gradually sinking into a fog. "You're so pathetic. You have to beat a woman up so that she'll..." was all she managed to mutter.

She looked up one last time into the eyes of a madman as he sneered down at her, greasy dark hair falling over his forehead as he grabbed her jeans with both hands and gave them a yank. The frigid air hit her legs, but she was already so numb with cold that she hardly felt it. She looked past his face into the night sky. The snowflakes that had fluttered about earlier in the evening were silently and steadily falling. Julianna blinked her eyes as they landed on her eyelashes like icy tears from heaven.

So this was it. This was how it was going to end. She closed her eyes to all that was around her, feeling numb. She thought about her cat Bella. Who would feed her? Who would love her? Would anyone notice when she didn't show up for work in the morning? Wait, this was Friday, so no work tomorrow. There was no one. No one to report her missing or even notice that she was. Similar thoughts went through her head - silly thoughts, meaningless thoughts, but she was sure they were her last thoughts.

Scream! Do something! Again her inner voice scolded her. *Open your eyes! Don't let this happen to you! You're better than this and you're certainly stronger than this!* But she didn't want to open her eyes. She wanted to wake up from this horrible nightmare and be in her own bed, in her own apartment surrounded by the green walls she had painted herself.

But she wasn't, and if she wanted to wake up in her own apartment ever again then she was going to have to do something about it herself, because contrary to the fairy tales her mother read to her as a child, there was no handsome prince or knight in shining armor on a big white horse. No one was coming to save her.

Julianna mustered all the strength she had and yelled a determined, "No!" which pierced the silence of the alley. She butted her forehead into her attacker's face, causing him to howl out in pain. He grabbed her by the collar of her coat and shoved her back down to the pavement before roughly flipping her over onto her stomach. Without even thinking about it she was up on her hands and knees, her jeans bunched around her thighs, clawing desperately at the ground, trying to get away. He grabbed her around the hips and pulled her back down, his weight heavy across her back.

Suddenly, he went still and they both heard it.

Footsteps. Someone was running. Were they running toward her or away? Julianna couldn't tell. She was completely disoriented and all logic was quickly fading. She tried to focus on what was going on around her but her head felt like it was going to explode and she wasn't even sure if she was right-side up or upside down. Excruciating pain radiated from behind her right eye and she whimpered softly as he straddled her, her body between his knees, the gun trained on her head as he listened to the footsteps, which were growing louder.

She heard someone yell something. Stop, she had definitely heard the word stop, but the rest was fuzzy. She was just so tired and wanted it all to go away.

A shot rang out in the arctic air, and all was suddenly very calm as Julianna felt strong arms lifting her upper body off the ground and cradling her against an equally strong body.

She momentarily struggled against him as a coat, which still carried the warmth of the person who had just shed it, was gently wrapped around her shivering body. A man's low and soothing voice, which seemed very far away, kept assuring her that everything was going to be okay and that help was on the way. She stopped struggling and fell against him as he held her. Maybe she was wrong and there *was* such a thing as a white knight. Or maybe this was all just a dream. In the distance she heard the wail of a siren.

That was the last thing Julianna remembered before darkness overcame her and she was left in a dark alley, with snow swirling all around them, in the arms of a stranger.

Chapter 2

Water was trickling into her mouth as something, a wet washcloth maybe, was placed to her lips. Julianna tried to raise her head, but found she was too weak. Where was she? Was she in a hospital? Every part of her body screamed with pain as the events came back to her. Someone had saved her life – a man – the same man who had sat by her bedside in the hospital for how long now?

She was in a bed, which was soft and warm, but it didn't smell like a hospital in here. She opened her eyes slowly, a bright light causing her to clamp them closed yet again. No, she had been in a hospital and had left and been taken where? She couldn't remember, and the more she tried to think the more her head hurt. Things seemed all jumbled up and nothing made sense.

"She's awake again," she heard a female's voice announce in clipped tones. The woman had a distinct British accent.

Footsteps padded quickly across the floor and someone leaned down over her. The light was suddenly switched off, but the room was not dark since there was a light on in the hall just outside the room.

"I need that light to see," the female voice objected.

"Good grief woman, this isn't an interrogation room. It stays off for now," a male voice stated firmly.

That voice, she had heard it before. Yes, this was the same voice she heard after the gun was shot in the alley and the same voice that had asked her questions in the hospital. Questions she had not been able to answer. Julianna opened her eyes again, terror shining in them, and tried to focus on the man to whom the voice belonged.

A navy thermal shirt was the first thing she saw. She looked up further and met sapphire blue eyes staring intently down at her. The man's dark brows were furrowed and he looked angry. Or was that worry?

Julianna struggled to sit up. "Whoa, hold on a minute. No one is going to hurt you; you're safe now," the man said as he gently pushed her shoulders back down onto the bed.

"Kilbourne, I need to talk to her alone," he said. Julianna wasn't sure she wanted this Kilbourne person to leave her alone with this man, but given the circumstances she didn't have a choice in the matter. He stood there with his arms crossed and glared at the thin blonde as she left the room.

He pulled a chair, which looked like it belonged in someone's kitchen, up to the bed. "Do you remember what happened?"

She shook her head, but the pain was so intense she closed her eyes for a few seconds. "Yes. No," she answered, her voice scratchy and not her own. "Maybe some of it."

"You've been seen by a doctor and he says you're going to be okay, albeit very sore for a while. You spent the night in the hospital and had a CT scan. You have a slight concussion, but no permanent damage. You might be dizzy for a while, and that headache is going to be around for a few days, but he gave you meds for it, so that should help. I'm Special Agent Will Delaney with the FBI," he explained.

His mouth softened into a slight smile, but it was still tight and his brow remained furrowed as he studied her face. "You're safe now. Everything's going to be okay."

"Where...am I?" Julianna asked, slowly and painfully, her voice barely a whisper.

Will paused before answering, "You're safe. The hospital discharged you, but you didn't have anywhere to go. You really don't remember any of this?"

Julianna didn't answer but furrowed her brow. Tidbits of information were there, she just couldn't reach them behind the cobwebs. And she was so incredibly sleepy.

"The pain meds have knocked you out, so that's probably why you feel a little foggy. Would you like some water?"

She nodded gratefully, but was well aware that he still hadn't answered her question as to where she was. She studied his face while he leaned toward the nightstand and poured a glass of water from a pitcher.

As she scooted up into a sitting position pain shot through every part of her body and her head throbbed so much that it hurt to keep her eyes open. She fought tears as she sat on the edge of the bed and with a trembling hand took the water he offered her.

While she drank the agent walked over to the window and looked through the blinds. He stood like that for a few quiet moments, just staring out, and then he turned around to face her, crossing his arms across his chest.

Julianna drank the water, feeling his eyes upon her, and then looked up to meet his gaze. Their eyes locked for several long seconds, but his expression remained unreadable.

"I don't..." she began, her voice ragged. She cleared her throat and began again, "I don't understand. What is happening? What does the FBI... I didn't do anything. I... damn it," she finally whispered as the tears started to fall. She wiped them away with the back of her hand and put her hand to her head. It hurt so badly. She just wanted to lie back down and sleep for a very, very long time.

The agent crossed the room and took the glass out of her hand and set it on the nightstand before moving to the bed to sit down beside her. Without saying a word he slid his arm around her and gently pulled her to him. She felt herself leaning into him as she closed her eyes, relaxed, and laid her cheek against his chest.

Through the material of his shirt Julianna could hear this man's heart beating and it was oddly comforting to her. She didn't know who he truly was or why this had happened to her, but she somehow felt she could trust him. After all, if he had wanted to hurt her he probably would have already done it by now. Maybe she was just delirious and this was all just some horrible nightmare.

There were many questions she wanted to ask, but she was so very tired and putting anything else into words seemed like an excruciating ordeal at the moment. The last thing she remembered before she drifted off to sleep was being laid gently back onto the bed and having the blanket tucked around her. The light from outside the room disappeared as the door was quietly closed.

"Well?" Kilbourne questioned when Will reached the living room.

"Well, what?" he responded, heading into the kitchen.

"*Well*, may I leave, your majesty?" Kilbourne replied sarcastically, standing in the doorway of the kitchen. "I told you earlier that my kid has a school thing tonight.

I've missed the last two school 'things' and both he and my husband are ready to disown me. Do you quite think you can manage things? She is finally coherent, so I believe we're past the point of panic here." Her voice had an edge of sarcasm that Will had discovered was the norm.

Will shrugged as he reached into the cabinet for a container of soup. He didn't reply until the soup was opened and had been poured into a large mug. "Do what you want, Kilbourne," he told her, his eyes narrowed and hard as he looked at her.

"Oh, don't be so irritable, Delaney. I believe that for one night you can put up with a solo babysitting job," she said, crossing her arms over her chest.

"Besides," she continued, "You should have left her at the hospital. Let's just wing it for the night. You should be an old pro at that by now. You're not exactly 'by the book' now, are you Delaney? I've been doing you a huge favor by being here and my pretty ass is on the line for this. Does the SAC even know she's here?"

Her gray sweater hung on bony shoulders, and overly processed blonde hair jutted out in all directions in one of those purposely scraggly hairdos of the moment. Just the sight of her standing there irritated Will, and he wanted nothing more than to see her leave.

"You know he doesn't. And you also know he was going to put Shepherd on her at the hospital, which, as we both know, is about the equivalent of putting a second grader on her. And what was I going to do? Camp out in the waiting room and hope no one comes after her? No, she's my responsibility, my case, and I'm not letting her out of my sight, mandatory leave or not. And besides, the hospital was itching to discharge her and she had nowhere else to go. You know how quickly they want to move patients in and out these days and I wasn't about to send her off to the apartment of one of her girlfriends just to have something happen to her."

"So you kidnap her and hide her here? You are going to be in a world of trouble over this, Delaney. This is every side of wrong. Ethically, professionally... What if you get called in to testify in this case? You will blow everything we're working for by being involved with her. It will be thrown out faster than that you can pack up your desk and haul ass down the elevator to a security job at the mall."

"I didn't kidnap her. She agreed to be signed out."

"She was barely coherent!" Kilbourne hissed at him.

"Where else was she going to go when they released her? She is safer here, and due to the marvel of pharmaceuticals she's resting and will heal faster. The perp is dead, so the SAC says we can't exactly put her in a safe house if no one's after her, but we both know that's not true. Look who the perp's uncle is. Hell, this has only just begun, but as shorthanded as we are I'm going to need more evidence to convince the SAC. As soon as she's able there are a lot of questions she's going to have to answer and I fully intend to be the one doing the asking. Just let me handle the specifics. I am sure as hell not going to jeopardize this case.

"So, by all means please leave, Kilbourne. Actually, I'd like nothing more. I'll handle this on my own; I work best that way." He gave her a tight-lipped smile and nodded in the direction of the front door, sarcastically motioning with his hand in case she couldn't figure out the way. *To hell with her*, he thought, turning his back on her as he set the soup in the microwave and pressed in the time for a minute and a half.

Kilbourne stormed over to him and jabbed a bony finger into his chest. "You think you are above reproach? You are an arrogant asshole, Delaney," she hissed, glaring up at him.

"That's what they say," he retorted calmly, removing her finger from his chest and glaring right back at her.

"You'd better watch out because the FBI doesn't like renegades. You aren't going to be able to fly under the radar on this one. I've heard rumors about what you did in the military, Delaney, and this isn't some clandestine operation. You have an agency to answer to on this one."

"And what makes you think I'm not going to answer to them, Kilbourne? I'm doing my job, the job I was sent to do, and that's to investigate Jackson Mattice, who led us to Julianna Brennan, and I can't very well do that if I don't have direct access to her, now can I?"

"There's an enormous difference between having access to her and harboring her in your own apartment, Delaney! You have most certainly crossed the line. I'll be surprised if you still have your job in the morning. Look, I told you I'd help out with her since I owed you one, but she's awake and coherent now, so I'm done with this. Do not involve me further in this, Delaney. Consider the favor repaid. You're on your own now unless Olsen is still foolish enough to stick around."

"Fine, you were never here," Will replied. Now head on out before you miss your kid's recital, or whatever it is. Doesn't he play the trombone or something?"

"Oboe. Good luck, Delaney," she said sarcastically, closing the door behind her as she left.

As the soup warmed in the microwave, Will leaned against the counter with his arms crossed, let out a long breath, and thought about the events of the past few days. He should have known something like that was going to happen. He should have been prepared, but instead he screwed up and Julianna Brennan had gotten hurt. He had been kicking himself over it ever since.

He had done his research on her and knew her every move. He knew exactly where she'd be that night, and he never should have taken his eyes off her. Something about this woman made him want to protect her. Sure, there was that sense of vulnerability, especially when one considered her background. But it was more than that. He felt inexplicably connected to her, and he hadn't felt connected to anyone in a very long time. Not since Sarah. Not really. And maybe not even with Sarah. Bitterness has a way of tainting reality. Or maybe actual reality was never the reality he thought it was. Damn, he was tired. He wasn't even making sense to himself anymore.

The microwave beeped, interrupting his thoughts. Will took the mug out and stirred it, then grabbed a napkin.

******

Someone was gently calling her name. She murmured something unintelligible and pulled the blanket more tightly around her.

"Julianna? I have some soup for you. Can you sit up and try to eat some of it?"

There was that voice again. Julianna opened her eyes slightly and promptly closed them again.

"...strength back." He was saying something, but she must have missed the first part of the sentence. Had she dozed off that quickly?

"You know, I think we might be able to manage this better by putting some more pillows behind you."

Will walked to the closet and got some pillows out, placing them behind Julianna's back and head as he leaned her forward as best as he could. She groaned as he moved her head. "You've still got a bitch of a headache, don't you?"

She nodded slightly, her eyes still closed.

"Okay, I'm going to give you something for that, but I want you to eat some soup first. Do you understand?" he asked, pulling a chair close to the bed and sitting down.

She nodded again, but she opened her eyes slightly this time and looked at him through her lashes.

"It's cream of potato. My mom always fed it to me when I was sick. Of course I was much younger then. And probably wasn't even sick half the time, unless you count not studying for a math test as an ailment."

As she ate Will kept his eyes focused on her and his tone light as he talked to her. He was going to have to gain her trust quickly because he was going to need it very soon.

When she had eaten about half of the soup, he gave her one of the pain pills they had prescribed at the hospital, and then took the pillows away, tucking her once again under the covers. By the time he had turned the lamp off, she was fast asleep.

Chapter 3

When Julianna awoke again the room was very dark, and although the curtains were drawn she could tell it was dark outside as well.

She wondered how long she had been there. And where is *here*, she wondered even more. Wherever she was, it was very quiet and she seemed to be alone. The only sound she heard was the faint ticking of a clock somewhere close by.

When her eyes finally adjusted to the darkness she looked around the room. There was a dresser with only a few things on top of it, but she couldn't tell what. A chair was beside the bed. She looked up and saw a picture hanging on the wall above the headboard. It appeared to be a print of New York City at night and was the only piece of art in the sparse room. The source of the ticking, an old-fashioned alarm clock, was beside her on the nightstand, stating the time as 7:32. Beside it was a stack of books but Julianna couldn't read the titles. Jewelry sat in front of the books and at a glance Julianna could tell it was her own watch, ring and earrings. She quickly reached up and let out a relieved breath as she realized the small gold heart was still in place on the delicate chain around her neck.

She momentarily relaxed back against the pillows, grateful that the severe throbbing in her head had been replaced by a dull ache, when reality suddenly hit her. Priority number two was getting out of here. Priority number one was finding a bathroom.

Julianna put her feet over the edge of the bed and slowly, shakily, got herself into a standing position. It was then that she noticed she was wearing only a man's t-shirt and her panties.

She looked around the room for her clothes, but she didn't see them anywhere. Across from her she saw a doorway leading into what looked like a bathroom. She stood beside the bed for a few moments, willing her body to cooperate and balance itself. Her legs were shaking and weak, and she felt dizzy, but she definitely had to get to that bathroom. She slowly made her way toward the door and upon reaching it, ran her hand along the wall just inside the door until she found the switch. The room was instantly bathed in light, and she snapped her eyes shut against the shock.

As her eyes adjusted to the light, she used the toilet and then headed toward the sink where she looked at herself in the mirror. The face that stared back at her was not her own. Her long auburn hair was a tangled mess and this new face had bruises and a sunken haunted look. Her bottom lip was slightly swollen and cut, her mouth dry and stale. She cupped her hands under cold running water and took several swallows. The water felt so good running down her scratchy throat. She looked around for some toothpaste or mouthwash. She desperately needed to remove the taste from her mouth, which was metallic, like blood.

She searched the top of the vanity but found nothing except a man's razor and other grooming implements. Everything was neat and very organized, but the contents of the bathroom were fairly sparse.

She opened the mirrored medicine cabinet and found both the mouthwash and toothpaste. Pulling them out, she shut the door to the cabinet and opened the tube of toothpaste, squeezing a line of it out onto the index finger of her right hand.

"I have an extra toothbrush if you'd like," a voice sounded behind her.

Startled and her heart racing, Julianna jumped, snapping her head up to look into the mirror at the face reflected behind her. Her eyes met the familiar sapphire of his, and for the first time she was able to really see the face to whom the voice belonged. The memories came rushing back. She could recall the doctor discharging her from the hospital. But she couldn't get in touch with any of her friends, and the FBI agent insisted that she could not go home. She had nowhere to go. He took her with him. She was tired, so very tired, that she didn't even care where they went. She had just wanted to sleep forever. She remembered all the questions. Questions she couldn't answer, didn't *want* to answer. She only wanted to crawl under the covers and forget. This man had taken care of her and given her that time, but now she was fully awake and wanted answers.

As he spoke, he reached behind the door for a white robe, which was hanging from a hook. He took a step toward her, because that's all it took in the small bathroom, and placed the robe around her shoulders.

"I'm sorry. I didn't mean to startle you," he said, standing so close to her that had she turned around her face would have been pressed against his chest.

Keeping her eyes on him in the mirror, Julianna nodded her head. "A toothbrush would be great," she answered.

He reached into a drawer and pulled out a package containing a green toothbrush. He opened it for her, removing the brush by the handle, and handed it to her. His task completed, his eyes once again found hers in the mirror.

Smearing the line of toothpaste from her finger onto the toothbrush, she began to brush her teeth. The man continued to watch her reflection in the mirror.

"Do you think I could have some privacy here?" she asked irritably, her voice muffled by the toothbrush.

He ignored her and instead asked, "Do you remember what happened, Julianna?"

She finished brushing her teeth, rinsed out the toothbrush and set it on the counter. "Where is my cat?" she demanded.

"Your cat is fine. Your neighbor is taking care of her. Do you remember what happened in the alley?" His voice was a little more impatient, a little less gentle.

She returned his gaze, her own expression guarded. "You were there; you tell *me*."

His brow furrowed slightly and he let out a frustrated sigh, but quickly regained his poker face. "We have a lot to talk about, but first you'd probably like to get cleaned up, maybe take a shower?"

"I'd rather go home. Where are my clothes?"

"You don't want them back. They removed your clothing in the hospital, but they sent you off in some hospital scrubs," he assured her as he reached under the sink and brought out a fluffy white towel and matching washcloth, handing them to her. "But Kilbourne put the t-shirt on you when we brought you back here, and she's the one who took you to the bathroom. We thought it would be easier without the scrubs. You don't remember any of this?"

Julianna shook her head slowly. "I don't know. Maybe some of it. There are bits and pieces missing. Where are the scrubs? I'll put those on and get out of your hair. I really appreciate all you did, but I have to go home now."

"I'm afraid I can't let you do that. You can't go home, and you said yourself that you have nowhere else to go."

"Why can't I go home?" she demanded.

"Look, take a shower and we'll talk about it afterward, okay? I promise you'll feel better."

She stood there staring defiantly at him. "You can't just hold me hostage here."

"I'm not holding you hostage. I'm trying to protect you," he stated calmly. I understand you have a lot of questions and confusion. I promise I'll explain everything to you, but please, take a shower. You look like hell, and I'm sure you feel like it too."

She opened her mouth to argue with him, but decided against it. "I don't remember your name," she said as he turned to leave the bathroom.

"Special Agent Delaney," he said. "But since you're standing in my bathroom and wearing my robe let's skip the formalities. Call me Will."

"Okay…Will." Julianna hugged the towel and washcloth to her body as she waited for him to leave.

"Make yourself at home," Will said as he backed out of the small space. "Everything you need should be in the shower."

"Thanks," she replied as she quickly closed the door behind him. Was she playing the stupid victim by trusting this man? She didn't even know him, or whether or not she could trust him. Her gut said she could, but instinct told her to be cautious. After all, she reasoned, he was an FBI agent and he had saved her from that man in the alley. He had taken care of her for…how long?

Of course she could have been dramatic and run around kicking and screaming and demanding to go home, but surely if this man was going to harm her he would have already done it, and he certainly wouldn't have saved her from being killed in that alley. She really needed to get in that shower and clear the cobwebs from her brain so she could think clearly.

When the water first hit her bruised and battered skin, Julianna winced with pain, but after a while her body adjusted to it and the warm water began to soothe her. She stood in the shower for a long time, letting the water run down her body. She washed her hair carefully, her scalp sore where her hair had been pulled. She looked down and saw bruises all along her legs, especially on her shins. Her hands were cut in several places and she vaguely remembered grabbing for a chain-link fence. The backs of her shoulders ached and she remembered hands roughly slamming her into that same fence.

As she thought back on the attack, she began to shiver as she remembered more from the incident. She turned up the hot water.

She was lucky to be alive, and she was pretty sure that thanks to this FBI agent she was. She could still hear the man's voice in her head. He had asked her for a memory card. What was on that card that he wanted so badly? And he had called her by name. And where had this FBI agent come from all of a sudden? How had he found her there in that alley? There were too many unanswered questions and the only way to find out the answers was to ask. Agent Delaney knew the answers, but he obviously wanted her to fill in the blanks. Was he testing her? The thought irritated her. Wasn't she the victim here? Fine, she'd just have to find out what he wanted from her and maybe he'd give her the answers she was looking for in return.

She turned off the water and stepped out of the shower and onto the thick bathmat where she toweled herself dry. Glancing at the sink counter she noticed a neatly folded clean t-shirt, so she put that on, along with the robe, wrapping it tightly around her and knotting the belt. It was a bit unsettling to realize he had been in the bathroom while she'd been showering, but she didn't want to think about that right now. She wanted to get out there and grill him for answers, just as she knew he was going to grill her.

She found a comb in the medicine cabinet and did the best she could with her wet hair. She didn't even want to think about what her face looked like. She had no makeup to cover the bruises or dark circles, and while the vain part of her cared, the realistic part of her didn't. She wasn't here to impress anyone, she silently reminded herself.

As she opened the door of the bathroom and stepped back into the bedroom she heard voices somewhere else in the house. One belonged to Agent Delaney, but the other was unfamiliar.

Julianna walked quietly to the door of the bedroom and opened the door as slowly as she could, careful not to make any noise. The door was almost open when it softy but recognizably creaked, announcing her presence. She winced, knowing there was nothing she could do but continue on through the door. And as she correctly assumed it would, the conversation abruptly halted and both men turned to look at her.

Julianna briefly studied the other man, who appeared to be about ten years Agent Delaney's senior and wore a dark suit with a grey wool coat. His polished appearance was stereotypical FBI, which was quickly confirmed.

"Julianna, this is Special Agent Paul Olsen. He went to your apartment and got some of your things," Agent Delaney told her. He took some money from his wallet and handed it to Agent Olsen, who quickly pocketed it.

"Why did you need to bring my things *here*? I need to go home tonight. I'm fine, *really*. I'll answer your questions as long as you answer mine, but after that I'd really like to go home." Julianna raised her chin defiantly and looked from one agent to the other.

The two agents exchanged a subtle look before Agent Olsen finally spoke, "Ms. Brennan, it's not safe for you to go home. Your apartment was ransacked and it's a pretty big mess, what's left of it anyway. It looks as though quite a bit has been stolen, and judging from the remaining cables it was probably the television, stereo and computer, but we're really not sure the extent of it until you file a claim. Quite clearly someone wants something that you have, and they're still looking for it. Your cat was hiding under the bed and it took me damn near forever to get her out. A Mrs. De Luca has been feeding her and said she'd take care of her until you could. She also helped me gather up what I could of your belongings, things to get you through for a few days. They're over there," he finished, pointing to several boxes, which sat in the corner beside the sofa.

"Julianna, it's best that you stay with me for a while. Whoever did that will be back, you can count on it. You'll be safe here," Agent Delaney explained. "I'm unable to get immediate authorization for a safe house, so your best bet is right here with me."

"So going home would be my option," Julianna stated, looking pointedly at Agent Delaney.

"That's not really an option," he disagreed.

"And why not?" she argued. "Am I in custody?"

"No," he answered slowly, dragging out the word. "But someone is clearly out to harm you and you're not safe. There's more."

"More what?" she moaned. "This couldn't possibly get any worse."

"Later," he promised firmly.

"But I want to leave. I want to go home. I'm standing here in a bathrobe, in a stranger's house, and I have no idea who I can trust!" Her voice was on the verge of hysteria and Delaney knew he needed to say something to calm her. Fast.

"It's going to be okay," was the only thing that came out. He knew it sounded lame the second he said it. The sideways look Olsen gave him confirmed that fact.

But the look Julianna gave him almost brought humor to the situation - almost, but not quite. "Is that all you can come up with?" she replied, shaking her head slowly, incredulously. "Fine, I'll stay, but only tonight," she agreed. "And I have one condition – I want to call my landlady and check on my cat." She looked pointedly at Delaney and arched a dark, perfectly groomed eyebrow at him.

"You can use my phone," he stated simply, and for the first time she saw the muscles in his jaw relax and his lips curve upward. The slight lines around his eyes deepened, and the blue of his irises seemed even brighter, clearer.

So the man actually smiles, she thought. Agent Delaney took his cell phone from his pocket and held it out to her.

As she took the phone from him her fingers grazed his hand and she felt...something. She was so startled by the sudden jolt of desire that she looked up at him, her green eyes widening with surprise. He was still smiling at her, his expression unchanged. She held the phone in her hand, too stunned and embarrassed, to even speak.

Special Agent Olsen cleared this throat, and Julianna realized she had almost forgotten he was standing there. "I assume you can handle the rest of this?" he asked Agent Delaney. "And I'll work on things we discussed earlier."

"We'll be fine and I'll see you tomorrow at the office. I don't think I can ride this out much longer; I plan on bringing her in with me. Thanks for your help today." Delaney had his hand on the door and seemed anxious for Olsen to leave.

"That's the job. Glad you're up and around now, Ms. Brennan," he said, directing his gaze to Julianna. "You're in Delaney's capable hands now."

Julianna nodded, "Thank you for bringing my things. Is my purse in there somewhere? I know it was there...in the alley."

"It's with the rest of your things," Agent Olsen answered.

"My phone?"

"There was no phone that we found."

"But he held it up. He had it. It's an iPhone with a red case. There's an owl on the cover." Julianna felt a little frantic. There were a lot of things on that phone she needed – contacts, pictures... She felt lost without it.

"I'm sorry," Paul offered. "Maybe it will turn up in evidence."

"Well, thanks," Julianna said, the disappointment evident in her voice. "I appreciate you bringing everything else."

"No problem. Enjoy your last night, Delaney, and be careful. You know what we're dealing with here," he added, closing the door behind him as he left.

Chapter 4

"Are you hungry?" Delaney asked as soon as Paul Olsen had gone.

At the mere mention of food, Julianna felt her stomach growl, but instead she answered, "What did Special Agent Olsen mean by 'Enjoy your last night?'"

"Mandatory leave. Standard procedure when you fire your weapon and someone is on the other end." To Julianna, Agent Delaney sounded as casual as if he were talking about taking trip to the dry cleaner's.

Delaney walked into the kitchen and Julianna trailed behind him.

"Doesn't that bother you?" she asked, incredulous.

"No," he answered simply but firmly as he turned to the counter where there was a brown takeout bag waiting. "Someone was going to die in that alley and it was either you or him. I chose him."

"Let's see what we have," he said, changing the subject abruptly while opening the containers of food that Special Agent Olsen had brought. "It looks like eggplant parmesan and something else. Ziti maybe? What do you think?"

Julianna looked into the container, "Ziti. What did you mean about there being more?"

"We'll get to that. First, we eat. I don't know about you but I'm starved."

Julianna knew he was clearly delaying something, so instead of fight it, because she was certainly not going to get answers out of him now, she'd let him run the show. For now anyway.

"You choose," Will said holding a container in each hand and moving first one box up and then the other, as if weighing the options.

"How about some of each?"

"Sounds like a plan. You haven't had anything more than soup for the past couple of days." Agent Delaney got two plates from a cabinet, and a serving spoon from a drawer, and piled some of each dish onto the two plates.

"Couple of *days*?" she asked incredulously.

"Well, it's been three as of tonight. You were in a lot of pain so the doctor gave you something for that and to help you sleep," he replied over his shoulder as he walked over to the refrigerator and scrounged around until he found half a wedge of parmesan cheese.

As she looked around the kitchen it was apparent that this was a kitchen designed for a chef. There were cooking implements of every sort gracing the walls and counters. The flooring was a medium brown tile, which was cold against Julianna's bare feet, and the walls were painted a warm golden yellow. The counters were black granite, and there was a pot rack over the island, from which hung several heavy pots and pans. With no one to cook for Julianna didn't find much need for fancy cookery, but she did recognize that everything in the kitchen appeared to be of excellent quality, which also meant it was pricey. She was pretty sure FBI agents didn't earn as much as this apartment appeared to have cost, but it was none of her business so she only gave it a passing thought.

Julianna realized she was still holding the cell phone Delaney had offered her earlier, so she set it down on the counter. After they ate she would call her landlady to make sure Bella was all right, but she wasn't really worried. Mrs. De Luca would take good care of Bella. She had cats of her own - neighborhood strays needing a place to call home. Mrs. De Luca had a heart bigger than the ample body it inhabited, and Julianna had been very fortunate to find a vacancy in her building a year and a half ago when she moved to New York. The rent wasn't cheap in the second story walkup, but she could just make it on her salary and still not touch her savings. And when something needed repair Mrs. De Luca had her son Antonio right on it. She knew that Antonio would secure her apartment after the break-in. The thought of someone going through her things... she would have to deal with the insurance company as soon as possible. Thanks goodness she had the wherewithal to attain renter's insurance when she moved to the city.

Will had the food plated and was using a small cheese grater to dust the entrees with parmesan. The cheese fell like snowflakes across the plate, just like *that night*, and her throat caught as she remembered why she was here in the first place. *Put it out of your mind, just for right now*, she silently told herself.

As she studied the details of the kitchen, she took a deep breath and focused on breathing, just one breath at a time, trying to force the rising panic back into the depths of her mind and body. She ran her finger along the edge of the cool granite of the counter, and silently counted to ten.

"This is a great kitchen," Julianna commented. Her voice sounded small and far away and she was beginning to feel dizzy. She could feel the panic attack begin its descent upward. Everything seemed surreal and she was having difficulty breathing, her heart pounding, her head throbbing. "I think I'm in the wrong line of work, though

– maybe I should have gone to Quantico instead of photography school," she joked. *Keep breathing. Deep breath in. Exhale.*

"Nah, I'd have never been able to afford this place on my government salary," Delaney said offhandedly. But he didn't offer anything else, so Julianna was left to speculate about just how he *did* afford to pay for this place. At the moment she didn't care. It was all just useless conversation, something to transfer her thoughts from the inevitable doom she was currently feeling.

She'd had panic attacks before, but she was usually by herself, with no one there as witness to her embarrassing display or the days it took to recover from the really bad ones. *Breathe. Inhale through your nose. Exhale through your mouth. Get ahold of yourself, Julianna,* she inwardly berated herself. *You're safe. There's nothing to be afraid of.*

"Would you like something to drink?" Delaney asked, changing the subject. "Water? Soda? I might have a bottle of wine somewhere, and maybe some juice in the freezer I could mix up. But with that headache you'd probably be best off without the wine."

His voice was low and very distant, and the thought of children with tin cans pressed to their ears flashed through her mind.

"Just some water would be great."

"There are some bottles in the fridge, and whatever else you'd like. Help yourself and grab an extra while you're in there." he had finished with the cheese and was headed to the kitchen table with the plates of food.

Julianna opened the refrigerator with shaking hands and examined the contents. There wasn't much in there besides beer, wine, condiments, milk, cheese, and some salad makings, which were in the beginning stages of mush.

She grabbed two bottles of water, continually willing herself to breathe one breath at a time. She could get through this. Maybe some water would help. She *had* to get through this. *Breathe.*

The room was suddenly spinning and Julianna's breathing became so labored she was almost gasping for her next breath. The bottles of water fell from her shaking hands and hit the floor with a thud, causing Agent Delaney to look up sharply from across the room.

Tears sprang to her eyes, but she quickly wiped them away. She didn't want to cry, not in front of this man – not in front of *anyone*. She looked frantically around for the closest place to sit down because she was in very real danger of fainting. Blind terror had welled up inside of her like a caged wild animal that was demanding to be released. She started shaking so badly that her teeth were chattering.

Delaney went to her and quickly wrapped his arms around her, enveloping her trembling body in his warmth. "It's going to be okay. I'm here now," he whispered softly. "You're just having a panic attack – I've seen this before. Breathe, Julianna. Slow deep breaths." He rubbed her back, his hands strong and reassuring.

Julianna continued to swipe at the tears that ran silently down her cheeks while Delaney tightened his hold on her. She felt his body press against hers – his thighs against her thighs, his torso pressed against her breasts. His breath whispered against her hair as he leaned down, talking softly to her, telling her that everything was going to be okay. She could feel the strong and steady beating of his heart against her cheek, and the rhythm of his breathing calmed her. She didn't want him to ever let her go.

She closed her eyes and concentrated on her breathing, just as the therapist had taught her to years earlier. And a few minutes later, amazingly, she began to breathe normally again. The trembling subsided, and slowly but surely the panic drained away from her. She felt so alone and wanted to hide in the protection of his arms forever. She held tightly to the front of his shirt, crying softly for several long minutes as he stroked her hair, her head tucked under his chin. Every so often he would say something reassuring – the kinds of things men say when they're not really sure what to say. She didn't know if she could trust him, but right now she needed to trust *someone,* and she really wanted it to be him.

Her panic attacks had started the day after she found out Josh was dead. Josh – she didn't want to think about him. Not now. She had to get through this. She couldn't afford the luxury of sleeping this off after taking the medication her therapist had prescribed. The panic attacks didn't hit her as often anymore, but every now and then one would creep up on her and she was a victim to its control.

Delaney's left hand cradled the back of her neck, his fingers entwined in her hair, still damp from her shower. He pulled her head back gently so she was forced to look up at him, and with his right thumb he tenderly traced down the side of her face from her cheek, and then slowly made his way across her lower lip. His jaw muscles clenched and those sapphire eyes burned intently into hers.

She gave a slight inward gasp and took a step backward, embarrassed and terrified for what she was feeling for this man, this virtual stranger, and even more terrified of what he was obviously feeling for her.

"Don't pull away from me," he said gently, lifting her chin so she was forced to meet his gaze, "It's going to be okay. You're safe now. I know you're afraid and you're not even sure that you can trust me, but you can. I promise I'm going to do everything I can to help you, but you're going to have to trust me."

"I know, Agent Delaney," she whispered, trying to regain her composure. "I trust you."

"I think we're a little past the point of 'Agent Delaney'," he said, his voice deep and husky. "Remember what I said about wearing my bathrobe. Not to mention the fact that you've been in my bed for days now." He gave her a small smile and released her.

"True," she admitted, giving him a small smile in return. "I'm sorry...for...falling apart on you." She was so embarrassed, mortified really. She studied his shirt, noting the wrinkles where she had clung to him in desperation. Maybe if she clicked her heels together three times she would be home, safely in her own bed, the nightmare over.

"No need to apologize. Please, come with me and sit down. We'll eat and then I'll explain everything to you," he said, gesturing toward the kitchen table where the food was growing cold.

Will retrieved the two bottles of water, which had rolled across the floor. He twisted one open and handed it to her. "Drink - you'll feel better."

She nodded and took a sip as he sat down across from her at the glass-topped table.

Will had retrieved his cell phone from the counter and was busily checking his messages as he ate. He was clearly both annoyed and disgusted by the majority of them. His mood had darkened and he chewed quickly, agitated.

Julianna felt a lot calmer now that she had some food in her, but Will's sudden change in mood was a little unnerving. She periodically snuck glances at him, but he didn't look her way as he continued to listen to each message.

Will snapped the phone closed and continued the meal in silence.

"Is everything okay?" Julianna ventured hesitantly after several minutes had passed.

Will stopped eating, his fork in mid-air, and glanced up at her quickly, as if he had forgotten she was even there. His face softened as he took a deep calming breath. "It's fine." He put the fork to his mouth and took a bite, chewing quickly, once again lost in thought.

The calls were none of her business, so she didn't press him. Finished eating, Julianna took her plate to the sink as Will got up to do the same. Without a word she washed and he dried their dishes. It was a mundane task that required no words, but as they stood side by side she felt comforted by the simple everyday task of washing dishes, especially washing dishes with this man. A man she had, for all intents and purposes, just met. But she felt something for him that she couldn't explain. Something that made her feel like she had known him forever. Something she felt she could trust, and she so desperately wanted someone she could trust right now.

Washing two plates, a serving spoon and two forks took about three minutes tops. Julianna was anxious to call Mrs. De Luca to check on Bella. "May I borrow your phone?" she asked Will. "I just want to check on my cat."

Will handed over the phone. "Just don't tell her where you are. It's not safe right now."

"I understand," Julianna nodded as she dialed Mrs. De Luca's number. Will left the room to give her some privacy.

Mrs. De Luca was very glad to hear from her and assured her that Bella was doing fine, and that she could stay there as long as Julianna needed her to. "Dear, I was so worried about you! Antonio and I still don't know how anyone got out of the building unnoticed with all those things of yours. We must have been down in the bakery. Are you sure you're okay? We were so frantic when you didn't come home after your apartment was burglarized. But that nice FBI man came and packed up some of your things and told me you were going to be okay. You *are* okay, aren't you? Are you in some kind of trouble?"

Julianna didn't know how much she should tell Mrs. De Luca, and she certainly didn't want the elderly woman to worry. "I'm fine, Mrs. De Luca, so don't worry about me. I'm staying with a friend for now, but I'll be home soon."

"Well, what's the number there? I tried calling your cell phone, but you don't answer."

"I can't find my phone, Mrs. De Luca. I think maybe I left it at the office," she lied. "I'm not sure what the number is here. It would probably be better if I call you when I can, okay?"

"Okay, dear. Be careful. The nice FBI man said it was okay, so my Antonio is going to get everything cleaned up for you. It will be all ready when you get back home. Don't worry 'bout nothin', dear."

"Thank you, Mrs. De Luca. I can't tell you how much I appreciate that. Give Bella a kiss for me." Julianna disconnected the call. It was time to get some answers.

She walked into the living room and hesitated, taking in her surroundings. The room was very stylish and neat, but masculine, definitely a bachelor pad. It was done in mostly black and white with touches of red here and there. There was a bicycle leaning against the wall next to the door.

Beside the large, black, leather sofa was a floor lamp, which illuminated the cozy room in a soft glow. Will was leaning back on the sofa with his hands clasped behind his head, his eyes closed. He looked exhausted. Julianna had vague recollections of him being with her during her time here, but there was nothing specific she could remember. She just remembered feeling comforted by his presence.

As she took the opportunity to study him she had to admit that he was definitely not hard on the eyes. He looked a little older than her thirty-two years, and if she had to pinpoint his age she would have guessed thirty-seven or thirty-eight. He was tall, at least 6'2" compared to her 5'6" frame. His dark hair was short, but messy and kind of spiky, like he had been unconsciously running his hands through it. She wasn't sure if that was intentional or not, but she liked it.

He was definitely in excellent physical condition judging from outline of solid muscle underneath a black t-shirt, which he wore tucked into blue jeans. His feet were bare. His facial features were strong, all angles and hard edges like the rest of his body, and he had the shadow of a beard where he obviously hadn't shaved for a day or two, but it just made him look sexier, rugged.

A faded black tribal tattoo was banded across his rock-hard, upper, right bicep, and the bottom of it peeked out from beneath his t-shirt. Julianna had never been one for tattoos, but this one somehow looked right on this man, decidedly sexy and a little bit dangerous.

A floorboard creaked on the hardwood floor, announcing her arrival as she walked closer to him and he opened his eyes slowly, smiling slightly as he saw her. "Everything fine with your landlady?"

She nodded, "Everything's fine. So, where exactly am I?"

"Officially, you're staying with a friend from work. Allegra, I believe her name is."

"And unofficially?"

"Chelsea. With me."

He patted the cushion beside him on the sofa. "Time to talk."

"Okay." Julianna sat down beside him on the sofa, curling one of her legs underneath her body and hugging one of the red throw pillows to her body in an unconscious attempt at comfort. Will leaned forward and turned to face her, resting his elbows on his knees and making a steeple with his fingers as he pressed them together.

He exhaled loudly as he searched for the right words. "Wow, where to start?"

Julianna waited, nervously rubbing corded trim of the suede pillow.

"First of all," he began, reaching toward the coffee table and producing his credentials, "As I told you before, I am an agent with the FBI. I just wanted you to see my badge and ID so there's no question," he explained, handing the wallet to her, which she opened, tracing her finger across the badge and studying the ID.

"I have been on this case for a few weeks now," he continued. "You work, or rather worked, for a man named Jackson Mattice. He was killed the day you were attacked. According to our sources it wasn't random or coincidence, but rather the work of trained professionals, contract killers. Unfortunately we don't have a line on the unsub, unidentified subject," he clarified. "But we're working on that."

Julianna looked straight ahead, desperately scanning her memory. She blinked a few times and chewed on her lower lip, deep in thought.

"You don't seem surprised," Will stated, his tone almost accusatory.

"I'm not," she replied, but her hands tightly gripped the pillow as she pulled it more tightly against her.

"But you're upset," he observed, his tone still cool.

"Of course I'm upset," she snapped, finally looking at him. Tears shone in her eyes, but she didn't let them fall. "He was my boss. He was my friend," she added more gently, sighing.

"Why did you say you're not surprised?" he asked, his voice still even.

"Is this an interrogation?" she tried to keep her voice calm in an attempt to stall as she frantically scanned her memory of the last time she had seen Jackson Mattice, desperately trying to remember every detail, every word that was spoken.

"No, we're just talking," he replied, but his tone was still all business and matter of fact. He sat up, leaned back and crossed his arms, while at the same time stretching his long legs out in front of him and crossing his ankles. Julianna was astute enough with body language to immediately sense that he was closing himself off to her, and that he believed there was something she wasn't telling him.

"Okay..." she paused. "I'm trying to remember. That day...it's a little fuzzy."

"Then start at the beginning," he suggested. "What was your relationship like?"

"Well, Jackson was like a father to me at times. I don't have a father – anymore. Jackson doesn't have any children and he sort of took me under his wing. We weren't very close outside of work, but I always knew that if I needed anything he would be there. He helped me with a lot of things when I first moved here; I was definitely a fish out of water. And I was personally a mess because I lost... someone important. And he promoted me pretty quickly when his senior photographer went back to London. We talked a lot...about relationships and such. He was having a lot of problems with his ex-wife. I think he got a pretty raw deal in the divorce settlement and was in financial trouble.

"He called me...that day...the day I was attacked...that morning. He wanted to meet, but wouldn't come into the office, which I found odd, so we met at a coffee shop near the newspaper. Jack had been on vacation so I was surprised to hear from him, especially when he said he was in town. He sounded really nervous on the phone, kind of desperate. His voice was strained."

"What did he say on the phone?" Will asked.

"He just said he needed to meet with me, and that it was very important, something he couldn't discuss at the office. He said to be careful and make sure I wasn't followed. He was acting really paranoid, but he's always been a little strange that way. I reminded him that this was New York City, and that it was going to be pretty difficult to tell if I was being followed. I thought he was joking, or just being his usual self. He's really into conspiracy theories and such. He loves spy movies, that sort of thing. I laughed it off until I heard the desperation and fear in his voice. He repeated to me that he was serious and would tell me what I needed to know at the coffee shop."

"What time did you meet him?"

She searched her memory. "It was around 2:30 when I got there," she finally answered. "I remember leaving shortly after 2:15 because Allegra – she's a co-worker – came in and asked me what time I was leaving work that day. It was her birthday that night and some of us were meeting for dinner. I wanted to go home first to feed Bella. I looked at the clock to see how much time I had because I needed to get back to the office to work on some photos before they put the paper to bed."

"Was Jackson at the coffee shop already or did you have to wait for him?" Will asked.

"He was there already."

"And...?"

"And I sat down, asked him what was so urgent, what was going on. He leaned in really close to me and put his hands over mine. He was talking in hushed tones and it was really loud in there, so we had to get pretty close in order to hear each other.

"He told me that he was in trouble, that some people were after him for some money he owed. I asked him what people, but he said it was better if I didn't know anything."

Will changed positions, sitting up again with his elbows on his knees, his hands clasped together as he listened to her.

She continued, "I asked him if there was anything I could do, like go to the cops. He said it was too late for that. He then asked me if I knew where the photos were that I had taken at the Mayor's Ball."

"Why would he ask you that?"

"I don't know; those photos were taken months ago. Of course I knew where they were, and he did too. I thought it was a really odd question."

"Did you express that to him, that you found it odd?"

"Well, in so many words. I said yes, and asked him why he wanted to know. It kind of caught me off guard because it was such an abrupt change of topic. He just looked at me. His eyes were really intense and he squeezed my hands and said that it was really important that I make sure nothing happened to them. He then asked about the backup system. We have everything backed up off-site to external servers. But he knows that, and he also knows that everything that's entered into any networked computer, and that means *all* the computers, are automatically backed up anytime any file is added or changed."

"Do you have access to those files?" Will asked.

"Which ones? The back-up copies or the ones on the newspaper computers?"

"Either. Both."

"I have access to the ones on the newspaper computers, but only through my computer at work. Once they're uploaded they're locked images. That's how they were set up, to keep anyone from stealing or copying them. We take a lot of pictures of celebrities and politicians at various events, and Jack is paranoid about someone using them outside of the paper. I don't have access to the ones stored remotely. I don't know if anyone does other than Jack and maybe his assistant."

"It doesn't matter," Will said, brushing it off with a wave of his hand. "I can get access to them. Can you remember exactly what he said when he asked you about the pictures?"

Julianna grimaced and closed her eyes, placing her hand on her forehead. "Do you want to take a break?" Will asked her.

"No, I'm fine."

Without a word Will got up from the sofa and came back shortly with another bottle of water and some pills. "For your head," he said, handing her the pills. Noting her dubious expression he added, "It's just headache medicine, nothing stronger, I promise."

"Okay, thanks." She put the pills in her mouth, drank some water and swallowed. Will took the bottle of water from her and set it on the coffee table. "From what I remember Jack asked me if I had the photos from the Mayor's Ball, then said something like, 'Look at the pictures.' Or, 'Make sure you look at the pictures.' Something like that."

"And what did you say?" Will pressed.

ARMS OF A STRANGER

Julianna scooted back farther on the sofa and pulled her knees up to her chest, hugging her legs against her body. She spoke deliberately, making sure she didn't leave out any remembered detail. "I told him I would. He said again to make sure I looked at the pictures, and I insisted that I would. That was pretty much it.

"He kept looking out the window of the coffee shop and it was starting to make me nervous. I asked him if someone was following him and he said that he thought so. I got the feeling there was something he wanted to tell me but now couldn't. I don't know. I was getting a little irritated by the whole thing, and nervous, but at the same time I needed to get back to the office. I told him he couldn't just lay all that on me without an explanation.

"I asked him if I was in any danger by meeting him there and he said no, that he had taken care of that. I asked him what he meant and he snapped at me and told me to stop asking questions and just listen to him, to trust him. I told him I was trying to do that, but he wasn't giving me anything. He was sweating by that time, even more nervous, if that's possible, and told me to be careful and to think about what he said. I asked him what he meant by that; what did he want me to think about? He told me I was smart and I'd figure it out.

"Someone had him really spooked, Will, and Jack isn't afraid of anything. He's a newspaper man – he could sit in a den of rabid lions and be totally unfazed.

"He started to say something more, but his cell phone rang and he looked down at the number and got this really 'freaked out', for lack of a better phrase, look on his face. He looked out the window again and I'm not sure what he saw, but he jumped up so fast he almost knocked his chair over. I grabbed it before it hit the floor. He told me not to follow him out immediately and then he said he was sorry."

"Sorry for what?"

"I don't know. He looked really forlorn and told me this was not going to end well, and that he was sorry, and hoped I wouldn't hate him. I didn't have a chance to say anything in response because he practically ran out the door."

"And that was it?"

"That was it. I went back to the office, finished my work that afternoon and left. I did take the time to look at the photos of the Mayor's Ball. I mean, that was obviously what he was trying to get me to look at, right? I glanced through them – there were over a thousand – but there was nothing there out of the ordinary. After that I went home, went to the restaurant with the girls...and you know the rest."

Will didn't say anything for a long time. He just sat there in the same position he had been in, tapping his steepled fingers against his lower lip, lost in thought.

"Is your head any better?" he finally asked.

"Forget my head! What is going on?" she demanded. "I answered your questions, and now I think you owe me some answers here."

He glanced at her sideways. "I know," he said, but he didn't offer anything further.

"You don't believe me. "Is that it? I told you everything, Will."

"I believe you."

"Then what?" she pressed.

He sighed and pinched the bridge of his nose. "Mattice was right, Julianna; this isn't going to end well."

"I don't even know what that means, Will. Look, I'm in this thing, so you have to tell me what's going on."

"I know," he repeated. "Damnit." He punched in some numbers on his phone. "Nick, it's Delaney. I need a favor." He got up and walked into the kitchen. Julianna could hear him pacing while telling the person on the other end of the line that he needed to get into the newspaper's files and wanted access to everything. Now.

She heard the phone snap shut and Will walked back into the living room and continued pacing. "It will take some time, but we need to look through those photos."

"Okay, but I'm not sure what we're looking for," she replied.

"I'm not either but that's clearly the key to this."

"Where is he?" Julianna asked quietly.

"Who?"

"Jack. Where is Jack?"

Will stopped pacing and pocketed his phone. "He's still in the morgue. His brother is here from Florida settling his affairs while he waits for the body to be released from the autopsy. He'll be taking Mattice back to Florida to be buried."

"I want to see him."

"That's not a good idea, Julianna."

"Why not?"

"Well, for one because it's not safe, and two, because it's just not something you want to see. Remember him the way he was, Julianna. Death is not a pretty thing, trust me."

"I know it's not, but I have to do this." She looked up at Will, her clear green eyes pleading with him. His jaw muscles worked while he looked away from her, staring straight ahead, thinking.

"I want to see him," she repeated.

"You're not going to let this go, are you?"

"No, I'm not."

"I'll see what I can do. No promises."

"Okay, no promises." But she cocked her head and arched that brow at him, which he was beginning to recognize meant she was determined to get her way.

"I don't want you involved in this, Julianna."

"I'm already involved, Will. Jack made sure of that."

"I know that. Damnit, I know." He let out a frustrated sigh and sat back down on the sofa beside her. "Look, I'm at a loss here. I know you want answers from me, but I'm still trying to figure this thing out. This thing involves the mob." He really hadn't wanted to tell her that, but he knew he had to because this thing was probably a lot bigger than either of them thought.

"The mob?" she exclaimed.

"Ever heard of Victor Ciccone?" Will asked.

"Of course – who hasn't? He was supposed to go to prison for tax evasion, money laundering, trafficking...there was an entire list of offenses, but he got off scot-free. Everyone says he had some judge in his pocket."

"I'm beginning to think it's bigger than that, someone higher up," Will said with disgust.

"Who?"

"We're not sure yet, but Mattice knew something, and that's what got him killed. Are you ready to talk about that night?" Will asked her gently.

"I didn't know I wasn't ready," she replied, receiving a dubious look from Will.

"Okay, so maybe ready isn't the word, but I'm as ready as I'm going to be," she admitted. She had pulled her feet under her body and hugged the throw pillow to her chest once more. She continued to hold the pillow tightly against her, like a shield, as Will gathered his thoughts.

"Ciccone," he began, "Had a nephew, Rico Cordova. His sister's kid, if you want to call a 28 year old man a kid. He took Cordova under his wing after the sister died when Cordova was 10. So, ultimately Cordova was like a son to Ciccone. There's no father in the picture because, well, Ciccone took care of that little problem when his sister showed up at his house with a black eye and a broken arm. Ciccone raised Cordova as his own."

"You said 'had'," observed Julianna. "Ciccone *had* a nephew."

"Yeah, that's because he's dead. He's the one who attacked you."

"And you killed him."

"Yes."

"Ciccone is going to want revenge."

"Exactly." Will looked down at his hands to find them trembling slightly. It had been a long time since he had taken a life. In his past he had done a hell of a lot of things he wasn't proud of, but they were for a greater good, or at least that's what he had been told when he was given the assignments. But who really knew? They gave him a job and he did it without question. Period. At the time he really didn't care; he just knew he had to get away from his life for a while.

He had been betrayed by two of the most important people in the world, and he was angry and wanted someone or something to take it out on. So when he was approached by a recruiter he found himself jumping at the chance to step into the life of another persona, someone who people didn't take advantage of, because *he* was the one in control. Or so he disillusioned himself to believe. Even with a personal life in shambles he had been a damn good Navy Seal, fearless, controlled, a team player, and someone had taken notice. Then suddenly he found himself doing covert ops for an agency that didn't know your name if you ever found yourself compromised. You were on your own, save for the men who worked side-by-side with you. It was just what he needed, and for a while he was back in the game. But soon, fearlessness turned to recklessness, and again, someone took notice.

A superior had taken him aside and told him to get out while he still could, before he ended up in a shallow grave somewhere in the Middle East or South America. Or worse, that someone else ended up there, due to the recklessness of one rogue operative.

With the promise of being able to return to the job when he got himself straightened out, he took that time off, did a lot of thinking and drinking on a beach in the Caribbean, and instead of turning back to the life like he once embraced, he joined the FBI.

There were times when he didn't think he'd come out the other side, but he had. His life as an FBI agent had been mundane at best, and he was perfectly happy that way. He had dated, sure, but he kept himself guarded and within arm's reach to pretty much everyone in his life.

But with *this* case, *this* woman, it all came flooding back, and had slammed into him with a force he didn't even know still existed. He knew he shouldn't, he *couldn't*, get involved with her, but somewhere deep inside his soul he felt himself waking up again. He wanted to protect her, and he wanted to save her from the past he knew she had tried so hard to heal from. Hell, maybe a part of him wanted her to save him, too.

He had done all the background checks on her, built up a thin file. She was just a girl from Tennessee who had witnessed the violent deaths of her parents at a young age, lost her husband of one year to a roadside bombing in Iraq, and now she was once again thrust into violence. Were Jackson Mattice not already dead he would kill him himself. How Julianna felt anything for this man who had so carelessly put her into the line of fire was beyond him, but he was not going to let anything happen to her, no matter what it cost. She was different, *real*. She was so unlike the women he usually dated, even the one woman he had once given his heart to.

He had never let himself feel like this except for with one other person – the person whose actions had started him down the collision course of self-destruction. He couldn't afford to go to that dark place again, but hell, he wasn't sure he could afford not to, if that's what it took.

Julianna tentatively reached out and placed her hand gently over his much larger one. Startled, he looked up and into her face. Her brows were furrowed, concerned. "Are you okay?" she asked softly.

"Yeah," his voice was husky, his eyes a mix of emotions she didn't quite understand.

"Your hands were trembling and you seemed a million miles away."

He turned his palm up and gave her hand a brief and gentle squeeze before letting go. "I'm fine; just thinking."

"Does he frighten you?"

"Who? Ciccone? No. Hell no."

"What then?" she pressed.

He stood up and once more started pacing. "This whole thing is my fault. You getting hurt – that's all on me. I should have stayed; I shouldn't have left. It was my job to keep you safe."

"What happened?" she asked softly, looking up at him expectantly.

He stopped pacing and walked over to the window, opening the blinds just enough to see out, but angling them so that no one could see in. He stood there staring out into the night sky with his hands in his pockets. Julianna could see his jaw muscles working once more as he contemplated his words.

"To start at the beginning, Jackson Mattice contacted the FBI a few weeks ago, saying he had some information that he knew we'd be interested in, but he wanted to meet with me specifically. When I asked him why me he said he had done some research on me and thought I was trustworthy. But when I met with him he wouldn't open up. Said he needed more time to investigate. I told him that was my job, not his, but you know Mattice. He insisted on waiting until he had rock solid information, but wanted me on 'standby', as he put it. I think he was feeling out the situation, making a decision as to whether or not he actually could trust me. "

"So why have you been watching me?" Julianna asked.

"Mattice finally revealed that when this went down it was going to be huge, maybe even political, and that if anything happened to him to go to you, that you'd have the information. He also said that if he turned up dead we needed to take a look at Victor Ciccone. That got our attention. We decided to stay one step ahead of him and put surveillance on you."

"But I don't know anything!" Julianna exclaimed.

Will gave her a sideways look. "If you really don't know anything, then there must be something you have access to that will reveal what Mattice died for. And obviously someone else, namely Ciccone, thinks you know what that is, too."

"Rest assured that I *really* do not know anything," Julianna replied icily. "I am, however, willing to help you look through those pictures, so whether you believe me or not, I'm telling you the truth. Now, what happened the night I was attacked?"

Will didn't respond to the implication that he didn't believe her. He knew in his heart that she was telling him the truth, but the agent in him had to get to the bottom of this investigation. "Olsen and I were at the restaurant – he on the inside and me outside in the car. Mattice had set up a meeting with me that day, paranoid that his phones were tapped, worried that something was going to happen to you, swearing he'd tell me everything if I promised to keep you safe. Mattice never showed to that meeting. Olsen thought he'd probably run, but I had a gut feeling that wasn't the case.

"Sure enough, as I sat there watching the restaurant I got a call a body had been found in Chinatown, and the driver's license identified him as Mattice. Olsen and I discussed it and decided that he would stay since he was already inside, and I'd run over to Chinatown, check out the situation, and come right back. You and your friends were nowhere near wrapping things up from the looks of it, so I figured I'd have plenty of time.

"Olsen," he continued, "Called me when I was about halfway back to the restaurant from Chinatown. He had seen a guy at the bar who we now know as Rico Cordova, looking nervous and suspicious. He walked out behind you and your friends, which Olsen knew wasn't coincidence. Olsen followed you and your friends up a few blocks, but when he got closer he realized that the woman he thought was you, was in fact not. He panicked when you weren't with them and calls me, telling me to get back to the restaurant immediately, because he'd seen Cordova back at the restaurant, but hadn't since. And when he realized he had been following the wrong girl..."

"I had loaned my hat and scarf to Allegra," Julianna explained. "She was getting a cold, and of course thinks fashion comes before common sense, so I insisted she take my hat and scarf. We both had on black coats, and our hair is similar."

"He knew that he had made a mistake, and that I had gone the opposite direction with Rico Cordova right behind me," she finished.

"Olsen asked the girls where you were. They, of course, didn't tell him until he showed them his badge, so he wasted precious minutes, but he eventually headed back in the opposite direction of where your friends had gone. I arrived about the same time and drove the same route. I heard you screaming... I think you know the rest."

"You saved me," she stated.

"I almost got you killed," he argued, turning to look at her.

"But you didn't. So what we need to do now is find the photo that is the center of this entire thing."

"We? No, there is no 'we' in this. There is a 'me' and there is a 'you', and *you* are no longer going to be a part of this. I'm going to get you into a safe house tomorrow."

"You are going to need me to help you with those photos," Julianna argued.

"I can handle the photos, Julianna."

"Rico Cordova was asking me for a memory card. Could the photos still be on a memory card? Or maybe Jack transferred them? Why would he specifically be asking for a memory card?"

"Maybe Mattice was threatening someone with information.

"Blackmail?" Julianna asked, incredulous. "I don't think Jack would ever do something like that," she argued.

"Nothing people do surprises me anymore, Julianna. People are capable of doing a lot of things we don't think they would do. It sounds like you didn't know Jackson Mattice as well as you thought you did."

"No, I guess I didn't," she said sadly. "What about the office? Did you find anything there?"

"Olsen pulled everything from your office and Mattice's, and there was nothing out of the ordinary that our team could find. No memory cards, no cameras."

She was almost afraid to ask, "What about the cameras in my apartment?"

"Gone," Will confirmed.

Julianna's face fell. She had saved for those cameras and lenses for years. Doing a rough calculation in her head she figured she had just lost close to ten grand in equipment. Sure, insurance would cover the loss, but nothing could erase the feeling of being violated like that. She didn't even want to ask about what other specific items had been stolen.

Aside from her cat, her cameras were the most important things in her life. They were her livelihood, her passion. They were an integral part of her past, and a vital part of her present. No matter what was going on in her life she knew that she could leave the cocoon of her apartment and become a part of another world; one that she often felt she was not a part of. The early loss of her parents, and then the more recent loss of her husband, had left her feeling isolated and timid about venturing out into parts unknown. Taking pictures was her way of integrating herself into those events and into the world that she wasn't sure she was fully ready to accept as her own.

It had taken all the strength she could muster to make the move to New York after her grandmother, who had raised her, had passed away. She had taken the small inheritance her grandmother had left her, sold the house she and Josh had turned into a home, put the items she couldn't part with in storage for when she actually had a place large enough for them again, sold the rest, and with a giant leap of faith applied for a job at a promising young newspaper. Miraculously, to her anyway, she had gotten the job, forcing her into a career that had turned out to be the best thing that had ever happened to her. She had gradually come out of her shell, had pushed her grief aside and was truly happy for the first time in a long time.

And now this. The one person she thought she could fully trust had put her in the middle of a nightmare.

"How long were you following me?" she asked Will. The thought of him being there, watching her without her knowledge, was a little unsettling, while at the same time comforting. Things could have gone a lot differently had he not been around.

"A few weeks," Will told her. "We were trying to locate Mattice and of course figure out the connection to Ciccone. Mattice would call me from a throwaway cell so we couldn't locate him. We needed him so that we could ultimately get to Ciccone. We thought you would lead us to him. He said he had something huge on someone important, but that he couldn't trust just anyone. You can't just call the FBI and start making accusations then take off. We have spent years on Ciccone, thousands of man-hours trying to put this guy away. Mattice obviously had something pretty big for Ciccone to want him dead, and if that something is still out there then I'm going to find it.

"Mattice said he knew Ciccone's guys were after him, but we had no identification for anyone in particular yet. In fact, Cordova didn't appear on our radar until the night you were attacked. He's a hack, a thug going around with nothing more than his uncle's name to throw around. Whoever killed Mattice was a pro. It wasn't Rico Cordova.

"The FBI has been building a case on Ciccone for a long time now, but every time we get close something happens – either he gets off on a technicality or we can't get enough evidence. His organization is so large that it's difficult to prove who exactly is behind what. We've sent countless associates of his to prison. He doesn't care because he has no loyalties to anyone other than himself. He just goes out and recruits someone else, pays them a hell of a lot of money or makes threats they can't refuse, and they do his bidding."

Julianna knew there was a lot Will still wasn't telling her, and couldn't tell her, about the case, but at least she had gotten most of the answers she had wanted.

"Are we safe here?" she asked him.

"For now. I told Mattice that I would protect you, Julianna, and I fully intend to keep my promise, no matter what I think of the man personally.

"I honestly think Mattice, in his own warped way, did what he thought was best. He thought we would watch you, catch the bad guys and call it a day, but unfortunately it hasn't worked out that way."

Julianna's mind was racing a mile a minute, racking her brain trying to think of what Jack could have known, and more importantly where was this elusive memory card and what the hell was on it? She suddenly felt overwhelmingly exhausted and drained from the events of the past few days. It was surreal. She had done nothing, absolutely nothing, yet she had the *mob* after her? Unbelievable.

"How about we get some sleep," Will suggested. "I think we could both use some." Julianna noticed that his eyes were red and the fatigue was definitely showing on his face.

"I insist you take the bed tonight," she offered.

"No way," he replied. "I'm actually quite at home on a couch since I spent a lot of time on the one at the office when I'm knee-deep in a case. But would you mind if I brushed my teeth and took a quick shower first?"

"Of course not; it's your place, so take all the time you want."

They walked into the bedroom together and Julianna sat on the bed while Will rummaged through his dresser drawers for the items he was looking for.

The situation was awkward at best – her sitting on this stranger's bed. "This is a nice apartment," she said, breaking the silence.

"Yeah, it's not bad," he agreed absently.

"It's a great bachelor pad," she rambled. "Very clean and masculine. Not a trace of a woman anywhere in sight."

"I have a cleaning lady come in every week," he explained. "As for women, no. Besides my cleaning lady women don't come here."

"Confirmed bachelor?"

Will paused before answering her, as if considering his words. "Bachelor, yes, but I wouldn't say 'confirmed' - I was married once." He pushed the dresser drawer back in with a bit more force than necessary, signaling that this was a touchy subject.

"I'm sorry," she said gently.

"Nothing to be sorry about," he assured her crisply. "It was a long time ago - another lifetime.

"Do you need to get in here before I get in the shower?" he asked, gesturing toward the door to the bathroom.

"No, I'm fine."

He nodded and went into the bathroom and closed the door.

Julianna stood staring at the closed bathroom door for just a moment. She suddenly felt helpless and alone without him. She had never felt so needy, and in fact prided herself on being extremely strong and self-reliant. What was the strong attraction to this man and why did she feel so drawn to him? Oh, she knew why, although she certainly didn't want to admit to being so foolish. He had saved her. That was it, pure and simple. He was the big strong hero to her damsel in distress.

She felt like an idiot – one of those silly needy women she despised in the movies. The ones who made her throw popcorn at the screen in frustration when the bad guy was killing the husband/lover/boyfriend while the pathetic woman stood helplessly screaming and whimpering instead of grabbing the nearest gun/knife/brick and saving the day.

While Will showered, Julianna went into the living room and rummaged around in her box of clothing that Agent Olsen had brought from her apartment until she found a nightgown and underwear, which she took back to Will's bedroom and put on. She had also brought her purse back into the room and dumped the contents onto the bed. Maybe Jack had hidden a memory card in her purse the last time she saw him. It was farfetched, but she searched the purse anyway.

She dumped out the contents of her makeup bag, but there was nothing there other than her makeup essentials and too many tubes of lip gloss. The rest of the purse contained nothing unusual either – notepad and pen, wallet with nothing missing, breath mints, some hair elastics and bobby pins, sunglasses, the keys to her apartment, a pair of silver hoop earrings and a mermaid necklace that Jack had given her recently after the trip he had just taken.

Julianna narrowed her eyes and stared hard at the necklace. Jack had given it to her the day she met him in the coffee shop. How could she have forgotten? Well, first of all, because the necklace was tacky and looked like it had come out of a junk store in Chinatown. It was definitely not something she would wear, although she thought it was sweet of Jack to think of her. The chain was gold-plated and gaudy, as was the mermaid. She had on a red bra top as well as red enamel scales and a row of rhinestones just below her belly button, fashioned like a belt. Julianna tried to remember what Jack had said about the mermaid. He had been at the beach and had seen it and thought of her, knowing how much she loved the ocean.

Could Jack have been in Florida then? Julianna's pulse quickened. She knew Jack had a brother who lived in Miami. Maybe he was visiting him, but she thought they were on the outs. She would talk to Will about it in the morning. If Jack's brother was here to take Jack's body back to Florida for burial, then the FBI could question him to see if Jack had been in Florida. Not that it really mattered at this point since Jack was dead.

Julianna put everything back into her purse, including the necklace, and crawled into Will's bed and turned off the light, deciding she would brush her teeth and use the toilet after Will had finished.

As she lay there, she thought about the events of the past couple of days. Where was she going to go? She couldn't stay here with Will indefinitely. Would the people that killed Jack eventually catch up with her? She didn't even want to think about the state of her apartment. She tried to think of what photo could be so important that people were willing to kill over it, and then racked her brain trying to think of where Jack would hide something like that, and how he had even come across it. Had he been the photographer? Had *she*, without even knowing it? The harder she tried to think the more drowsy she became, and she soon found herself drifting off.

Will opened the door quietly, but Julianna was awakened anyway. The light from the bathroom filled the bedroom with its glow. "You can leave the light on. I'm going to brush my teeth," Julianna explained sleepily.

As Will walked from the bathroom, Julianna could see that he wore only a pair of light blue striped pajama bottoms. Still damp from the shower, his torso was bare, exposing the hard muscles that his form-fitting t-shirt had hinted at earlier. The faint aroma of lime from the same soap she had used earlier wafted across the room as he crossed it.

She got up from the bed and headed into the bathroom, keeping her eyes averted. She didn't dare look at him. He might know what she was thinking, and what she was thinking was definitely not something she wanted him to know.

"Sleep well, Julianna. If you need anything I'll be just on the other side of the door on the sofa."

"Good night, Will," she answered.

Minutes later, when Julianna came out of the bathroom, he was gone, the door to the bedroom closed. She got back into bed and pulled the soft comforter tightly around her. As she lay there alone in the dark the tears started to fall. Her body ached from the effects of the attack, but at the moment her heart ached even more, and she felt utterly alone. She fell into a restless sleep, filled with dreams of running, searching, frantically looking for something, for someone. She finally came to a dark alley and cautiously opened a heavy wooden door, ancient with rotting wood and spider webs. The door slowly creaked open, and she gasped in horror to realize that everyone she had ever loved was dead on the other side, and she was forever alone.

Chapter 5

The next morning as dawn began to break, Julianna padded softly to the bathroom to freshen up, noticing that the boxes of belongings from her apartment had been moved into the bedroom and were stacked neatly beside Will's dresser.

The house was completely silent, so she opened the bedroom door quietly and walked softly into the living room where Will was still asleep. His blanket had fallen to the floor, so she crept quietly over, picked it up and gently covered his sleeping form.

He was breathing softly, his right arm thrown over his forehead as he lay there on his back. His legs were no match for the length of the sofa. She really should have insisted that he take the bed last night. There was no telling when he had last had a decent night's sleep, and that was made even more apparent when she looked over at the desk and saw photo printouts, in the newspaper's standard proof form of 30 photos per page, scattered across it. She could tell even from a distance that they were the photos of the Mayor's Ball. Doing a quick calculation in her head she figured there were at least 35 or more sheets of paper since there were well over one thousand photos in the bunch.

He had obviously gotten into the online backup system and had printed out every photo that had been taken.

She looked back down at Will to find him watching her. He smiled lazily up at her, "G'morning. Sleep well?"

She shrugged her shoulders. "I've slept better, and from the looks of it so have you."

"Nah, it wasn't so bad. How are you feeling?"

She ignored his question and nodded toward the photo printouts. "Did you find anything?"

"Nothing unusual," he replied. "Just a lot of schmoozing among New York's elite. I'd like for you to take a look again, see if you see anything unusual now that we know there's actually something we should be looking for."

Julianna nodded thoughtfully. "There has to be something there, otherwise Jack wouldn't have made a point of those pictures being important."

"How are you feeling?" Will asked again.

"I'm okay. I think something for this headache would help, but otherwise I'm just stiff and sore, nothing that some pain meds won't cure. I was actually just headed to the kitchen for some water. Want me to make coffee?" Julianna started to walk toward the kitchen but Will reached out for her hand to stop her.

"You were crying last night."

"Was I?"

"Bad dream?"

She nodded. "I think it's all catching up with me, but I'll be fine, especially once this is all over. I just want this to be over."

"I know," Will said gently. "Want to talk about it? The dream, I mean."

"No, not really. I barely even remember what it was about," she lied. He was still holding her hand and showed no sign of letting go.

"Look, Will, I know you have a job to do, and I really appreciate it. Truly I do. But you don't have to babysit me. I have been taking care of myself for a long time and I am quite capable. I can't stay here forever. What if Victor Ciccone, or whoever it is who wants those pictures is never caught? I have a life, I have a job, I have a home. And you have all of those things too. You can't have your job invading your personal life. In fact, I'm not naïve enough to think that my being here isn't going to affect your career entirely. I can't stay here."

"My *job* right now is you – to keep you from whoever killed Jackson Mattice and who also, need I remind you, nearly killed you." Will stated, letting go of her hand. "And this," he said, waving his arm around the apartment, "is my personal life. This is it. Let me worry about the rest of it."

"Do you normally bring your 'job' home with you like this?" she asked sarcastically.

Will ran a hand through his hair in frustration. "I didn't mean that you were a job to me, Julianna, at least not anymore. It's more than that," he said, moving to the edge of the sofa so he could reach her hand once more. "I mean, it's *become* more than that.

I know you probably think this has happened quickly, but for me it happened weeks ago when I first saw you." There, he had said it and now there was no turning back.

Yesterday when he had held her in the kitchen she had taken his breath away. The scent of his soap on her, her hair softly curling as it dried. He had wanted to hold her like that forever, kiss her until they both couldn't breathe, but he couldn't. He also knew he had a job to do and pursuing her was wrong on so many levels, but he saw the fire in her eyes and knew she wanted him as much as he wanted her.

He reasoned that his job was to protect her, and keeping her close would definitely accomplish that. Last night he had heard her crying in bed, *his* bed, and he had gone in to check on her. He had stayed with her, sitting on the chair beside the bed, until the dream had passed and she was once again sleeping soundly.

He pulled her closer so that she was standing between his knees. He saw a flash of surprise in her eyes, but it was gone as quickly as it had appeared.

"I don't even know you," she said softly. "You've been nothing more than a sleeping pill induced dream for the past few days – a comforting voice, a gentle touch. You've made me feel safe. You're doing your job. That's... that's all this is."

"Not to me," he said, his voice low. "I know this seems really fast to you, but don't you feel something too?"

The corners of her mouth turned up ever so slightly, in a barely perceptible smile, as she reached her hand out to softly touch his cheek. Closing his eyes briefly, he savored the feel of her touch. He brought her hand to his lips and his blue eyes seemed to darken as he kept them intently on hers while softly kissing the palm of her hand, then the underside of her wrist. He heard her breath catch and felt her body tense slightly.

Standing up, he murmured, "Come here," offering his hand to her, palm up. Julianna reached out and tentatively placed her hand in his.

"Just let me hold you." he said, pulling her against him and tenderly kissing her forehead.

She closed her eyes and rested her head against his bare chest, her sigh the sweet sound of contentment. They stood like that for what seemed like several long minutes.

Taking a step back so he could see her face, he ran his finger along her jaw line, and then across her full bottom lip. She opened her eyes then and looked up at him, her mouth slightly open, her questioning eyes burning into his.

"Are you okay?" he asked her. "I mean...is this okay?"

Pulling back slightly she tentatively put her hands against his bare chest and nodded. He covered her hand with his own and slid both their hands to his pounding heart. "Wow," she whispered.

"Wow indeed." His conscience screamed at him to stop this before it went any further, but ignoring common sense Will tenderly cupped her delicate face in his large hands and gently kissed her bruised lips for the first time. She kissed him back, hesitantly at first, small soft kisses. Then her hands were around the back of his neck, in his hair, pulling him hungrily into her as she made soft mewling sounds.

He angled his head to deepen the kiss and wrapped his arms tightly around her, one hand on her bottom pulling her against him. She parted her lips to his tongue, which he used to trace her lips slowly before exploring her mouth.

His inner voice of reason once again chided him for being so stupid, for letting things go this far. But pushing those thoughts deeper into oblivion, Will continued to kiss her.

Just then his cell rang, startling them both. "Damn!" Will cursed under his breath.

"Delaney," he answered quickly, his voice husky. As he listened to the person on the other end he kept his eyes on hers.

"Are you positive?" he suddenly exploded, turning away from her and switching the phone to his other ear. He began pacing the room. "Get dressed," he mouthed silently to her, motioning toward the bedroom with his head. "Yes, yes, I'm listening. I understand," he spoke to the person on the phone.

Julianna went into the bedroom and rummaged through her boxes of clothes until she found a bra, some jeans, a black sweater, and socks and black boots.

She was finishing getting dressed when Will walked into the room and went to his closet, pulling out two duffel bags. "Pack what you'll need for a few days," he told her, handing one of the duffel bags to her and placing the other one on the bed where he began tossing his own things.

"What's happened?" she asked worriedly, clutching the bag against her chest.

"We've been compromised and there's a hit out on me, probably on you too, but we're still getting information. We're going to the office, and then to a safe house. Pack." He began pulling on jeans and a light blue button-down shirt, his shoulder-holstered gun going under a black leather jacket.

Julianna hastily began packing, grabbing items out of the boxes, trying to find anything that matched. Thankfully Mrs. De Luca had also packed her makeup bag and a bag of toiletries, both of which went into the duffel.

Will had packed in record time and had headed into the living room. When she joined him there he was shoving his laptop computer into a case, along with an iPad and the stack of photo printouts, which he tapped on the desk in an attempt to straighten them.

"Can you get those?" Will indicated to his items on the coffee table. Julianna scooped his badge, wallet, cell phone and watch into her purse, and together they headed out the door and down the elevator to the basement parking garage where his vehicle was parked.

Chapter 6

As Will's black Tahoe screeched out of the parking garage, he glanced over at Julianna. She had been silent since he had told her they were going to the safe house. "You okay?" he asked her.

"I'm not going to be able to see Jack now, am I?"

Will sighed, "It's not a good idea."

"That didn't answer my question."

"It's not safe."

"Please, Will. This is the only chance I'm going to have."

Will chewed on his lower lip and furrowed his brow, contemplating. Once on the street, he was forced to slow down as traffic inched along.

"Did you grab my phone?" Will asked Julianna.

Julianna reached into her purse for Will's things, handing them to him one at a time as he drove.

"Thanks," he glanced at her, giving her a tight-lipped smile and pressed in some numbers. "This is FBI Special Agent Will Delaney and I need to take another look at the body of Jackson Mattice. I'd appreciate it if you could have everything ready when I get there. I'm on an extremely tight schedule."

He waited while the other person spoke, and then answered, "Yes, now." He kept his eyes on the road, his brow furrowed and his left hand gripping the steering wheel tightly.

"Thanks," he said, ending the call and glancing over at Julianna, who had grabbed her makeup bag from the duffel and was applying concealer to her bruises.

"We'll be there in a few minutes, but we've got to make it quick," Will told her. "I'll be there with you. In case you're nervous," he added.

"Okay," she replied nonchalantly, keeping her eyes on the mirror as she blended the concealer. "But I'm not nervous. I've seen a dead person before, Will, so you don't have to protect me."

"All right, tough guy," he teased her, but he didn't smile. "It's all right to be nervous. I'll be right there with you."

"I'm not nervous," she insisted, turning to look at him.

"Oh yes, you are. I can see it in your eyes," he observed as he glanced over at her, his own brow furrowed.

"Your eyes are supposed to be on the road," she replied, turning toward the passenger seat window.

"It's also in your voice. You forget that you are dealing with a trained professional here, Julianna," he joked, finally giving a hint of a smile.

"Do you mind if I turn the radio on?" she asked, changing the subject, wanting to get her mind off of the entire thing, at least for the moment.

"Whatever makes you happy."

Julianna flipped it on, and then exclaimed, "I love this station. 80's music is so..."

"Ridiculous," he finished for her.

"Yes, exactly! Rarely did the lyrics ever make sense, but somehow it all worked. Oh, and the love songs, those were the best," she closed her eyes and leaned her head back against the tan leather seat.

Traffic moved at a snail's pace in typical New York City style. Car horns blared, cabbies yelled. The only ones who seemed to be making any progress were the pedestrians as they hurried past, heads down, bracing themselves against the winter chill. A young Hispanic woman, likely a nanny since the girls resembled her in no way, walked quickly past with two identical blondes in tow. Both had on bubble gum pink coats with matching scarves, hats and gloves. Little brown monkeys holding bright yellow bananas were appliquéd at the lower left hem of each coat. One sister carried a green backpack and the other sported red. The girls, who looked to be around six or seven years old, were clearly not interested in going to school on this cold morning. The nanny had each of them by the hand and was practically dragging them down the street. One of the girls turned around and made eye contact with Will as they hurried past. Will smiled and wiggled his fingers at her over the steering wheel in a childish wave, and was not surprised when she stuck out her tongue at him in response. He chuckled to himself as they disappeared around the corner of the next block.

Will tapped his fingers impatiently against the steering wheel and watched Julianna from the corner of his eye. She was so beautiful, her auburn hair falling in soft waves around her face. Her skin was pale and smooth, its only flaws being the bruises that were still clearly visible. Her lips were a full rosy pink, which were darkened by the blows she had sustained. She put on a brave front, but it hid a vulnerability that he knew existed under the facade.

"What kind of movies do you like, Jule?" he asked, turning the volume on the radio down a few notches.

"What?" Julianna seemed startled by the question, clearly wrapped in her own thoughts.

"Movies. What kind of movies do you like?" Will repeated.

"Um, I don't know. Old movies are good...Fred Astaire, Ginger Rogers. I also like action stuff like James Bond. Romance is always good, too. It sort of depends on my mood," she answered, her eyes still closed.

"I love Bond. No one could beat Connery. He was the best."

"Absolutely," Julianna agreed. "He had such class, although Pierce Brosnan wasn't hard on the eyes either. And Daniel Craig - he's definitely the reason my friend Allegra goes to Bond movies. You'd make a great Bond, you know," she teased, opening her eyes and looking over at him, one eyebrow raised mischievously.

He chuckled, "I doubt it, but thanks for the vote of confidence. It sure would be fun to play with all those toys and stand around ordering martinis all day, though."

"Not to mention all the women," she added.

Will didn't say anything but she noticed he had tightened his grip on the steering wheel and had furrowed his brow again.

"So you like martinis?" she asked, changing the subject.

"Not really, just the olives," he replied, his expression softening. "I'm not much of a drinker. Anymore. I went through some stuff, drank too much, and found out I didn't like that person very much. I like to be in control of myself."

Julianna nodded. "I know what you mean. That night...the night you found me, my friends got pretty wasted. That's not really my thing."

Will noticed Julianna stiffen as they pulled into a parking space at the morgue. He took the key out of the ignition and turned to her. "Are you ready?" he asked.

"Yes," she said, but she was staring straight ahead and her hands were clasped tightly on the handle of her purse.

"You don't have to do this, you know," Will reminded her.

She turned to look at him, "Let's just get this over with."

Chapter 7

The day had been warm, but as the evening progressed a chill had fallen, as was typical with autumn in Tennessee. There was an old joke in Tennessee – if you don't like today's weather, just wait until tomorrow because it will likely be completely different. It was true. Tennessee weather did tend to change on a dime.

Ten-year-old Julianna had worn her best outfit for dinner out with her parents to celebrate her mother's birthday at La Paz, their favorite Mexican restaurant. A little bit of salsa had stained the front of her Kelly green dress, the dress her mother said looked so pretty with her eyes, making them appear even brighter and greener than they actually were.

Julianna dabbed at the stain with a spit-covered finger, but the stain didn't budge. Her mother had a knack for removing stains, no matter how impossible they seemed, and Julianna knew she could tackle this one, but how she hated to have marred her beautiful green dress, especially so early on in the evening. She worried about it for the duration of their meal, looking down often at the dark red stain. Her mother kept assuring her that the stain was not permanent and they'd take care of it as soon as they got home. Julianna felt that all eyes were upon her in the restaurant, silently chastising her for her sloppiness, though in reality no one noticed.

Julianna was almost relieved when the meal was over and they left the restaurant. As they turned south onto Hillsboro Pike in the upscale Green Hills community of Nashville, she listened to her parents discuss their upcoming Disney World trip for Julianna's Fall break from school. Julianna didn't have the heart to tell them she was getting too old for Disney World. This was their annual tradition, and she was beginning to think her parents enjoyed the trip more than she did.

That's okay, she thought to herself. Let them have their fun. It really didn't matter where they went as long as they were together. They were the Three Musketeers, closer than any of her friends were to their parents.

"You're awfully quiet back there, pumpkin," her father said, looking at her in the rearview mirror.

"I'm fine, daddy. Just thinking. Can we go to the beach when we go to Florida?"

"Of course. You know your mother would never allow us not to." He winked at her and she smiled back at him. "Did you get your homework finished this afternoon?"

"Yes, I just had a book report – Little Women – I finished it."

"Good girl. Maybe we can do some work in the darkroom then. Develop those pictures we took last weekend?"

"Sure! I want to see how my pictures of Jennifer and Nicole turned out. They should be good. I worked really hard on my lighting like you taught me."

Julianna's father was a portrait photographer, and she had inherited his keen eye for bringing out the best in people through the lens of her camera. She loved taking pictures of her friends, who would pretend to be fashion models as they posed for her. What she didn't tell them was that she preferred the photos that weren't posed, the ones where they were laughing or just being themselves.

Wise beyond her years, she realized that people's true personalities came shining through when they didn't know the camera was on them, when they were most vulnerable. These were the pictures Julianna was most proud of. These were the pictures that her father knew would turn her into a talented photographer someday, if she so chose.

He could say with all honestly that she was probably more talented than he, or at least she would be once she gained more confidence and honed her skills. He was exceedingly proud of her and exhibited her photos on his studio walls. It was a rare talent for a ten year old to have, and he fully intended to help her make the most of it.

"Hey, maybe we could go shopping tomorrow for some frames for your pictures." Julianna's mother said. "I'm sure Jennifer and Nicole's mothers would love to have them."

"Okay, but I want to make sure they're good enough to frame first. They might not be."

"They'll be great, baby, and if they're not then you'll try again." That was her mother, forever the optimist.

Julianna stared out the window of the car as the traffic past the shopping center and restaurants thinned out. They were on a two-lane road, traveling alongside the large estates of the wealthy, the lots growing larger, until they came to farmlands.

The sun had already set, the days getting shorter. The stars glittered brightly in the sky. Julianna could see the Big Dipper, or was it the Little Dipper? She always got them confused. It was hard to believe they were so close to the city.

She leaned her head against the cool glass of the window and closed her eyes, the car ride lulling her gently to sleep.

Suddenly she heard her mother cry out and opened her eyes in time to see headlights, very bright headlights, directly in front of them.

"Oh my God! He's in the wrong lane!" her mother screamed.

Julianna's father swerved the car to the right, trying desperately to miss the oncoming vehicle, but it was too late. Tires squealed as car slammed into car. The horrifying sound of metal on metal screamed into the still night air.

And then they were rolling, rolling, rolling. Julianna couldn't utter a sound as she was slammed into the roof of the car, back against the seat, then forward against the back her mother's seat in front of her. She desperately tried to find something to hold on to as she squeezed her eyes tightly shut and willed it all to go away.

Then as suddenly as it began it was all over. Julianna opened her eyes and suddenly found her voice. "Daddy!" she screamed. "Mom! Mommy!" But the only reply was the sound of her own voice and the pounding of her heart.

"Daddy! Mom!" she screamed again. She was frantic now, screaming in the pitch black of the night. But no one answered.

She frantically tried the door, but it wouldn't budge. Her knees were pressed against the seat unlike they had been before. She tried to unlatch her seatbelt but it wouldn't budge. Julianna screamed and cried until her cries became whimpers and then ceased altogether.

For seventeen hours Julianna was held captive in the car with the bodies of her parents before she was discovered and rescuers could get her out. And when they did she didn't utter a word. In fact, it was a very long time before she spoke again. The trauma of it all was too great for her, the loss too intense. She had gone to live with her maternal grandmother, but her grandmother was in poor health, and while Julianna knew she was loved, she also knew it had not been easy for her grandmother to rearrange her entire life to accommodate her orphaned granddaughter. Her grandmother had never complained, and she had done the best she could, but it had been hard on them both and Julianna somehow felt responsible for being a burden.

With therapy she learned to cope and the pain lessened, but never quite left. She also developed an extreme case of claustrophobia. But the worst part was the loneliness. She thought she could never become too attached to anyone ever again. Life was often cut short and those you loved were gone in an instant. She could never bear that kind of grief again. But she did when she lost Josh, and she vowed to never become so attached to another person that she couldn't imagine her life without them, because quite possibly she would have to do just that.

She would later learn that the driver of the other vehicle had been drunk and came out of the tragedy with barely a scratch. The entire front end of her parents' car had been compressed against the seat, killing them instantly. Everyone said it was a miracle anyone came out of that car alive. To Julianna it was a cruel twist of fate that she had survived.

Chapter 8

Julianna walked purposely down the hall of the Medical Examiner's Office, her head and shoulders erect, her purse clutched to her side. On the outside she appeared confident, but Will watched the tightness of her face, the purse of her lips, and knew that she wasn't as cool as she appeared.

"Are you sure you're okay with this?" he asked her.

"I told you I've seen death before," Julianna reminded him, continuing to stare straight ahead, her expression unchanged.

"I remember what you said," Will replied, and let it drop.

They took the elevator in silence, and when the door opened Julianna seemed rooted to the floor. She stared at the open doors, at the long hallway on the other side, and swallowed.

"You don't have to do this," Will said softly.

"Yes, I do," she replied after hesitating for a breath of a second.

Will stepped out of the elevator and offered his hand to her. She met his eyes as she took his hand. "It was my parents." Her voice was so quiet that Will almost didn't hear her, and wouldn't have had he not been looking directly at her.

He waited, seeing if she would offer more, but she didn't. "I know," he said gently.

"Why didn't you say something?" she asked him.

"I thought it was something you needed to tell me on your own. I know your background, Julianna. It's my job."

She nodded absently, her thoughts a million miles away. "Yes, of course you would. And you probably know about Josh, too."

Will nodded. "Look, Julianna. I know you feel some sort of obligation toward Jackson Mattice, but he wasn't your father, and you do *not* have to do this. In fact, I would highly recommend that you don't."

Julianna didn't reply, but she tightened her grip on his hand, squared her shoulders once more and began walking.

When they reached the morgue Will walked in ahead of her, giving her hand a squeeze. "I'm right here," he reminded her.

Julianna was trying very hard to be strong about this and she kept reminding herself that it was just a body, an empty shell. This was not Jack. He was in a better place now. She hoped. With all the crap Jack had pulled who knew? Even still, she wanted to turn and run away from this place and go back to Will's apartment where she felt safe.

Will pressed a button on the wall and a young blond guy with a ponytail walked out into the room where Julianna and Will stood.

"Hey, Nick," Will greeted him. "This is Julianna Brennan. Is everything set?"

"Sure is, Delaney. Haven't seen you in a while – how's it going? Nice to meet you, Ms. Brennan," Nick greeted them in a thick New York accent, his words tumbling out like someone who had indulged in a bit too much caffeine.

"It's going," Will answered.

"Something always is," Nick replied as he started walking ahead of them. He turned around and addressed Julianna. "You ready?"

She nodded gravely as they reached the body of Jackson Mattice. She thought the room would be full of sheet-covered bodies resting on metal tables like they showed on television, but Jackson's was the only body in the room and everything was covered from the neck down.

Keeping a distance, she looked down into the face of the man who had been her mentor and her friend. *Why did you do this, Jack?* Julianna thought. *Why did you think involving me in this was okay?*

She was not about to shed tears for this man. She was pissed. No, she was angry, but not necessarily pissed. Anger was better. Pissed meant she had to do something about it. She was also confused as hell, hurt, and scared. Yes, definitely scared.

She stared at his face and suddenly felt the room begin to spin around her and her legs started to sway. She closed her eyes and took a deep breath, then looked down at Jack's face once more. Will gave her hand a gentle squeeze. He hadn't said anything the entire time they had been there. In fact, no one had. They were giving her time to say goodbye. But the clenching of his jaw and the stormy look in his eyes spoke volumes.

It was Julianna who finally broke the silence. "That man is not Jackson Mattice," she said.

Chapter 9

"Are you sure?"

Julianna had lost count of how many times Will had asked her this and her answer hadn't changed. "I'm sure, Will. Absolutely, without a doubt, willing-to-bet-my-life-on-it sure. Like I told you in the morgue, Jack has a scar above his right eyebrow."

"From a childhood run-in with a barbed wire fence, I know, I know." Will replied irritably. "Shit. Shit!" He slammed his hand on the steering wheel of the Tahoe and started the engine. "So, not only does he almost get you killed, but he gets his brother killed. That son of a bitch is unbelievable.

He'd better be glad he wasn't standing beside Cordova in that alley, because I might have had to waste two bullets on both their sorry asses."

Julianna was silent as they drove. Jackson Mattice had been her friend and he had clearly betrayed her. Long gone was the feeling that he must have had a good reason. She didn't care what his reason was at this point. The man in the morgue was obviously his brother Ray. She had never met Ray so she was surprised to see how eerily alike they looked, but even with the pallor of death she knew that wasn't Jack. The scar above the eyebrow just clinched it. But they were similar enough that anyone who didn't know Jackson as well as she did would be fooled.

They stopped at a red light and Julianna watched a homeless woman pushing a shopping cart at the crosswalk in front of them. The woman looked like a fish trying to swim upstream. She seemed to be going in the completely opposite direction from the rest of the world, as they ignored her and pushed past her hurriedly, impatient to get to their destination. Julianna knew how she felt for she, too, felt like a salmon swimming upstream. Nothing was as it seemed, and there seemed to be more questions than answers, questions which were growing by the minute.

"What is it like, killing someone?" she blurted out.

The question took Will by surprise. "It sucks," he stated simply.

"But it's easy? With someone like Rico Cordova, I mean."

"No, it's far from easy, Julianna, but I did what I had to do. He was going to kill you. I told him to drop his weapon and he went toward you. I had a shot and I took it. That guy was bad news. He's a suspected murderer with a rap sheet a mile long, but because of who his uncle is he was still on the street. I'm not a cold-blooded killer, Jule, but when an innocent civilian is involved I do what I have to do. It's my job."

"That simple?" She asked.

"Yes, it's that simple."

"I wasn't completely honest before. I never actually saw my parents' bodies after they died. They got me out of the car first. I wish I had seen them."

"No you don't."

"I do. Maybe then I could get over it, move past it. I lied that night, told my parents I had already done my book report. I hadn't. If I had just taken the time to do it we would have been later going to the restaurant and they wouldn't be dead."

"For God's sake, Julianna – you were a kid! It wasn't your fault. It was the fault of that scumbag drunk driver."

"I know. I sometimes just wonder..."

"Well don't," he interrupted her. "You can't go back in time and change things. It happened. Shit happens to good people every day. It sucks. It's life." Will's voice had taken a hard edge, and Julianna sensed he wasn't only referring to her past, but to his own as well.

"You're right, but my parents didn't deserve for someone to cut their life short, and neither did Jack's brother," she said.

"Jackson Mattice knew the consequences of dealing with Victor Ciccone, Julianna. He made choices that have put everyone around him in danger. He's going to have to pay for that, one way or another."

"I know, but that doesn't change the fact that Ray is dead. He has a family. He had a life. He still didn't deserve to die."

"You're right. He didn't. But he's gone now and we have to deal with what's at hand. I have to find Jackson Mattice and find out what's so damn important that people are willing to kill for it. I also have to find out how the hell his brother ended up in Chinatown when he lives in Miami."

Will parked the Tahoe at Federal Plaza, but didn't make a move to get out. "Julianna," he began, turning toward her. "I don't know what's going to happen with this case and I might not have a job when we get in there. I haven't exactly been 'by the book' on this one. They're going to take you to a safe house. I'm not sure what they're going to do with me yet, but I'm going to fight like hell to keep my job because right now that's the only way I know to keep you safe. I'm sorry if I jeopardized your safety by becoming personally involved in this."

"I won't go anywhere without you, Will."

"Yeah, you will, if that's what it takes, because your being safe is the priority here. Once we walk in there this is out of my hands."

"I know," she said tightly, looking straight ahead. There was so much more she wanted to say, more she wanted to ask. She was embarrassed by the way she had practically thrown herself at him this morning. She felt so damn needy, and that was unlike her. She had vowed never to need anyone again because once you did, once you let them have that power, they disappeared from your life and you were left trying to gather up the scattered pieces of your heart.

She also wanted to tell him how sorry she was. Sorry that Jackson had gotten them all into this mess. Sorry that he might lose his job. Sorry that she couldn't bear the thought of spending a moment away from him because she was terrified and just wanted to hide under the covers like a child until this all went away.

But she didn't say any of those things as they each grabbed their duffels and she followed him into the building.

Chapter 10

"We have a problem," Will announced to Special Agent Paul Olsen as he tossed his duffel bag down beside his own desk and took off his leather jacket, tossing it across the back of the chair.

"No, you have the problem. Simpson has been storming the building looking for your sorry ass. Where've you been, man? I called you over an hour ago."

"M.E.'s office," Will supplied offhandedly he flipped through stacks of messages that had been tossed onto the pile of paperwork that littered his desk.

"What?" Olsen asked incredulously. "Simpson is already threatening to tear you a new one. You were supposed to come straight here."

"Yeah, well don't be so quick to judge. Turns out, Jackson Mattice has a barely perceptible scar above his right eyebrow. The poor man lying on a slab at the M.E.'s office – no scar. *Not* Jackson Mattice."

"Shit."

"Exactly."

"The brother?" Olsen asked.

"Ray Mattice. Younger brother by a year."

"Shit." Olsen said again.

"Yeah. So that means Jackson Mattice is still out there. He could be long gone by now, especially with his brother's passport."

"We'll need to get someone in touch with the wife, see what she knows. Hell, does the woman even know her husband is dead? We'll have to get someone down to Florida."

Julianna, who had been standing there quietly in an attempt to remain unobtrusive, suddenly spoke. "Ray has money – a lot of it – which means if Jack is using Ray's identity he will have plenty of resources with which to disappear. And maybe Ray's wife is even helping him. Her name is Carla. Jack talked about them having a house on the water, but I'm not sure where exactly."

"I'll call the Miami field office – get someone on it," Agent Olsen said, picking up the phone.

Will nodded and turned his attention to Julianna. "Would you like some coffee or anything?" he asked her. Will thought she looked a little flushed realized that she was probably exhausted. She had, after all, just spent the last several days in bed recovering. This was too much for her so soon. He looked through his desk and finally found a granola bar, which he offered to her.

"Do you have hot tea?" she asked, waving away the offer of the granola bar.

"I'm sure I can find some. Here, sit down," Will said, holding onto the back of his desk chair.

Julianna gratefully sank down onto the chair as Will left the room in search of tea. She half listened to Agent Olsen talking to the person on the other end as she closed her eyes and let her mind wander. She was suddenly really, really tired.

"So, how are you holding up?" Agent Olsen asked, startling her. She hadn't realized he had ended his call and had swiveled his chair around to face her.

"I'm okay. I really appreciate you getting my stuff. You did a great job getting exactly what I needed."

"Glad to help, but it was mostly your landlady who gathered everything up." Olsen continued to look at her as if he wanted to ask her something, but he didn't.

Julianna just nodded, not sure of what else to say. She clasped her hands nervously and was relieved when Will returned a few seconds later with two steaming cups. He handed the tea to her and kept the coffee for himself.

"I took the liberty of adding some sugar and milk, just the way you like it," Will told her.

Julianna looked up at him with surprise, wondering how he knew what she liked in her tea. "How did you know?"

Will just shrugged and concentrated on chugging his own coffee.

Will's desk was fairly utilitarian. Nothing on it seemed personal, whereas the other desks in the vicinity had photos of children, a spouse, pets or any combination of the three.

As she looked around the room she noticed a bulletin board on which were pinned various photographs. She got up from the chair and walked over to it as she noticed with surprise that some of the photos were of her. There were also some with various other men she didn't recognize, and as her eyes traveled across the board, she noticed that several were of a crime scene. It took a moment for her to recognize that they were of Ray

Mattice, and upon that realization her eyes widened and she took a step backward, looking quickly away from his photos. His resemblance to Jack was eerily uncanny, and the thought that he had died in place of his brother made her stomach lurch. What was he even doing in New York when he lived in Florida? Jack said that he never saw his brother due to some falling out they had years ago. Could Jack have lured him here to take the fall? If so, he was not the person she had known and cared about. It had become quite apparent that nothing about Jackson Mattice was what she thought.

She continued looking at the various photos, pointedly avoiding the crime scene photos of Ray Mattice, when something else caught her eye and she stepped closer to study the picture on the board.

"What is it?" Will asked, walking up beside her.

"I think I recognize this man," she replied incredulously. "Who is he?"

"We think he works for Victor Ciccone," Agent Olsen said. "Where have you seen him?"

"I'm not sure...somewhere. I don't know," Julianna wracked her brain trying to remember.

"Do you remember if you ever saw him talking with Jackson Mattice?" Will asked.

Julianna shook her head slowly. "No. It seems like it was outside, on the street maybe. Somewhere. I see so many people, come in contact with so many people every day. I can't remember specifics, just that his face is familiar."

"Any trace on the call regarding the hit?" Will asked Olsen.

"Nope. Throwaway cell, but the caller was male, which should really help us narrow things down," Olsen stated sarcastically. "Here's the transcript of the call," he said, handing Will a piece of paper.

Will silently read the transcript.

Caller: "I need to speak to an agent on the Jackson Mattice case."
Agent: "This is Special Agent Hanover. How can I help you?"
Caller: "I don't have much time here because I'm standing in quicksand, so to speak, but I have reason to believe that Special Agent William Delaney is in danger, as is the girl he's protecting – Julianna Brennan. We're talking mob here, so tell Simpson to get them into protective custody immediately."
Agent: "What is your name, sir?"
Caller: "You know I can't tell you that, Agent. Just pass the information along to Simpson as soon as we hang up."
Agent: "Sir, I'm going to need more information. Don't hang up."
Caller: "What do you want me to do, hand it to you on a silver platter? That is all the information I have right now. Do what you want with it, but take it seriously. Victor Ciccone never plays games. He's out for revenge on his nephew's death."
Agent: "Sir, how did you come across this information?"
Caller: "I came across this information because I am the one who is supposed to carry out the hit." (end call)

"So, the caller uses the phrase 'supposed to'. Doesn't mean he's going to actually do it," Will said.

"Doesn't mean he won't either. You wanna take that chance?" Olsen asked.

"Not with her," Will replied, nodding his head toward Julianna. "But I'm not about to go into hiding. We haven't even come close to unraveling this thing."

"What are we having – a party?" a voice boomed from behind, startling the three of them. "Delaney, where the hell have you been? I had Olsen call you in almost two hours ago! My office. Now." The man stormed away from them as quickly as he had arrived.

Will turned to Julianna. "Will you be okay here for a little while?"

"I think the better question is, will *you* be okay in there with *him*?" She arched an eyebrow, her expression one of concern.

"Don't worry about me. His bark is bigger than his bite. But if anyone asks, you've been staying – "

"With my friend Allegra, of course." Julianna finished.

Will turned to Agent Olsen. "I think we'd better get her official statement and I think you'd better be the one to do it."

Agent Olsen nodded. "Absolutely, and if you still have a job after Simpson finishes with you, you can take out your frustrations on Victor Ciccone. They're bringing him in."

Will swallowed the last of his coffee and tossed the empty Styrofoam cup into the trash can beside his desk. "Good," he replied, stepping over to Julianna and squatting down in front of her. "Are you going to be okay?" he asked, reaching out to move a lock of her hair off her face.

"She'll be fine," Agent Olsen said tightly.

"I'll be fine," she agreed, giving him a small smile. "Good luck in there."

Will sighed and stood up. "Yeah, I'll need it."

Chapter 11

"What the hell were you thinking?" Special Agent in Charge Walter Simpson boomed for at least the tenth time. His salt and pepper hair had begun to recede years earlier, making him appear older than his fifty-four years. "You're one of my best agents and you go all renegade on me!"

Will had gone over the details of the case with his superior several times, deciding that honesty was probably the best policy here. He had made the decisions to pursue the case in his own way, and yeah, he probably *had* gone 'all renegade', as SAC Simpson had accused. But at the end of the day he knew he had done the right thing under the circumstances. At least he hoped so. He was fully prepared to accept the consequences of his actions, but he hoped it wouldn't come to that, because if it did he was still going to work this case, badge or no badge.

"I was *thinking* that I had to protect Julianna Brennan, which is exactly what I did!" Will shot back. "Look, we can go round and round about what a renegade I was, how I screwed up and got too involved, but the fact of the matter is that I did my job. I kept her safe and I'm progressing with the investigation. Jackson Mattice is out there somewhere and he has the answers. If you'll put me back on the case I can find him and get to the bottom of this."

"As you well know, Delaney, there's a hit out on not only you, but on Julianna Brennan. This is organized crime we're dealing with, so she's going to a safe house."

"Fine, then I'll go with her and work the case from there."

"No, you won't. You're going to a different safe house, far, far away from Ms. Brennan. And by the way, you're off the case. Olsen can handle it from here with Jankowski and Rodriguez."

"With all due respect..."

"You know I hate that phrase, Delaney," Simpson interrupted. "It's usually followed by a complete *lack* of respect."

Will took a deep breath and weighed his statement carefully. "You're right, sir. I mean absolutely no disrespect. I just feel that it would be in the best interest of this case if I stay actively involved. I have already put weeks' worth of work into this, and I know the players inside and out. If you want to put Jankowski and Rodriguez on it I think that would be beneficial, but please, sir, I'm asking you to not remove me from the case. I am an asset and you can't afford to lose me. Not now."

SAC Simpson was quiet for a few moments. He took off his glasses and rubbed his eyes wearily. "Don't make me regret this, Delaney."

Will waited while his superior gathered his thoughts. It seemed like an eternity before Simpson spoke again.

"First of all, I want this by the book, you understand?"

"Yes, sir," will agreed.

"And second, you will not be accompanying Ms. Brennan to the safe house." Simpson looked pointedly at Will, his eyes narrowed.

"Sir," Will began.

Simpson held up a hand to stop him from continuing. "This is non-negotiable. You are getting personally involved in this case and it has clearly clouded your judgment. Ms. Brennan will be going to a safe house with Jankowski and Rodriguez, and you will be working from an undisclosed location, the details of which we will have to figure out."

"Yes, sir," Will agreed. As long as Julianna was safe he could handle the rest. He knew Simpson was correct and that his attraction to Julianna was clouding his judgment. He couldn't take that risk with her. He would have to trust that the other agents would keep her safe.

"You do anything else to jeopardize this or any other case, Delaney, and you're out of here, you understand?"

"Yes, sir, and thank you, sir."

Simpson waved his hand, "Don't thank me, Delaney. Just do your job."

"I will, sir."

"I assume we've gotten Ms. Brennan's official statement?"

"Agent Olsen is working on it now."

"When he finishes up I want you both in there with Ciccone, then you're going to say your goodbyes to Ms. Brennan."

Chapter 12

Agents Delaney, Olsen and Simpson walked down several hallways and corridors until they came to the interrogation room.

"Did you get a statement from her?" Their boss demanded as they walked.

"Yes. I just finished up," Olsen told him.

"Good, we don't need that hanging over our heads. Not with Ciccone in there demanding some answers as to why his nephew was supposedly shot in cold blood. Cold blood my ass. I don't need to remind you two that this is going to be high profile, what with Ciccone being in all the papers these days."

"We know, sir. It won't be a problem," Will answered.

"Has she given you any answers about the memory card, Agent Olsen?"

"No sir. Nothing other than the photos Agent Delaney discussed with her already – the ones from the Mayor's Ball. I had her look through them again and we still haven't found anything unusual."

"Did you get the statement I faxed over this morning?" Will asked.

"Yeah, yeah, I got it. I just thought she might have *remembered* something later," Simpson said sarcastically.

Will ignored his remark, but Paul spoke. "She's not like that, sir. We watched her for three weeks. She doesn't know anything, trust me."

"Trust you? *Trust* you?" The only thing I trust is results, and so far I haven't seen any. You two have screwed up this case from day one. I want you to get your collective ass in there and get some answers!" Simpson demanded, indicating the interrogation room.

"Call it," Paul said before Will opened the door to the interrogation room.

"Bad cop," Will answered irritably.

"You always are," Paul remarked as he followed Will into the room.

***

"Victor Ciccone!" Will loudly greeted the infamous mob lord as he stormed into the room and slapped a tape recorder down onto the table. Ciccone looked smug as he eyed the recorder, but he appeared much older and weary than the pictures which had graced the newspapers recently depicted.

Paul, in his role as the good cop, took the chair at the end of the table where the attorneys usually sat, except in this case there would be no attorney as Ciccone had specifically denied his rights to one.

Will took the chair directly across from Ciccone and clicked on the tape recorder. "It's Thursday, February the tenth, eleven thirty-two a.m.," he stated in a semi-bored tone, consulting his watch for the time.

"This is Special Agent William Delaney, and also present is Special Agent Paul Olsen. We are questioning Victor

Salvatore Ciccone." Will turned toward Ciccone. "Will you please state your name for the record?"

"Why?" Ciccone answered. "You just did."

"Because I told you to."

"Of all the...oh, fine. My name is Victor Salvatore Ciccone," Ciccone boomed loudly.

Will continued, "Mr. Ciccone, will you please state for the record that you have denied counsel for this questioning?"

"I have denied counsel for this questioning," Ciccone repeated, sounding bored.

"Mr. Ciccone, did you hire someone to kill Jackson Mattice?" Will asked.

"Yes," Ciccone stated simply.

Will looked quickly up at Ciccone, his shock at the quick admission evident, but he held onto his composure.

"Is this the man you hired? Will asked, slapping a photo of Ethan Fray, who they believed had hired the hit, down onto the table in front of Ciccone.

"Could be, could be not. I don't generally get headshots of my employees."

"Cut the bullshit, Ciccone," Will said, his voice low. "Is this the man you hired? Yes or no?"

"As I just stated, I. Do. Not. Know. It might be. It might not be. You would have to ask my nephew Rico who he hired. But now you *can't,* can you?"

Will ignored Ciccone's last comment and moved on, "Why did you place a hit on Jackson Mattice?"

"He has something of mine. I wanted it back," he stated simply, his large stubby hands clasped together on the table.

"If he had something of yours that you wanted back why would you have him killed? Is this the usual way you collect your belongings?"

"Usual way, there is no usual way. We don't follow a guidebook, agent. I will have to check Barnes and Noble, but I'm pretty sure there is no *Strong-arm Collections for Dummies.*" Ciccone laughed at his own joke, the sound loud and arrogant.

"Mattice was weak," he continued. "He tells me about this woman who works for him. Tells me she has my property for safekeeping in case something should happen to him. I don't care for scumbags who don't take responsibility. I also don't care for liars. He needed to be eliminated. The woman would probably agree," he reasoned, shrugging his shoulders.

"Did you order a hit on the woman...Julianna Brennan?" Will asked.

"No, of course not. She's a woman, I thought she'd be easy. I didn't need to waste money on her so I just sent my nephew, Rico, to rough her up a little. He's a babbo, but what can I say, he's my nephew, he's family."

"He was going to kill her," Will stated calmly, but with anger clearly visible in his voice.

"He just got a little rough," Ciccone shrugged.

"He was going to *kill* her," Will repeated.

"She didn't give him what he asked for. He has a temper," Ciccone stated simply.

"So do I, Mr. Ciccone," Will agreed, staring him in the eye.

"You...you...barbarian," he spat, "You didn't have to kill him."

"Yes, I did," Will shrugged.

"My sister Teresa, she's all torn up about it. I do what I have to do to vindicate Rico's death," Ciccone stated, staring back at Will.

"And what does that mean?" Will demanded.

"You ever read the Bible, agent?"

"What are you saying, Ciccone?"

"I'm asking if you ever read the Bible."

"Get to the point, Ciccone. I'm not playing games with you, you scumbag."

"Matthew 5:38 - 'An eye for an eye.' It's right there in the Bible," Ciccone stated.

"I believe the entire quote is closer to this," Will declared, his gaze even with Ciccone's. "'You have heard that it was said, An eye for an eye, and a tooth for a tooth. But I say to you, do not resist him who is evil; but whoever slaps you on your right cheek, turn to him the other also.'"

"Don't think for a minute that I haven't heard that one before, Ciccone. Not that it really matters; I don't think we came here to quote Bible verses to each other."

"No, but it's something for you to think about."

"Let's cut the cryptic bullshit, Ciccone. What do you want me to think about?" Will asked, clearly weary of the way the questioning was going.

"An eye for an eye. You killed my nephew, Mr. Delaney. I can't let that go without punishment."

"Oh, I see how you're going to play it. Okay, punishment, fine. What do you want?"

"It's not what I *want*, *Agent* Delaney. It's simply vindication for my sister, whose child was taken from her."

"Your sister's *child,* who was 38 years old by the way, was a known criminal with a rap sheet longer than the GWB."

"Maybe so, but that makes no difference to my sister. We all pay for our sins, *agent.* My nephew paid for his sins with his life, just as will you."

"And what's that supposed to mean?" Will asked calmly.

"It means I had a little nest egg," Ciccone said cryptically.

"You've hired a hit on me."

"Something like that."

"Do you realize how much trouble you're in, Mr. Ciccone?" Will could not believe how willingly this man admitted his crimes.

"Of course I do, agent. It doesn't matter. I'm old, I'm broke, I've got a bad heart and I'm dying of cancer. Might as well go out with a bang!" he said, slapping his fist against his palm, his eyes wide.

Will got up and began to pace the room, thinking, as Ciccone sat there calmly, his meaty arms folded across his massive chest.

"So where does Julianna Brennan fit into this, Ciccone? My sources say that a hit has been put out on her as well."

"I don't know nothin' about that," he answered defiantly.

"Oh really? And why should I believe you? It seems like you've got your name written all over this case."

"Why would I lie to you, agent? I have nothing to lose. I've already told you everything else. Obviously I'll be going to prison, where I will no doubt die before the year is up. There's no reason for me to lie. That woman is nothing to me, but you'd better make sure she's not pulling the wool over *your* eyes too, agent."

"She wasn't *nothing* three days ago, Mr. Ciccone. She was very much a part of your plan to get a memory card back, which is what we're talking about here, right? Let's cut through the crap, Ciccone. Why the sudden change of heart?"

"Think what you will, young man. I have nothing to hide. I'm an old man and I'm tired of playing the game so I'm throwing in the proverbial towel. Happens to the best of us, I suppose," he shrugged, then added, "It's always such a shame when the life is snuffed out of one so young."

"You're tired of playing games, huh? That's bullshit, Ciccone, and you know it. You *live* to play the game."

"I just love watching people squirm, agent, especially when it's justified."

"Okay, let me get this all straight," Will began, ignoring Ciccone's last comment. "You hired a hit on Jackson Mattice. You hired a hit on Julianna Brennan, and now you've hired a revenge hit on me. Is that correct? It's been a busy week for you, hasn't it Ciccone?"

"No busier than usual, but no, I did not hire a hit on Julianna Brennan. On you and Mattice, yes, but not the girl. Good try, though."

"Well, *someone* did!" Will observed.

"Wasn't me. You should check your sources more carefully, Mr. Delaney."

"Call off the hit on the girl, Ciccone," Will demanded, leaning down into Ciccone's face and grabbing him by the collar of his shirt.

"You can't call off a hit, Mr. Delaney, especially one that you didn't contract in the first place," Ciccone calmly retorted, his face growing red as Will tightened his hold.

"Delaney!" Paul warned. "I think Mr. Ciccone has had enough for the time being."

Will let go of Ciccone's shirt, but his rage didn't subside. He wanted to throw Ciccone through the two-way glass that separated them from his boss and whoever else was looking on.

"You should listen to your partner, *agent*. He seems to have more sense than you have, especially in the area of women. Do you always take your work to bed with you or is Ms. Brennan a special case? If I were her I'd get as far away from you as possible. I can't guarantee that she won't get caught in any crossfire. You understand, *agent*?"

"You leave Julianna Brennan out of this, Ciccone, or you *will* go to your grave regretting the day you ever crossed my path." Will was truly afraid that if he didn't leave the room he would kill Victor Ciccone with his bare hands, so he shoved his chair backward against the wall and stormed out of the room, leaving Paul to finish the interrogation.

"What the hell are you doing storming out of there like that?" SAC Simpson demanded as he met Will in the hall. "You pull another stunt like that and I'll pull your ass right off of this case!"

"The hell you will!" Will yelled. "I am *not* leaving this case!"

"You're too close to this, Delaney. Don't think we didn't all see you lose it when he started talking about the Brennan woman. You're so far out of bounds on this that you've crossed more lines than a 3-year-old's crayon." Simpson was clearly pissed, but Will was even more so.

"Send her to a safe house. I won't see her again until after this case is closed."

"That's the first sensible thing you've said, Delaney. Look, you've got to play the rest of this by the book. I've got a boss to answer to also, so you're putting my ass on the line, too. You're a good agent, one of my best, and until now you've never done anything to disappoint me. You can work the case from a safe house."

Paul suddenly came out of the interrogation room. "He's not talking. He clammed up the second you walked out the door."

"I'm not going to a safe house, Simpson. I'm staying on this case and I can't do a damn thing from a safe house and you know it."

"There's still the matter of Julianna Brennan," Paul interrupted, reminding Simpson. He maintains he doesn't have a hit on her, but the anonymous caller contradicts that."

"So who do we believe – the anonymous caller or Ciccone?" Will asked. "I don't buy it one bit that Ciccone doesn't have it out for her, but I'm still not sure why he'd lie about it when he admitted to hiring the hit on Jackson Mattice."

"And you," Simpson reminded him.

"So then who's got the contract out on her if not Ciccone?"

"Don't know, but we're going to play it safe. Jankowski and Rodriguez will take Ms. Brennan to a safe house out of town," Simpson said, looking pointedly at Will.

"And I'm going to find Jackson Mattice," Will returned.

Chapter 13

"I don't want to leave you, Will," Julianna pleaded after he told her what was happening.

"It won't be for long, I promise," he told her, hoping he could keep that promise. "I won't see you for a while and they aren't going to tell me where you are," he admitted. "It wouldn't be safe and Simpson won't want me to know…" his voice trailed off as he saw the tears in her eyes. He wrapped her in his arms and held her there for a very long time, feeling like this might be the last time he ever saw her.

"I'm scared, Will," she spoke in a very soft voice as she clung to him.

"I know you are, Jule. I am too," he admitted.

"I'm afraid for you. Please be careful."

"It's going to be okay," he said, reaching down to take her face in his hands as he looked into her eyes. "I promise. I'm going to do everything in my power to get to the bottom of this as quickly as possible." He leaned down and kissed her gently on the lips. For all too brief a moment the world seemed to stop spinning and time stood still.

He wrapped her in his arms, holding her tightly to him, praying it wasn't for the last time, memorizing her scent, the way she felt against him, the sound of her breathing. "I never meant to fall in love with you," he breathed into her hair.

She held onto him tighter, tears falling onto his shirt.

There was a soft knock on the door, and then Paul came in. "It's time, Delaney."

He took the duffel bag out of her hand and carried it for her as they walked down to the waiting agents who would take her to the safe house.

As the van pulled away Julianna looked back as Will's form became smaller and smaller. He stood in the middle of the parking garage, hands in his pockets, watching her leave. She pressed her hand up against the dark tint of the glass, but he didn't wave back.

The van finally turned the corner out into the New York City traffic and Will was gone. Julianna had never felt so alone in her life.

Chapter 14

As he watched her leave, Will felt a lump in his throat and wondered if he would ever see her again. He started to head back upstairs to his office but as he stood there waiting for the elevator he changed his mind and walked to his truck instead.

Pulling his cell phone out of his pocket, he called upstairs to his office and spoke into the phone, "Paul, I'm leaving for the day. Tell Simpson thanks but no thanks on the safe house. I'll be fine. And call me after you talk to Florida regarding Carla Mattice."

"Sure, Will," Paul replied. "We're going to catch these guys, you know."

"Yeah, I just hope it's not too late when we do," Will replied, his voice low.

"Keep your guard up, Will. You really should have taken Simpson's advice about that safe house," he admonished.

"Thanks, I'll consider it," Will replied before hanging up.

As Will pulled out of the garage, he headed south on Lafayette Street, then turned left onto Duane. As he adjusted his rearview mirror, he noticed a silver Porsche 911 Turbo following closely behind him. He felt paranoid for doing so, but he changed lanes, then again, pulling in front of a city bus. The Porsche followed closely behind. Okay, he thought to himself. Maybe I'm not so paranoid.

Will followed Duane Street into Centre but instead of turning left onto Canal, he turned right, the Porsche hot on his trail.

Traffic. Will was suddenly stuck. There was nowhere else to go so he just sat there, watching the Porsche in the rearview mirror, tapping his fingers impatiently on the steering wheel.

The driver of the Porsche blew his car's horn and flashed the headlights. On. Off. On. Off. Will continued to watch in the rearview mirror. "What the hell?" he mumbled aloud.

The traffic began to move again. Will turned down the next street and parked in front of a row of brownstones. The Porsche pulled in behind him and Will watched as a familiar figure unfolded himself from the car. Gun in hand, he walked toward the passenger side of Will's Tahoe. Will motioned for him to get inside.

Will turned to his passenger. "What took you so long?"

Chapter 15

Special Agent Leo Jankowski watched Julianna in the rearview mirror as they drove silently toward the safe house.

"How far away is the safe house?" Julianna asked.

"Not too far," Special Agent Isabel Rodriguez answered.

As they drove, Julianna watched the city disappear and suburbia surround her. She wondered what would happen to her when this was all over, assuming she was still *alive* when this was all over. When she had told Will goodbye she had been terrified. But now she just felt numb and the houses out the window of the van seemed very surreal. To think that people were inside them living normal lives was completely foreign to her. When would *her* life ever be normal and not full of loss and loneliness?

Completely lost in thought, Julianna was startled when Special Agent Jankowski spoke. "We should be there in about ten minutes," he informed her meeting her eyes in the rearview mirror.

True to his word, Jankowski pulled into the driveway of a normal looking house about ten minutes later. Julianna had expected a safe house to look a bit more...industrial, but it didn't. It looked like someone's house.

"Home, sweet home. For now anyway," Agent Rodriguez said.

The agents cleared the house, making sure nothing had been compromised, and showed Julianna to a small bedroom in the middle of the house.

"We'll need to go through your bag and purse," Agent Rodriguez stated. "Do you have on you or in your possession a cell phone, laptop computer, iPad? Anything that accesses the internet or a mobile network?"

"No, nothing. Just my clothes and toiletries in the duffel and whatever is in my purse, but I don't have any of those things."

Nodding, Special Agent Rodriguez proceeded to place the duffel onto the bed and quickly go through it, placing the contents beside the bag as she went. She then moved on to Julianna's purse.

"Everything checks out. There's food in the kitchen, bathroom's across the hall," Rodriguez told her, turning to leave the room.

"Thanks," Julianna said, placing the items back into the duffel bag and her purse. When she was finished she sat down on the bed, the springs creaking, and ran her hands through her hair. It was all so overwhelming and she hated sitting here doing nothing, relying on someone else to figure out this entire mess.

She was suddenly completely and utterly exhausted. *I'll just lie down and close my eyes for a few minutes*, she thought. Within seconds she was fast asleep.

Chapter 16

"Everything was falling into place. Now that Will knew Julianna was in the capable hands of Agents Jankowski and Rodriguez he could concentrate on finding Jackson Mattice. He thought he'd put on a decent performance for everyone and no one was the wiser. They'd all unknowingly played their parts in the exact direction he'd wanted them to. Now the rest was up to him.

Olsen had called him with the news that Carla Mattice was alive and well in Miami. To their trained eyes she hadn't seemed all that shocked to discover her husband was dead when the agents from the Miami Field Office questioned her. They were looking into recent bank transactions and financial records to see if they could get a pinpoint on Jackson Mattice's whereabouts. "Carla Mattice might not know where exactly he is, but she's definitely funding his disappearance," Olsen had said.

"And there's a yacht," he continued. It's a seventy-two footer named the *Carla Ray*. Still trying to get a location on where it's supposed to be docked, but I'd bet my next paycheck it's not there."

"Want me to notify The Coast Guard and the Mexican authorities?" Will asked.

"Already done," Olsen answered. "The Bahamas, too, but realistically he could be headed to South America."

"Or he could be right in our own back yard."

Chapter 17

Julianna awoke with a start to the sound of a gunshot. Momentarily disoriented, she realized with great relief that it was only a dream. She reached for her watch, which she had laid on a chair beside the bed. The room was almost completely dark, save for a small spot of moonlight which brought a soft glow to the room. It was almost midnight. She had been asleep for hours.

After using the bathroom she went into the living room where Agents Jankowski and Rodriguez were. Rodriguez was reading a book on a digital book reader while Jankowski paced the floor.

"Sleeping Beauty is awake," Jankowski announced.

Without looking up Rodriguez turned off the book reader, set it down on the sofa and stood up. "You must be starving," she said.

"Yeah, I guess I am."

"Come on in the kitchen and let's see what we can find."

Jankowski stayed in the living room while the two women headed to the kitchen.

Rodriguez opened up refrigerator and peered inside. "There are drinks in here – some sodas, water, juice. And there's coffee, of course. As for food there's soup, PB&J, cereal, and I think I saw some of those microwave mac and cheese meals. My kid likes those," she smiled for the first time.

"Thanks. The soup is fine," Julianna said, taking the can off a shelf.

Rodriguez opened a drawer and took out a can opener, handing it to Julianna. "So, have you thought any more about this mystery memory card?" she asked Julianna.

Julianna opened the can and poured the soup into the bowl Rodriguez had set on the counter. "Yes, I've thought about it," she said, sighing. "But I still can't come up with anything."

"Mmmhmmm," Rodriguez said, cocking her head sideways as she studied Julianna.

"Do you think I want to be here? If I knew anything I would have told Agent Delaney or Agent Olsen."

"No, no, I believe you. I just think you might know more than you think you know. People usually do. It's the little things in conversations – the things that make you smack your forehead and realize maybe you had the answer all along."

"Maybe," Julianna answered. "I've replayed every conversation I've had lately with Jackson Mattice, and I can't come up with anything concrete. In fact, very little of what he actually *did* say makes sense to me."

The microwave beeped, indicating the soup was ready. "After you eat something we can go over your statement again, if you're up for it," Rodriguez said.

"I'm up for it," Julianna replied, blowing on the soup before she took a bite.

Chapter 18

"**S**o how'd you convince Simpson to let you hop a plane to Miami?" Olsen asked.

Will switched the phone to his other ear and took a long swig of overpriced airport coffee. "I told him I'd be safer if I got out of town," he laughed.

"I've got a lead on Ethan Fray," Olsen told him. "I'm on my way to check it out with the SWAT team."

"Good luck. I'd love to see us bag a hit man for the most notorious crime family in New York."

"Yeah, so would I. Have a safe flight."

"Will do," Will said, ending the call and swigging the last of the coffee.

Chapter 19

Knocking. Someone was knocking. Julianna opened her sleepy eyes, and turning over saw Agent Rodrigues peek her head inside the bedroom door. "Julianna, Agent Delaney is on the phone for you."

Julianna stretched and got out of bed, glancing at her watch. It was 9:30 a.m. already. She felt stiff and her back ached. In black leggings and a grey t-shirt, she padded barefoot down the hall, smoothing her hair as she followed the agent to the front of the house.

"Agent Delaney?" she answered tentatively when Rodriguez handed the phone to her.

"Hey, how are you holding up?"

"I'm okay. Where are you?"

"I'm boarding a plane to Miami."

In the background Julianna could hear a woman over an intercom announcing a flight boarding. "Did you find Jack?" she asked.

"Not yet, but I'm working on it. I just called to ask you if you know anything about Ray Mattice's yacht."

"Didn't you find Ray's wife?"

"Yeah, but she's been less than forthcoming. I wondered if maybe you had heard Jackson talking about the yacht, where it was docked for one, we would know if she's being honest. The Miami Field Office is convinced she's lying. I haven't talked to her yet. I wanted to get your impressions before I did."

"I think it's called the *Carla Ray*. There's a picture in Jack's office of Jack and Ray standing in front of it. He said it was the last picture he had of him before their falling out."

"Did he ever tell you why they stopped speaking?"

"No, but I assumed it had something to do with money. Jack always seemed bitter about how much money Ray had."

"Hmmm..." Will murmured.

"Does that help?" Julianna asked.

"Everything helps."

Neither said anything for a few seconds. "Will?" Julianna spoke quietly into the phone.

"I'm here." He said crisply, his voice all business.

"I...I wish there was something I could do to help. I feel like there's something I should know, but I can't quite wrap my brain around, you know?"

"Don't worry about it, Julianna. Look, I've got to go," he told her.

She didn't want to hang up the phone. Where was the Will who had held her and told her everything was going to be okay? She wanted to hear that Will's voice before she hung up the phone.

"I miss you," she ventured softly.

"I miss you, too, Jule," he answered, but he sounded distracted and very far away. Then the line disconnected and he was gone.

"You're playing with fire there, girlfriend," Agent Rodriguez said, taking the phone from Julianna's hand.

"I know," Julianna sighed. "I'm beginning to think I'm making a huge fool of myself."

"The heart wants what it wants," Rodriguez shrugged.

"What, no reprimanding me for falling for the knight in shining armor, Agent Rodriguez?"

"Isabel," Rodriguez said quietly. "Just don't tell Jankowski I said you could call me that," she said rolling her eyes toward the living room. "And no, I'm not going to reprimand you. It happens. I'm just telling you that I can relate."

"Don't tell me you saved some guy in an alley too," Julianna joked.

"Not quite," she said with a small smile. "But I did fall in love with someone I was working a case with. He's NYPD.

"That must have gone over well."

"No one really knew until after the case was over. Just be careful, that's all I'm saying."

"Careful about keeping things quiet, or careful about falling for Agent Delaney?"

"Either. Both. You don't know him very well, do you?"

"Apparently not if you're warning me about him," Julianna replied. "Is there something I should know?"

Rodriguez shrugged. "Not really. There's just talk – that's how it is in the Bureau. We all come from different backgrounds and everyone speculates about people's past. Delaney was a Navy SEAL, from what I hear. Kind of a badass, kind of a ladies' man. I don't know any specifics – this is all just gossip among the boys, you know?"

Julianna chewed on her lower lip. "I'm beginning to get the picture. What happened after he joined the Bureau?"

"Nothing. He does his job, he goes home. Something changed, I guess. He keeps a low profile. Doesn't really fraternize with anyone outside of work, not that many do anyway, but he makes a point not to.

"I'm sure he's a nice guy and all," Rodriguez continued. "Don't let me dissuade you. It's just that I see girls like you all the time. They fall in love with the handsome FBI agent. It's easy to do – hero worship, I mean. He saved you, you're a woman, you want the fairy tale."

"I just want someone who doesn't leave," Julianna said softly.

Rodriguez's face softened. "Yeah, I read your file about your family. I can't imagine not having anyone. I come from a huge Puerto Rican family and my husband is Dominican. When we get together I swear there are *too many of us.*"

"You're very lucky. I'd give anything to have a family – large, small – doesn't matter."

"I am very fortunate. And it will happen for you, Julianna. My advice is to wait it out, see if there's anything there after all this is over with. If so, then trust your heart and don't be afraid to follow it."

Chapter 20
Four weeks earlier...

J ackson Mattice sat at his desk, his fingers flying over the keyboard with absolute certainty. He had been Editor-In-Chief of the New York Chronicle for twelve years now, and was regarded highly by his peers and staff. Over his forty-nine years, he had worked his way up in the newspaper business and knew every in and out of the industry. It thrilled him to go to work each day, now more than ever.

Two years ago his wife of twenty-three years had suddenly filed for divorce and moved in with her much younger lover, whom she had met at the gym where she worked out. The divorce had been messy and Jackson had been required to pay a hefty sum in alimony to her every month, which he resented with a passion. She has the affair and he has to pay – go figure. Clearly she had the better attorney, and he ought to know because he had to pay her also.

He and the former Mrs. Mattice had never had children so now he lived alone, which was fine by him. He would much rather work at the paper every day than go home to a nagging wife.

As he hit the send button on an email, he fingered the envelope that sat on his desk. The envelope contained ten thousand dollars in cash, same amount as last week and the weeks before that. All he had to do was print a simple ad on the front page of the newspaper once a week. It had been an easy way to make that alimony payment every month and had even offered him a few "extras" that he would have never been able to afford on his own. But most of it sat untouched in a safe place, which he had a feeling he would need to access very soon.

It had all started out innocently enough. Most people posted their cryptic little messages in the personals, but if someone wanted it on the front page he was more than willing to take their money under the table.

He had received the first envelope approximately five months earlier in his interoffice mail. The envelope contained two hundred fifty thousand dollars cash and instructions on what to print when, and how to receive future payments of ten thousand dollars each. Each time there would be different instructions and he willingly and carefully followed them. It had been an offer he couldn't refuse, but he had been given the choice, with instructions on how to return the money if he so chose.

He was tired of living paycheck to paycheck and supporting his ex and her boy toy. He envied the life of his brother Ray, who had made his fortune early on in the dot com industry and now spent his days fishing on his boat or lounging poolside at his Miami mansion. Had Ray ever tried to help him out when money was tight? No! In fact, Ray had pointedly *not* helped his older brother, telling Jack that he had gotten himself into the mess with Mona, and he'd just have to bail himself out.

So that was exactly what Jack had decided to do until he started putting two and two together and realized that these ambiguous messages were something far more sinister. Jack had a love for puzzles, and the seemingly innocent ads he printed every week started to pique his curiosity. He had printed them all out and spent days pouring over them at home.

He had a meeting in half an hour and then was getting out of here and calling the FBI. He wasn't sure exactly how much he was going to tell them, because he had, after all, accepted cash under the table for printing these ads, but he knew he needed to tell them something. He also knew he'd end up losing his job over this, and he'd probably have to disappear for a while, too, maybe indefinitely.

Julianna Brennan stuck her head in his door as he was glancing at the clock. "I'm finished editing and uploading the proofs for the museum fundraiser spread," she announced. "I had to do a lot of extra cropping on Eric's shots," she said, referring to their new junior photographer. "He's getting the hang of it, though, and is going to work out fine."

Julianna was very good at her job as the paper's senior photographer, but she also pitched in wherever else she was needed at the small paper. Jack liked her a lot and trusted her implicitly. He found he never had to question her judgment or proof anything she did. She was an asset to the staff. Her only downfall was that she had no personal self-confidence. Where work was concerned she was a piranha, but when it came to personal matters she was shy and reserved. He had tried setting her up on some dates with the few men her age that he knew, but she wasn't interested. As far as he knew, she just went home to her cat every night then came back to work the next day. It didn't seem to be much of a life for a young woman, but Jack minded his own business most of the time.

"If you want, I can take your meeting this afternoon," she offered. "I'm pretty much finished for the day." She twisted her hair up into a knot and secured it with one of those plastic claw things women seemed so fond of using these days.

"Really? I'd hate to make you stay late. Don't you have any plans tonight?" he asked, for once hoping she didn't.

"No, no plans," she admitted. "You know I love my job far too much to clutter it with *plans*," she laughed.

"That would be great, Julianna, if you're sure, of course." He answered, trying not to appear too anxious.

"I'm sure. Go! Get out of here. You've been jumping at the bit all day."

As Julianna turned to walk out the door Jack grabbed the envelope full of cash and stuck it in his briefcase, hurrying out the door.

Chapter 21

"Yes?" the voice answered, ripe with irritation.

"So he called the Feds."

"Yes."

"Not so smart, that newspaper man of yours. I'm going to have to deal with this."

"So deal with it."

"I've got my associate on it. We need a little more time."

"Don't take too long, but find out if he's distributed this information to anyone. And deal with his office and apartment."

"My associate knows what to do. We've got plenty of ears on him."

"Don't call me again until you have something more concrete."

"And don't *you* forget that you're working for *me*."

The line went dead.

Chapter 22

Talking to Agent Rodriguez had left Julianna with more questions than answers. She literally ached for Will, and the feeling of loneliness was overwhelming. She had such strong feelings for him, and she hated to admit it, but she felt even more attracted to him than she had her own husband.

Josh, how she missed him. She immediately chastised herself for even thinking like that, comparing her feelings for Josh to another man. She had loved Josh with everything she had. He had been good to her and had loved her unconditionally, as she had him. Their marriage was short, but filled with many good memories. They had made so many plans for the future – a family being first and foremost on Julianna's mind. Josh had promised her they'd start working on it as soon as he finished his tour. He was just as excited about it as she was.

He had bought them a tiny house in Clarksville, close to Fort Campbell, and had painted the rickety old fence white, just for her. She had always wanted the white picket fence, the rocking chairs, the babies in her lap, the *dream*. It wasn't meant to be.

When she learned that Josh was gone, a part of her died too. She couldn't bear the thought of going on with her life without him. She spent days holed up in her house, lying in bed staring at the walls or watching sad movies. For weeks she couldn't seem to stop crying. Then one day the tears abruptly stopped and she could cry no more. The anger and grief were too much and she felt like she couldn't breathe without the release of tears.

Her mother-in-law tried to get her out of the house, or at least to turn off the sad movies, but Julianna couldn't. She took a small bit of comfort in the fact that there were other people out there who had lost someone and were grieving too, even if they were fictional characters being portrayed by actors.

At the urging of Josh's parents she sold the house, put the furniture in storage, and moved in with them. They and Josh's sisters were all she had, but they were dealing with their own grief. The daily reminders of all she had lost were consuming her and she couldn't function.

It was a Sunday when she packed up her things, told them she needed some time, and moved to New York. Her calls to them had grown farther apart until they rarely spoke. It was a part of her life that she wanted to put behind her.

She had lost the four people in her life who had meant the most to her. Maybe she was meant to be alone. She rarely got close to anyone. She went to work, occasionally went out with friends from work, but didn't try to develop those friendships. She kept everyone at arm's length. Until she met Will Delaney. She had practically thrown herself at him, and he had reciprocated by doing all the right things – holding her the way she longed to be held, kissing her the way she had always dreamed of being kissed, telling her that everything was going to be okay. It had been a very long time since someone had actually been concerned about her, listened to her, and looked at her with the fire of desire in his eyes that Will had when he looked at her.

Hero-worship, as Agent Rodriguez had called it, was definitely clouding her judgment. She needed to get ahold of herself and forget about him. Maybe if he still wanted her after this was all over she'd reconsider, but for now she needed to get her head out of the clouds.

She heard voices in the living room of the safe house and walked in to see Agents Rodriguez and Jankowski shrugging into their coats as two others removed theirs.

"You're leaving?" Julianna asked them.

"We'll be back late tonight," Rodriguez assured her. "These are Special Agents Jane Kilbourne and John Shepherd. They'll take good care of you."

Kilbourne – Julianna remembered that name and this woman with the short, over-processed spikey hair.

Kilbourne saw the look of recognition in Julianna's eyes. "You're looking quite better than the last time I saw you," she said in her clipped British accent.

"Thank you," Julianna replied. She looked at the other agent, John Shepherd. He looked bored as he sat down on the sofa and pulled out his smartphone and began playing solitaire. She saw a look pass between Rodriguez and Jankowski as they noticed it, too.

"Take care of her, guys. We'll see you later, Ms. Brennan," Jankowski said as they closed the door.

Kilbourne sat down in a chair across from the sofa and began to flip through a file folder while Shepherd continued to play solitaire. Julianna noticed a small stack of magazines on a shelf in the corner and picked up a well-worn 2009 issue of *Instyle*. It was either an outdated fashion magazine or 7 copies of *Guns and Weapons for Law Enforcement*.

Jennifer Garner smiled at her from the cover, which promised to double her wardrobe and share 48 of the best-kept beauty secrets – escapism at its best. Julianna grabbed a bottle of water from the refrigerator in the kitchen and took it and the magazine back to her room.

… ARMS OF A STRANGER

Chapter 23

Will boarded the plane from Miami International Airport back to New York. The interview with Carla Mattice had been a total bust and he had a feeling Walter Simpson was going to be furious with him because of it. They had located the yacht, but there was no sign that Jackson Mattice had used it.

He hated to admit that he had been wrong, but he didn't think she knew anything. What he had found out, however, was that Jackson Mattice had called his brother Ray, telling him he was in trouble and needed to get out of town. According to Carla, Ray, hearing a desperation in his brother's voice that he had never heard before, had worried himself sick all night long and had gotten on a plane to New York the next morning. That was the last time she saw him. She claimed Jackson had not contacted her, and her phone records backed that up.

Will grilled her for three hours over every conversation Ray had had with Jackson in the past year, of which there had been few. She didn't know the specifics of the conversation that had ultimately moved Ray to travel to New York, but she knew it had been bad, and that Ray was very afraid for his brother.

Will leaned back in the seat and closed his eyes. Exhaustion was beginning to take its toll on him. He couldn't remember the last time he had the luxury of a full night's sleep. *You'll sleep when this is over, Delaney*, he thought to himself.

Chapter 24

It was late, almost midnight, as Julianna sat in front of the television in the dark, watching reruns of old sitcoms. Agents Kilbourne and Shepherd had told her she could move the small television into her room from the living room. They clearly didn't want her in the same room with them, which was fine with her.

She half listened to the perfectly timed canned laughter, which poured from the screen. Her mind was racing and she felt agitated and helpless. She wanted to *do* something. She felt panicky, claustrophobic, like she needed to get out of the house, but she knew she couldn't. She was beginning to feel like a caged animal and the thought both frightened and irritated her.

Letting her thoughts drift to Will, she wondered where he was and what he was doing. She remembered all too well how his arms felt around her and she longed for them now.

Julianna flicked the off television and got up to put an oversized sweatshirt over the t-shirt she wore. The temperature outside had dropped significantly and the house was drafty and cold. Julianna decided to sleep in the leggings she had worn all day, as well as the sweatshirt and thick socks.

After brushing her teeth in the bathroom across the hall, Julianna slipped under the icy sheets and blankets, her chattering teeth the only noise in the house. How she missed the comforting sound of Bella's purr to lull her to sleep. As lonely as Julianna was, she knew she could always count on the comfort and companionship of her sweet Bella. Curling up into a ball and hugging herself for warmth, Julianna finally fell into a fitful sleep.

Someone was chasing her. She was running, running as fast as she could. She came to a dead end against a brick wall. She felt the cold metal of a gun against her cheek, and saw the eyes of Rico Cordova boring into hers. She struggled to remove herself from his grasp, but he simply sneered at her and grabbed her hair with his other hand, forcing her to hold still as the gun pressed against her cheek.

Suddenly, Rico Cordova turned into Will! No, it couldn't be Will. Why would Will be holding a gun to her? She pleaded with him to let her go. He just smiled and pressed the gun harder against her cheek, not saying a word. She heard a scream, then another. Where was the scream coming from? Then she heard a series of gunshots. She was suddenly falling, falling, falling – down into a large body of water. She tried to struggle to the top, gasping for air. She couldn't breathe! She clamped her mouth tightly shut against the water that threatened to pour in.

Her eyes flew open and sat up in the bed, breathing heavily and trying to shake herself out of the nightmare.

Then she heard it. It hadn't been a dream. Someone was actually screaming! Then there was a crash, and all was once again silent. There was just enough light to barely make out the time on her watch – 3:17 a.m.

Julianna sat there in the dark listening, her heart was beating wildly. She licked her lips, which were trembling and took several silent deep breaths to calm herself.

Julianna didn't know what to do. Should she hide? Go out and investigate? She looked around the room for somewhere to hide. There nothing in here to hide in or under, so she would either have to sit here and wait or leave the room. If she waited and something *was* going on, then she was a sitting duck. She really didn't have a choice, so she got up from the bed and crept quietly to the door, opening it slowly.

The house was deathly quiet and there was a strange odor in the air. She peered around the door, looking both ways, but she didn't see anything unusual. She slipped quietly into the hall, staying close to the wall, in the shadows. Her heart was racing so fast that if there *were* an intruder in the house, he would surely hear it.

She started slowly down the hall, toward the other end of the house where the other bedroom was. Every couple of steps she would stop and listen for any unusual noises. Still, all was quiet. Had she imagined the scream? She didn't think so, but after all, she *had* been dreaming. As afraid as she was, she knew she would have to check it out. She wanted to call out to the agents, but something told her not to.

She was almost to the middle of the house, where the front door and living room were. Suddenly a tall dark figured strode directly toward her! Julianna leaned back against the wall and held her breath. It was dark, but Julianna thought she could see something in his hand. Oh God, she thought. What is happening and where are Shepherd and Kilbourne?

The stranger kept walking. He appeared to be looking directly at her, but as he reached the foyer, he turned left toward the front door. Julianna heard the door open, and then click shut. He must have gone out the door, but she couldn't see it to be sure.

She waited for a moment and then headed toward the door herself, staying low and in the shadows. He could still be in the house and just have pretended to go out the door. Maybe he saw her and was simply toying with her, trying to trap her. She squatted down and peered around the corner to where the door was, but there was no one there. She rushed over to it, intending to lock it but realized that the lock had been broken. Where were Shepherd and Kilbourne?!

She contemplated going outside and looking for the agents, but was afraid to go where the stranger had gone. If he had been in the house, then something must have happened to the agents, she reasoned.

She made her way to the living room. When she had gone to bed the lights had all been on. Why were the lights were off, and why was the house *so* dark? She glanced toward the kitchen. Then she realized – the microwave's clock and night light on the refrigerator no longer glowed. The electricity was off!

The hairs on the back of her neck bristled and she froze with the realization that something bad had happened to the agents. She didn't know what to do. *Think, Julianna, think!* She forced herself to move, continuing on toward the living room at the front of the house.

It was completely dark and she could barely see what was in front of her in this section of the house. She felt her way slowly along the edge of the wall, staying close to it. She focused on keeping her breathing quiet, the adrenalin fighting against her.

Her socks suddenly slid against the wooden floor and she gave a small gasp of surprise and pressed her hand harder against the wall to keep herself from falling.

She paused briefly and let out a controlled breath in an attempt to calm herself as she reached the doorway into the living room. Her right hand continued to glide against the wall, with her left stretched out in front of her to keep herself from running into something. Or *someone*, God forbid.

Her hand suddenly felt something wet against the wall and she jerked it back as if she had been burned. She stopped cold, paralyzed with fear.

The metallic odor of what she now realized was blood clung to the air. She had to get out of here! She turned and ran back toward the front door and right into a hard body.

She opened her mouth to scream as a gloved hand clamped tightly over her mouth and the familiar metal of a gun pressed against her head. He was breathing hard, as if he had been running. She could smell the leather of his glove as he kept his hand firmly over her mouth. She gripped his arm with both hands to keep herself balanced, but stopped struggling against him and focused on breathing through her nose.

His breathing slowed, but he was still winded as he whispered to her, "Are you going to scream if I remove my hand? Keep in mind, I still have a gun to your head and I won't hesitate to use it."

Julianna shook her head slowly to indicate no.

He removed his hand from her mouth, but kept the gun against her temple. Her shoulders pressed against his chest as he loomed over her. She stood there silently, waiting for him to make the next move. Her heart was pounding in her chest and her breathing was beginning to quicken. *Oh God, please don't let me have a panic attack now*, she thought frantically. Her temple began to throb, but she reasoned that it was due to the fact that a gun was pressed against it.

"I have to get out of here," she whispered. The odor of blood and...something else, was making her dizzy and nauseous. "If you're going to kill me, just do it."

The man reached behind his back, feeling for the door. With his right hand he opened the door slightly so that there was a bit of light shining in from the street light in front of the house. He removed the gun from her temple and pushed her gently away from him. "Turn around take 3 steps backward. Slowly," he said coldly, his voice low.

She did as she was told and met his eyes in the half-dark. As she had imagined, he was very tall and very muscular. His dark features didn't quite match his shaggy blond hair. He looked dangerous as the light from outside obscured the right side of his face. They stared at each other for several seconds before he finally spoke. "Do as you're told and you won't get hurt, Julianna."

"Did... did you kill the agents? Where are they?" she asked, her voice trembling.

He didn't answer, but glanced around the room behind her. She turned to see what he was looking at and gasped as she saw the body of Agent Kilbourne sprawled across the sofa in a pose that even in the darkness Julianna could tell was humanly impossible in life.

Julianna instinctively took two steps away from the man, and suddenly felt herself falling as she stumbled over... something. The man reached out for her, but it was too late. She gasped again as she came face to face with the dead Agent Shepherd. She struggled to get to her feet, but she kept getting caught in the arms and legs of the dead agent. She suddenly felt a strong hand clamp around her upper arm as she was jerked roughly to her feet. Pain shot through her arm as his grasp tightened. "Make the slightest noise and you will be just as dead as those agents," he warned her, his voice still low and menacing.

He stood there for a few excruciating moments, as if deciding what to do, then pulled her by the arm to the bedroom she had occupied earlier. Letting go of her arm, he pointed the gun once more to her head. "Take off your clothes," he ordered, his voice soft. He put his finger to his mouth to indicate that she remain quiet.

"Wha...? No," she whispered. "Please don't." There was just enough light coming through the curtains that she could make out his face.

He gave her an exasperated look. "Woman, I'm not here to assault you." He looked around the room and then made a beeline for her duffel bag, grabbed jeans and a sweater and threw them at her. "Put these on. Now. You have twenty seconds."

Her hands were shaking so badly that it took her closer to a minute, but she took off the bloody clothes and changed into the jeans and sweater. "Take off the socks, too," he told her.

She did.

"Now stay close to me," he told her, latching onto her arm once more.

Crying and shaking Julianna said nothing as he pulled her down the dark hallway to the front door, then hoisted her over his shoulder and made his way quickly down the street to a dark sedan.

As they reached the back of the car, he opened the trunk, and pulled something out of his pocket. Julianna struggled against him, but before she knew what was happening, she felt a sharp sting in her arm. The man quickly set her in the trunk and looked down at her.

"You'll be fine. It's better if you don't fight it," he said, slamming the door of the trunk quickly, leaving her in complete darkness.

Julianna immediately began to panic and her breathing came out in short gasps. The last time she had been trapped in a car was when her parents had been killed.

She closed her eyes tightly and concentrated on inhaling and exhaling. The last thing she remembered was the car's engine starting. And then she felt nothing.

Chapter 25

As he merged onto the Hutchinson River Parkway, Ethan Fray tossed the blonde wig out the window. He drove at a respectable speed that was neither too fast nor too slow. He didn't want to attract any attention, which was why he had chosen the non-descript black Ford out of the mall parking lot earlier that evening. He had then driven a short distance to an apartment complex and had switched the license plate on the Ford with the plate on a car there.

His black-gloved hand reached out and flipped on the radio, and instantly the car was filled with the lively sound of the fiddle in the Charlie Daniels song about the devil who went down to Georgia. Ethan snorted at the appropriateness of the song. Most people would probably consider him somewhere on the same stratum as the devil, and he would certainly have to agree. It wasn't that he necessarily *enjoyed* it, but it was where his life had taken him.

When he had been driving for about an hour and a half, he exited off to a gas station that also housed a large and brightly lit convenience market a with sign announcing that they were open 24/7.

As Ethan was replacing the nozzle onto the pump, he noticed an elderly couple getting out of a huge RV, which they had parked on the right side of the store, alongside a row of small fir trees. That side of the lot was more dimly lit than the rest of the area. He walked to the back of the Ford and quickly removed the license plate, slipping it under his black leather jacket.

Ethan entered the store, and along with the fuel he purchased a bottle of water and a granola bar. He then exited the store and walked over to the fir trees while sipping the water. He glanced around, making sure no one was paying any attention to him, but there weren't many people there at that time of the early morning. It was just after five a.m. and the moon was still shining in the early morning darkness.

Ethan quickly removed the tag on the RV and replaced it with the one from the Ford, noticing the *We're Spending Our Grandchildren's Inheritance* bumper sticker on the back. He despised bumper stickers, especially those designed to provide humor to passing motorists. And right now he definitely didn't see anything humorous in the self-proclaimed selfishness of two old people bragging about how they weren't giving their children squat, but were instead riding around the country in their gas guzzling trailer house on wheels, their exhaust fumigating everyone they passed. He knew he was just in a bad mood. Seeing blood spill from four Federal Agents had a way of doing that to him.

He walked casually back to his car and had just sat down in the driver's seat when the elderly couple, in their matching green coats and hats, returned to their vehicle with a small bag of groceries and two cups of coffee, the steam from the cups rising in the cold morning air. He knew it would probably be quite a while before they noticed that their Florida tag had been replaced with one from New York.

Ethan got back onto the highway and then pulled over to the side of the road, attaching the Florida tag to the Ford, and then opening the trunk. "You okay?" he asked Julianna, who was huddled there in the darkness. He didn't really care if she was okay or not, but for some reason he felt he should ask.

She was silent, but he could see she was still breathing. He knew the dose of Lorazepam he had given her back in Larchmont would keep her calm and quiet for at least the next hour or so until he could get her to his place.

Ethan drove for another forty-five minutes, and then exited off and headed to the ski village of Windham. It was early Saturday morning, and as usual the place was packed with people who were there for the weekend. It was six o'clock, and he needed to hurry before the disgustingly happy skiers, their rainbow-striped scarves trailing behind them, were out and about for the day. For the time being everyone was still inside the resort, the parking lot full of SUVs but no people.

Pulling the Ford into an empty parking space at the south end of the lot, Ethan killed the engine and exited the vehicle. He walked around the rear of the car and opened the trunk, removing a black duffel bag, which he slung over his shoulder.

Julianna was still curled in the fetal position. "Get up," he ordered, his voice low.

She groaned and shielded her eyes with her hands, but she didn't make any move to get out of the trunk, so he reached down, put his arms under hers and lifted her out. She leaned unsteadily against him, making a slight whimpering sound.

He then slammed the trunk shut, pulled her along with him, and together they walked down the row of cars until they reached a black Mercedes SUV, which he unlocked by remote control.

Just as he was settling Julianna into the seat, he heard a woman's voice speak behind him. "Is she okay?"

Ethan turned around to see an attractive young woman and her male escort, both ensconced in colorful ski garb.

"She's fine," Ethan grinned sheepishly, his voice friendly. "I'm afraid she had a bit too much to drink last night and wouldn't you know it, fell down and twisted her ankle. Not sure what hurts more, the ankle or the hangover." He chuckled, "Time to head home, I suppose. Such a shame, too since we're here on our honeymoon."

The skiers shook their heads sadly, as if they understood and sympathized. "Well, congratulations and good luck," the young man spoke as they started walking again.

Ethan's smile disappeared as quickly as it had appeared. He buckled Julianna's seatbelt, then closed the door and walked to the other side, getting into the driver's seat and heading toward the cabin, which was just outside of Windham and sat on twenty-five gloriously secluded acres in the heart of the Catskills.

Chapter 26

At two minutes after 4 a.m., Will sleepily reached over to his nightstand and answered the ringing phone.

"Bad news, Delaney," Walter Simpson barked into the phone. "Your girl is gone."

Will's heart froze. "What do you mean she's *gone*?" he demanded, instantly alert.

"She's gone. Safe house security was breached and we've got three bodies out there and one critical in the hospital.

Will was silent as he held the phone in his shaking hand. "Is she...?" He couldn't bring himself to utter the word.

"No, Delaney. She's not dead. Aren't you listening? She's *gone*, as in *missing*! She's not there!" Walter fumed. "The Crime Scene Unit is out there now. I called Olsen on his cell and he's on his way there now. You need to get out there pronto! He gave Will the address and added, "Call me when you get there and let me know what you find, understand?"

"Yes, of course," Will responded as he hung up the phone, quickly dressed, and then ran out the door and down to his Tahoe.

What the hell had gone wrong? He wondered as he drove out of the city at breakneck speed.

When he arrived at the safe house, the place was lit up like a Christmas tree with external lighting. Police cars and FBI agents littered the street, and crime scene tape appeared to be everywhere.

Olsen was just stepping out of his Taurus as Will arrived. He got out of his Tahoe and together they surveyed the scene. There was a vehicle parked across the street from the house and agents buzzed around it, taking photos. Will and Paul walked over to the vehicle. "What happened here?" Will asked a young red-haired woman who was speaking into a recorder. She pushed the pause button and turned to Will.

"Who's asking?" she demanded, her face unfriendly.

"Special Agents Delaney and Olsen. This is our case," he replied, his face equally unsociable.

"Oh, sorry. We were told you'd be here soon," she apologized. "I'm with the Crime Scene Unit. Here's one of your guys," she said, indicating the dead man, who Will quickly recognized as Special Agent Jankowski, still seated in the car. This one was shot in the head at point blank range. The woman was also shot in the head, but probably not as close up. She's in surgery now, but it's iffy if she'll make it. My boss is right over there. You really should be talking to him."

"We will," Paul affirmed, as he and Will walked toward the house where the agent was standing.

"What do you think, Olsen?" Will inquired.

"Not sure, but it looks like they were taken by surprise."

"Or knew their killer," Will added.

"Exactly," Olsen agreed.

"Special Agents Delaney and Olsen," Will greeted the man the female agent had indicated.

"Margolis, Crime Scene" he replied curtly, his impatience clear. "I understand Julianna Brennan was involved in a case of yours."

"*Is* involved in our case," Will corrected.

"Sorry, I meant *is*," he corrected, clearly annoyed by the interruption of his crime scene.

He handed Will and Olsen each a pair of latex gloves and continued quickly, his words punctuated in short bursts. "We have four victims – one agent in the car, one agent outside the car, and two agents in the house. Our preliminary findings show that at least one of the outside agents was shot at close range, and then the intruder entered the house, shooting the two agents inside. Apparently they were coming in to change shifts. Someone was likely watching the house to know that.

Agent Rodriguez has been taken into surgery, but she's in very critical condition. We're hoping to question her, but it's not looking good. The doctors are pretty sure she's not going to make it through the night, but you never know; we might get lucky."

"What about Julianna Brennan?" Paul asked.

"She's gone. No sign of her here," Margolis said, his tone matter of fact. "Any chance she could have done this?"

"No," Will stated coldly. "And don't even insinuate that in your report."

Margolis heaved a sigh and gave Will a cutting look. "We're also looking into a possible kidnapping, among other things."

"What 'other things'?" Will asked.

Margolis shrugged, "Don't know yet, but you'll read all about it in my report."

"Why aren't the lights on?" Olsen asked as they moved to the inside of the house.

"Power was cut," Margolis answered. "They're still working on getting it back up, but we've got a generator out here we're using to run power inside.

"What about the security cameras?" Will asked. He knew the safe house was equipped with surveillance cameras inside and out.

"Those were taken out, too. We've got a technician working on it to see if it caught anything before they were disabled. Someone knew what they were doing," Margolis said.

Will noted the Luma-Lite. "What have you found?" he asked Margolis.

"Lotta blood, lotta fingerprints," he answered vaguely.

"Any of the blood belong to Julianna Brennan?" Olsen inquired.

"Won't know 'til we've analyzed it, but see how the blood is smeared across the floor here next to Agent Shepherd?"

"Someone was dragged across the floor," Will said.

"Or was sitting here," Margolis said. "That impression there – in layman's terms it's a butt impression. Like someone fell or was pushed down beside the body. Or maybe there was a struggle between her and Agent Shepherd before she shot him, and the blood is from Agent Kilbourne. We just don't know yet.

"We collected bloody clothes from the bedroom," Margolis continued. "Like to tell me why a kidnapper would have his victim change clothes before dragging them out of here? Julianna Brennan was not the victim here."

Will's jaw, as well as his fists, clenched. "She's the victim here, Margolis. Don't even try to go anywhere else with this. There's a logical explanation for the clothes. Maybe the perp didn't want blood in his car."

Margolis rolled his eyes and shook his head in disbelief. "This your first rodeo, Delaney? Because it's not mine. It's my job to find out what happened, Delaney and I'll go where the evidence leads me, and right now it's leading me straight to your girl. However, she didn't act alone, so if you don't mind, I'm going to get back to my job and I suggest you do the same." Margolis turned to walk away.

"That's my intention, Margolis. We're going to take a look around," Will stated.

"Just stay out of the way and don't touch anything,"

Olsen gave Margolis an irritated look as he and Will walked down the hall to the left of the foyer.

When they reached the room that contained Julianna's things, the two agents stood in the doorway for a few moments taking everything in.

"The bed has been slept in but not disturbed in such a way that would indicate a struggle," Will noticed. "I have a feeling Julianna heard something and then left the room."

"I agree," Olsen said as he glanced around the room.

"There doesn't seem to be anything else in here other than her personal belongings. It all appears neat and orderly, but we can't know for sure if anything is missing," Will said. "Maybe the perp had her come back in here and change clothes before he took her out."

"Maybe. We need to get back to the office and get an APB out. This is going to be huge. You know there will be a press conference and Simpson is going to want you to do it," Olsen said.

"I doubt that. I'm not exactly in a favorable position with Simpson right now," Will reminded him.

"Well then, this is your chance to redeem yourself," Olsen said tightly. "And besides, you look better on camera than I do," he added, only half joking.

"Call me if you get anything from Rodriguez," Will called over his shoulder as he walked to the Tahoe and headed back to the city.

Chapter 27

Julianna felt herself being lifted up and carried somewhere by strong arms, but she was too dazed to care. She rested her head against a man's chest. She was so tired! *Why* was she so tired? She felt like she couldn't wake up. She was set down onto a soft bed where she turned over on her side, curled up and closed her eyes. She dozed for what seemed like many hours, but her mind was racing the entire time, trying to free itself from the cobwebs that smothered her rationale.

I must be at Will's, she reasoned. That's right, she reminded herself, relieved. Someone had been after her with a gun in an alley and Will had found her. No, wait, that wasn't right. She had been at the safe house. Oh, God, the agents! What happened to them? Her mind started piecing things slowly back together. Someone had shoved her into a trunk after sticking her with a needle.

She opened her eyes, praying that she would be at Will's and this had all been a horrible nightmare. Her eyes focused slowly on the room around her. The walls were dark, paneled in some sort of wood. There were paintings of landscapes all over the walls. They looked expensive but Julianna couldn't be sure. There was a tall chest of drawers, nightstand and cheval mirror, all crafted of the same dark wood as the paneling. Julianna sat up slowly, feeling dizzy, and sat on the edge of the bed for a few moments before looking around the rest of the room.

She had been laid upon a wooden sleigh bed, which was covered by a quilt patterned in plums, blues and greens. Behind her was a sitting area with two overstuffed chairs, which were upholstered in a coordinating green fabric. Between the chairs was a small wooden table with a few books stacked neatly on top. There was a fireplace next to the chairs, but it wasn't burning.

Julianna needed to use the bathroom but she was afraid to get up. Where was she? Finding herself in strange places was becoming commonplace for her these days, and she certainly didn't like it.

She walked over to one of the four windows in the room and looked outside. Everywhere she looked there were trees. She wasn't even in the city anymore! Without warning, the door opened behind her and she spun around, almost losing her balance in her dazed state.

"You're up," a man stated, his tall and muscular frame completely filling the doorway. Julianna gasped as realization struck. This was the man whose photo she had seen in Will's office, however his hair was different. It was now dark brown and much shorter, although still scruffy, and he was casually dressed in a plaid flannel shirt and well-worn blue jeans. He might have looked normal, even handsome, to anyone else, but to Julianna he looked like the devil himself.

"Where am I and who the *hell* are you?" Julianna demanded angrily, trying unsuccessfully to hide her fear.

"You're at my home, Julianna. Well, one of them," he told her.

"How do you know my name? And I asked you before, who *are* you?"

"You don't have to be afraid of me," he stated, his voice calm.

"You...you shot FBI agents," Julianna accused him.

"You think I did that?" he replied, narrowing dark eyes at her.

"Of course I do!" she snapped.

"I didn't, but I would have if I had to."

"What do you mean you didn't? I *saw* you! You were *there*!" she argued, her rage building.

"And so were you, but you didn't do it. Or did you?"

"Of course not!"

"Then you can't be sure *I* did it either."

"Do you think I'm stupid? No one else was there!" She gestured wildly in the air.

"How do you know that, Julianna?" He casually crossed his arms and leaned against the door frame. "We can talk about it later, but first, if you want to shower or use the bathroom, it's over there," he said, indicating a closed door on the other side of the room.

Julianna stood there for a moment, trying to decide what her next move should be. However, she *really* had to go to the bathroom so she turned and walked into it, closing the door firmly behind her, noting the absence of a lock.

When she came out of the bathroom, he was standing there waiting for her.

"Please come with me," he requested, although Julianna knew it wasn't actually a request.

Julianna narrowed her eyes angrily at him, but she followed behind him as he led her down a hall and into a very large living room. She wanted to attack him, shoot him. If only she had a weapon. Why would a killer leave his back exposed? Simple, it was confidence. He knew he'd win. She hated him, and her eyes bore into his back like lasers.

The place was beautiful, which surprised Julianna. So far, the entire home looked as it if had come straight out of a magazine. It was rustic, but elegant. The sofas in the living room were buttery soft tan leather, and the entire room was bathed in morning light from the windows that wrapped all the way around. Because there were so many windows, there was little artwork, but what was there was exquisite, and some even looked familiar to Julianna. Were they originals, she wondered? The entire place reeked of money. The floor was covered with hardwood, but on top was a heavy wool rug of striped earth tones.

"Like what you see?" he asked. Julianna noticed that his expression never changed. He seemed calm and cool no matter what was said.

She shrugged noncommittally.

"Please have a seat."

Julianna sat down on the sofa closest to the window and perched on the edge. He sat across from her on the other sofa, which faced the window, and stared at her for several moments. Julianna stared right back. She wasn't going to let this man know how much he intimidated her, although she was terrified and he probably knew it. Of course he did. He had killed Federal Agents and had threatened to do the same to her. Why hadn't he? What did he want?

Finally he spoke. "I didn't kill those agents. It's important that you know that."

"I don't believe you." She scooted back on the sofa and tucked her hands under her thighs so he wouldn't see them trembling.

"I'm telling you the truth. You can choose to believe it or not, but I'd rather you did."

"Why should I believe you? You put a gun to my head, gave me a shot of... something, shoved me in a car and kidnapped me."

"Yes, I did do those things to you and I readily admit that. That said, why would I lie to you now?" he asked, leaning forward with his elbows on his knees, his hands clasped, and his chin resting on his knuckles as he gazed calmly at her.

Julianna didn't say anything for a few minutes. She sat there thinking, looking at his chin so she didn't have to see the dark eyes that were intensely watching her every move. She concentrated on the ticking of the grandfather clock that stood against the wall beside the sofa she sat on, trying to match her pounding heart rate to the steady cadence of the clock.

"If you want to know the truth, I actually saved you," he explained.

"*Saved* me? From...?"

He cocked his head to the side and shook his head slowly, the kind of head shake one gives someone who is either mentally challenged or completely delusional. "From the man who actually *did* kill the agents, Julianna."

"And who might that be?" Julianna asked sarcastically. "The one-armed man?"

He ignored her. "I don't know – he ran away and I couldn't catch up with him."

"Uh huh, sure. So why didn't you kill me, too?"

"I'm not sure," he mused, rubbing his chin thoughtfully. "Maybe because it's been a loooong time since I've had a woman here." He grinned at her with very white, perfectly even teeth, the corners of his eyes crinkling. His looks were movie star handsome, but then again so were Ted Bundy's, Julianna reminded herself.

She jumped up and ran across the room and out into the hall, looking frantically for a door from which to escape.

"Julianna," he called after her, getting up calmly to follow her. "It was a joke, clearly a bad one."

Julianna finally saw the front door and ran to it, grabbed the knob and turned it. It was locked. She quickly fumbled with the handle and managed to unlock it with shaking fingers, then turned the knob again. Still locked! She looked up and noticed that it had a deadbolt, which would require a key to open it, but there was no key. She was trapped and the panic hit her hard. Everything that had happened to her in the past few days was suddenly boiling over and she was powerless under its force.

She began to sob uncontrollably and pound on the door with her fists. She wanted to scream, and run as hard and fast as she could while doing so. Her fists ached as she continued to pound the door. She could feel her nails boring into the cuts on her hands from the metal fence of the alley just a few days ago. Why did this keep happening to her? Why had Jackson Mattice gotten her into this mess? She hated him! She ignored the pain in her right wrist as it hit the metal of the deadbolt lock.

He came up behind her and grabbed her by her wrists, pulling her hands behind her against her back with one of his own large ones. "Enough," he said, leaning heavily against her, which pushed her left cheek up against the door. Julianna continued to stand there, sobbing as he held her wrists behind her with his right hand, his left braced against the door above her head.

They stood like that for some time and when she stopped struggling against him, he took a step back so that he wasn't leaning directly on her. She pulled back slightly from the door and he felt her body go limp. As he let go of her hands, she slid to the floor and leaned against the door, crying softly.

He squatted down beside her and took her face in his right hand, pulling her chin up so she was forced to look at him. "Don't do that again," he warned.

He then stood up and walked over to the doorway that led back into the hall, leaning against its frame, his arms crossed. He stood there watching her for about thirty seconds before he spoke again. "I'll be in the living room. Pull yourself together. I trust you can find your way back." Then he turned and walked away.

Julianna continued to cry until she couldn't cry anymore. She dried her eyes on the sleeve of her sweater. She felt completely defeated and didn't care whether she lived or died at this point. She had no idea what this man wanted from her. Maybe he was just biding his time because he knew he had her here indefinitely.

When she had looked out the window she had seen nothing but trees. There were no other houses or signs of civilization. They were obviously in the mountains, probably in either Pennsylvania or New York. No one would ever find her out here. Of that she felt certain.

She got up and walked back to the living room and stood in the doorway. "I'm going to go take a nap," she announced quietly.

"No, you're going to eat breakfast first."

"Thank you, but I'm not hungry," she answered politely.

"You're going to eat breakfast," he repeated.

He got up from the sofa and took her by the elbow, pulling her with him as they walked down the hall toward the kitchen.

He pulled out a chair at a small dining table and pushed her down into it before he walked over to the fridge and rummaged around until he found some eggs. Before long he had placed an egg white omelet in front of her, along with a tall glass of orange juice.

"Eat." He commanded.

Julianna picked up her fork and poked around at the omelet. He sat across from her and began to eat his own omelet, glancing at her with irritation because she wasn't eating.

"Just eat the damn omelet."

The food is probably poisoned, Julianna thought to herself. She took a bite of the egg, almost hoping that it was poisoned so she could get out of this nightmare. At once she felt like vomiting, but she managed to swallow it and then took a sip of the orange juice to wash it down.

Maybe the orange juice was poisoned. He hadn't drunk any of his yet. Yes, that must be it. The orange juice was poisoned and any minute she was going to drop dead. She sat there and waited for the moment to arrive, but it never did so she took another sip. Maybe she just needed a larger dose.

"I didn't poison the food," he said casually, as if reading her mind.

"I wouldn't care if you did."

"You know, I think I liked you better when you were feisty and aggressive."

"Sorry to disappoint you."

He gave her an amused expression and continued his omelet.

"I know you're going to kill me, so why don't you just go ahead and do it?"

"Maybe, but wouldn't it be best to wait, take your chances?"

Chalk it up to stress, lack of sleep, or whatever drug he had given her, but she was suddenly pissed. Everyone else seems to have control of her life right now. *Everyone except her.* She was tired of sitting here and letting him make all the decisions. If he was going to kill her, then she wanted him to go ahead and get it over with. She leaped up from her chair and lunged toward him, her fork in hand. He grabbed her wrist and wrenched the fork out of her hand as Julianna kicked at him and tried to hit him with her free hand. She felt like a wild animal and she didn't care. Common sense and logic was no longer a part of her and she didn't feel capable of thinking clearly or rationally, or maybe she just didn't want to right now. What she *did* want was for this to be over with, and one way or another she wanted to be the one to end it. "Go ahead! Kill me!" she screamed. "You're going to do it anyway! Go ahead! Do it! *Do it!*"

He grabbed her around the waist and hoisted her, kicking and screaming, across his shoulder. He carried her down the hall to the bedroom she had occupied earlier and tossed her roughly onto the bed. She jumped up and scrambled after him, but he got to the door first, exited and closed the door quickly behind him, leaving her inside. She heard a click and tried the knob, but the door had been locked from the outside.

Julianna ran to the window and tried to open it but it wouldn't budge. She then looked around for something to slam into the window, but she didn't see anything in the immediate vicinity so she walked over to the sitting area hoping to find something there. When she turned around, he was standing behind her, syringe in hand.

"No!" she exclaimed, backing up. Whatever he was going to do to her she wanted to be cognizant and aware, so that she at least had a chance of putting up a good fight. If he was going to take her out she at least wanted to give him a good scar or two across that smug face of his.

"The windows are shatterproof and bulletproof, by the way," he stated, walking toward her. "I thought you were smarter than this, Julianna. You're really leaving me no choice but to sedate you again."

"Why don't you just kill me the old-fashioned way!" she screamed at him. "What, you want to rape me first? Is that it? You rape women before you kill them?"

"I have no intention raping you or anyone else, Julianna. Once you calm down we might be able to have a rational conversation."

"Rational?! *Rational?!* Nothing in my life is very *rational* right now, least of all me!" she continued to yell. "You want me to sit down with you and have a *rational* conversation? How about we have tea? We can talk about the weather. Or hey, how about we discuss which version of CSI is better?! I'm betting you're a Vegas kind of guy."

"Are you finished?" he asked her, his voice just as calm as it had always been.

Julianna didn't answer, but instead crossed her arms defiantly.

"Because when you're finished we'll go back to the kitchen and have a normal conversation."

He stood there leaning against the door frame waiting for an answer from her, but she said nothing. "I can stand here all day," he warned her.

"All right," she reluctantly agreed. "But you're going to answer *my* questions, not the other way around."

"Okay."

She walked purposely out the door and down the hall to the kitchen and sat down in "her" chair. Let the games begin. She would play nice and pretend she was a guest in this sick criminal's home. If he wanted polite conversation she'd give him polite conversation.

"It's New York," he said as he followed her down the hall. "That's my favorite CSI. In case you were actually interested."

Julianna didn't respond.

"So, what do you do for a living, Mr....? I'm sorry, you never told me your name," she asked politely when he had joined her at the table.

"It's Ethan," he answered, "Just Ethan. And I do a variety of things."

"Oh really? What sort of things, *Just Ethan?*" she replied sarcastically.

"You really don't want to know the answer to that question. Let's talk about something else," he suggested.

"Okay, what is your favorite color?" Julianna asked.

"Green."

"Why won't you answer my question?" she pressed.

"Because you're better off not knowing."

"I'll be the judge of that."

"Okay, fine. I work for Victor Ciccone," he said, searching her eyes for a reaction, which he got in the form of two very wide green eyes. For someone who tried so hard to be tough and unreadable her expressions were completely transparent. This was a woman who would have a very difficult time concealing a lie, he mused.

"So you're a..."

"Trained killer? Hit man? Assassin? Contract Killer?" he finished for her.

"Yes."

"Yes," he agreed.

"Is Ethan your real name?"

"Yes."

"Does Victor Ciccone know you as Ethan?" she asked.

"No," he stated simply.

"So why tell me?"

"I don't know," he replied. And he didn't. He *never* told anyone his real name, so why had he told her? And he certainly never told anyone about his profession. Something about mentioning he was a professional killer tended to frighten the hell out of people, and it was definitely a relationship killer. Not that he ever actually told anyone what he did, but he wasn't naïve enough to assume differently. The kinds of women who found him attractive were also the type to write letters to convicted serial killers. He needed to get himself in check before he totally blew this thing. Julianna Brennan needed to be afraid of him and everyone else she came in contact with, for very good reason. He wouldn't make the same mistake twice. There was a reason he kept to himself and didn't form relationships. Relationships made him sloppy, and sloppy got you or someone you love killed.

He looked down and realized his hands were shaking. He glanced at Julianna and saw that she realized it, too. She gave him a puzzled look. Doing the only thing he could do, he grabbed his plate and threw it across the room, satisfied as it crashed into the cabinet and shattered into a million tiny pieces.

Julianna sat there stunned for a split second, her mouth slightly agape. He narrowed his eyes at her and gave her a look that spoke volumes. It was a Jekyll turned Hyde moment that he knew would intensify her fear of him. He leapt up from his chair, sending it backward, its wooden back slamming against the tile floor, and stormed out of the room.

Julianna sat there, numb and terrified. This man seemed to run hot and cold. One minute he was kind, almost gentle, and the next he was menacing and violent. Was one of those personalities an act or was he really that volatile? Attacking him earlier had perhaps been the most irresponsible thing she had ever done. She needed to maintain composure around him. She had no doubt that he was watching her every move, maybe even testing her.

She walked over to a small pantry, found a broom, and began sweeping up the mess he had created.

Chapter 28

"Isabel Rodriguez made it through surgery," Olsen said as he walked into the office at around 10 a.m.

Will breathed a sigh of relief. "Thank God. Is she able to talk?"

"No, they've got her in a medically induced coma while she heals. They aren't sure what state she'll be in when she comes out of it. The bullet entered her head from the back right side and exited out the front. The surgeon said had it gone lower into her brain she'd be dead."

"What are you doing back here? I thought you were going to stick around the hospital?"

"Simpson wanted me back here to go over the case with you again, see if there's something we're missing. There's nothing I can do there since she's in a coma. We've got two agents on her – one in her room and one at the door. They'll call us once she's awake. It could be days, or even weeks."

"I'm going over the recorded conversations we had with Jackson Mattice," Will told him. "See if I can find something. I don't know what else to do at this point. It could be a while with the crime lab. I still don't know how someone in the area didn't see something."

"It was the middle of the night, Delaney. Everyone was asleep." Olsen reminded him.

"Sure, but I also have to wonder if people just aren't coming forward. This is a high-profile case, a lot of bloodshed, a lot of fear."

"And you know how people like to be in the middle of these high-profile cases, get their 15 minutes. Someone will come forward," Olsen assured him.

"Maybe," Will answered thoughtfully.

"Look, Delaney, I hate to bring this up, knowing how touchy you were over this with Margolis last night, but do you think she could be in on this with Mattice?"

"No." Will stated firmly.

"Come on, Delaney. We've got nothing to go on here. All fingers point to her on this. There's no sign of her. Don't you think she'd be dead too, right along with Jankowski, Shepherd and Kilbourne?"

"Not if someone took her."

"Why would someone take her? If she knows something they would have killed her, too," Olsen reasoned.

"Maybe they only think she knows something, and they need to find out what she knows."

"It wouldn't matter what she knows. If she knows something they're going to want her dead."

"They're still looking for this phantom memory card and they think she knows where it is." Will said.

"Do you think she does?" Olsen asked.

"No, she's told us she doesn't. I believe her. I *still* believe her."

"Do you like Jackson Mattice for this?"

"He's a good possibility."

"And knowing his relationship with Julianna Brennan you can still say with all honesty that you think she's an innocent bystander in all this? Get a grip, Delaney. Personal feelings aside, admit that there's at least a possibility she knows more than she's saying."

Will let a few moments pass before he spoke. "Okay, there might be a small chance she knows more than she's admitting, which is why we have to find her, and find out who is behind all this."

"Agreed. So, after the press conference I'm going to go back to Larchmont and re-canvas the neighborhood around the safe house."

"I'll head to Riker's and give Ciccone another go," Will said.

He put on the headphones and resumed listening to the last recorded conversations he had with Jackson Mattice. He had already listened to the tapes countless times and had the written transcripts in front of him, but he kept listening to them, trying to determine voice inflections, listening for background sounds, *anything* that would somehow put this thing together.

Something about the conversations was niggling at him, but he couldn't exactly place what it was. Either Jackson Mattice was a little off his rocker or he was missing something. He replayed the section that was bothering him and read along with the transcript as it played.

SA William Delaney: "Look Mattice, you're going to have to give me more than that. I can't start an investigation based on what've told me so far."

Jackson Mattice: "I already told you everything I know! What more do you want?"

SA William Delaney: "What I *want* is for you to be honest with me, Mattice. Either tell me the whole story or stop calling me with your conspiracy paranoia. You're a credible guy, which is why I've believed you up until this point, but you're not giving me anything. I can't continue this without more information. So, take it or leave it. What's it going to be?"

Jackson Mattice: "You want me to put it on the front page of the paper, Delaney? You know what? Just forget it. I'll take care of this myself. Just do me a favor, Delaney. Keep Julianna Brennan safe. Can you do that one thing without giving me grief? I did a stupid thing and I'm going to pay for it, but I don't want her to pay the price."

Will could hear the desperation and frustration in the man's voice at various points in the conversation. He had told Will very little about who and what this entire thing was about, only that they needed to look at Victor Ciccone, but that this was "even bigger" than him. Had Mattice actually given him something that he had missed? It was always very noisy where Mattice called from, obviously a pay phone, but he had listened carefully to the call and there were no gaps in the call, or any interference whatsoever. Mattice kept his voice low during all the conversations, but certainly not low enough to be heard. So why did he insist that he had already given Will the details?

Will looked at the clock on the wall and realized it was almost time for him to be at the press conference. He quickly finished the cold cup of coffee that had been sitting on his desk for the past two hours, grabbed his jacket, his stomach churning with dread, and headed outside.

Chapter 29

After Julianna finished cleaning up the mess Ethan had made she walked around the kitchen checking the windows. They were all locked and appeared to be made out of the same weird glass as the bedroom Ethan had put her in. Bulletproof and shatterproof, she realized with frustration. There appeared to be nothing but woods in every direction she looked. She wondered where on earth she was and why this man had taken her. So far he had asked her nothing, demanded nothing of her.

Unlike earlier, when she had felt panicky and irrational, she now felt calm and extremely tired, her body still aching from the attack in the alley days earlier.

She walked back to the living room where she thought Ethan might be but he wasn't there. Padding quietly down the hallways in her socks, she peered into rooms, wondering where he was. At the end of the hallway she opened a door, which led down a flight of stairs. She slowly descended.

When she came to the bottom, there was a glass door, and beyond it was the most beautiful indoor pool she had ever seen. Opening the door, the familiar scent of chlorine assaulted her nose. The floor was tiled in a beautiful Mediterranean pattern of blues and greens mixed with terra cotta. Around the pool area were a few lounge chairs with overstuffed cushions. This was no ordinary cabin. A setup like this must have cost a fortune. The front of the room had French doors leading outside, but the walls on the other three corners were concrete as if the house had been built into a hill. She had seen many basements like this back home in Tennessee, but never before had there been a setup like this in any of them. Pool tables, yes, but swimming pools – never.

Julianna squatted down beside the pool and ran her hand through the water, which was warm. She then stood up and walked all around the edge. In the left back corner of the room, underneath the stair area was a glassed in wall, behind which was an exercise room.

Inside, Ethan was working out on a piece of equipment, doing what she vaguely recognized as butterfly resistance training. She walked over to the room and watched from the window. He had changed into a pair of gray knit shorts and a royal blue t-shirt, and in this outfit, Julianna could see just how muscular he really was. As she stood watching him, his eyes never left hers, his expression angry as his arms rhythmically worked the exercise machine.

Julianna turned and walked back toward the stairs. She was exhausted and looked up at the top of the staircase, wondering if she would ever make it that far. The last time she had slept well was at Will's. Will. The thought of him brought tears to her eyes. Was he looking for her? Was anyone?

She put her hand on the railing of the stairs and took a step up. Suddenly, she felt a hand clamp down on her shoulder and she jumped, losing her balance, but catching herself before she toppled backwards. "Where are you going?" Ethan asked, his hand still on her shoulder. How did this man creep around so silently? she wondered.

"I'm going to take a nap – I'm really tired," she replied, hoping he would let her go. His moods seemed to be incredibly unpredictable.

"Okay," he said simply, removing his hand.

Julianna trudged wearily up the stairs with Ethan following behind her. She could still feel the weight of his hand on her shoulder, even though he had removed it.

When she reached "her" room he paused at the door, waiting for her to enter, then he closed the door and she heard a click. He had locked her in.

Damn him, she thought, but really she was too tired to care. She crawled into the bed and pulled the covers over her, but as exhausted as she was, she found she couldn't sleep. Every time she closed her eyes, images of the Rico Cordova and the dead agents burned into her retinas. There had been so much blood, and even though she hadn't been able to *see* it very well, she could smell it and feel it. Julianna would never forget that raw metallic scent and the veil of death that hung in the air.

The hours on the clock ticked slowly by as Julianna was consumed with her thoughts and fears, unable to sleep. By late afternoon, shadows were darkening the room, which only frightened her more. "Will, where are you? I need you," she whispered into the darkness.

A few minutes later she heard the door's lock click. She waited to see if Ethan would enter the room, but he didn't so she snuggled deeper under the covers, wishing she could disappear.

A short time later she saw a sliver of light cross the wall, and when she looked toward the door Ethan was standing there watching her. "Please come into the living room," he requested, his tone matter-of-fact.

Julianna sighed, but stood up and followed him, squinting as her eyes adjusted to the brightness of the light. Maybe she could get some answers.

When they reached the living room he indicated for her to sit down while he sat across from her on the other sofa. "Those are for you," he indicated a bag, which was there on the sofa beside her.

Julianna cautiously opened the bag, glancing at the contents. Inside were several toiletry items, such as a toothbrush, toothpaste, soap, deodorant, shampoo, and conditioner. "I'm not staying here," she informed him.

"Let me know what else you need and I'll get it for you," he said, ignoring her statement.

Julianna was silent as she set the bag back down on the couch. She kept her eyes averted from his, afraid that if she looked at him she would cry.

"Who is Will?" Ethan asked her pointedly.

Julianna looked up, startled. Ethan waited for her to answer, his eyes narrowed. Why was he asking about Will? Julianna wondered. Had Will found out where she was and he knew it? She wasn't sure how or even *if* she should answer him so she kept her silence.

"Who is Will?" he repeated, this time impatiently. "I heard you say his name in your room."

How could he have heard her *whisper* Will's name? "You have my room bugged?" she asked incredulously.

Ethan gave her a look. Of course he had her room bugged.

"He's...a friend," she answered hesitantly.

"Does this friend have a last name?"

"Why would I tell you that? So you can go and kill him, too?"

"Would this happen to be Special Agent Will Delaney?" Ethan asked, ignoring her questions.

Julianna didn't answer, but her non-response gave her away.

"I know a lot about you, Julianna, and I also know he was assigned to your case."

"*Is* assigned to my case," she corrected. "And if you know so much then you wouldn't have to ask me who he is. You know exactly who he is."

"Is, was...it doesn't matter. I'm sure he's moved on by now," Ethan mused, "and even if he hasn't, he'll never find you here."

"You don't know anything about Will. He *is* going to find me."

"I know more than you think I know, Julianna, and I certainly know more than you *want* to know," he informed her cryptically.

"What is *that* supposed to mean?" she asked, her voice becoming angry.

"Let's just say that there's more to Will than meets the eye."

Julianna sat there, waiting for him to continue but he just sat there looking at her smugly. He's probably just seeing what kind of reaction he can get out of me, Julianna thought to herself.

Seeing that she wasn't going to prompt him, he continued on his own. "I knew him...a long time ago. In fact, I got to know him fairly well, learned he had quite the reputation as a ladies' man."

Seeing the hurt look in Julianna's eyes, he continued. "He had a reputation for being, how shall I put this nicely...a hustler. Lots of women, lots of booze, you get the idea."

"I don't believe you," Julianna stated quietly.

"That's okay. You don't have to believe me, but I thought you might find it interesting to ponder." He looked into her eyes and saw tears.

"Let me guess," he continued. "You fell for him, too?" He already knew she had, he just wanted to toy with her, hurt her. "Did he offer to cook dinner for you in that fancy apartment of his? It's a typical ploy of men of that caliber."

"He's not like that," Julianna defended.

"Oh, come on, Julianna. Has he been just a little *too* helpful? *Too* considerate? *Too* understanding? Guys like that always are. Think about it."

"He *is* considerate and caring! You, on the other hand, are not."

"Julianna, I know this guy and a hundred other guys like him. He's a taker. He'll take what he wants, then toss you out, just like all the other women. I'm only telling you this for your own good."

"Not that it's any of your business, but I am not his girlfriend, therefore he doesn't owe me anything.

"Furthermore, it doesn't really matter what there is or isn't between Will and me because I am here and you haven't exactly been offering to drive me home." Julianna stood up to leave the room. She was suddenly feeling very uncomfortable with the direction the conversation had taken and she certainly didn't like the way Ethan spoke about Will. She didn't want to even *think* about questioning Will's motives or intents. Will had been good to her and she trusted him. She *knew* she could trust him. Her head began to hurt. This was all too much...too much to think about...too much to deal with. She just wanted it to be over, but she knew it was far from it.

"Don't get so uptight, Julianna. I was just offering some advice. Maybe you are correct in your assumptions about Will. It *has* been a few years since I saw him last," Ethan explained, his voice light, but he could see doubt on her face and knew he had done his job.

"You must be hungry. It's been a long time since breakfast, which you barely touched, I might add."

Julianna didn't say anything, but she didn't leave the room either. Ethan took that as a good sign. "Come on, let's go to the kitchen," he encouraged. "I have a surprise for you."

"I'm not hungry."

"Sure you are. You just don't know it yet. Come see what I've prepared for us."

Julianna dutifully followed him to the kitchen. It was just easier this way. She wasn't sure how he'd react if she refused. When they reached the dining area, Julianna's heart froze. There were flowers on the table, and a candle flickered in the dimly lit room. Ethan looked at her, noting her reaction of uneasiness, and grabbed her shoulders as she turned and tried to dart out of the room. "I thought girls liked this sort of thing. I don't mean anything romantic by it," he assured her.

ARMS OF A STRANGER

As Ethan propelled her into a chair, Julianna was filled with dread. Her head hurt and she felt like she couldn't breathe. What could this man possibly want from me? She wondered.

Ethan banged around over by the stove for a minute or two, and then carried two plates to the table, setting one down in front of Julianna and then taking his own seat. Under normal circumstances, the meal of baked chicken, rice pilaf, and steamed asparagus would have been lovely, but these were definitely not the right circumstances.

"Eat," he ordered. "I know you're hungry."

But she wasn't hungry. She was just scared, and mentally and physically exhausted. However, her hand shaking as she moved the fork to her mouth, she took a bite to please him, but felt sick the moment she did. The room seemed to be spinning and she was having a difficult time focusing. Ethan's voice seemed to come from very far away and it was like he was speaking very slowly as he moved toward her, saying her name. As Julianna stood up, her body swayed and she braced her hands against the table. Ethan was saying something to her, but it wasn't making any sense. What was happening to her? Had he somehow drugged her again?

As a sharp pain flickered in her head, Julianna closed her eyes and touched her hand to her brow and as she did so, Ethan picked her up and carried her down the hall. She fought him, afraid he had drugged her again and was going to do something terrible to her, but he set her down gently on the bed. It was the first time he had not tossed her roughly onto it. He then left the room and came back with a small black bag. He pulled out a needle and drew something out of a tiny vial. "No..." Julianna whimpered, knowing what it was.

"It will help you sleep. You are exhausted, Julianna. You've dealt with an extreme amount of stress the past few days and it's catching up with you."

He injected the medicine into her arm, and then brought out another vial of something that smelled like a combination of rotten eggs and funeral flowers. Darkness was overcoming her as she closed her eyes and began to drift off into unconsciousness. She had the vague sense of something being applied to various parts of her face, but she was too tired and weak to care.

"That's right," Ethan was saying in a surprisingly soothing voice. "Close your eyes and sleep, Julianna, sleep."

Chapter 30

"I was telling the truth before," Ciccone alleged. The old man had somehow aged about five years since Will had seen him last. His days were obviously numbered.

"Cut the crap, Ciccone. I'm not in the mood for games today. We've got 3 agents dead, the other in the critical condition, not to mention someone has abducted the girl we were to protect and I think *you* have something to do with this!" Will fumed, standing over him.

"Have you found the memory card yet?" Ciccone asked.

"We haven't exactly had time for that thanks to you. Why?" Will snapped.

"Because I think all of your answers might be there."

"Why don't you save us the trouble and give us the answers yourself?" Paul interjected.

"Because I'm not sure exactly what's on the card."

Will gave him a humorless laugh. "I'm sure you don't."

Ciccone crossed beefy arms and leaned back in his chair. "I know and I don't know," he admitted.

Will slammed his fist on the table. "No more of this cryptic crap. Tell me what you know!" he yelled angrily.

"It doesn't matter anymore," he shook his head sadly, his meaty hands waving in the air. "The doctors, they say my cancer has spread to my lymph nodes. I don't have much longer."

"So now you want me to feel *sorry* for you?" Will scoffed. He stood up and began pacing the small room in a futile attempt at releasing some of the frustration that had built up inside him for the past few weeks.

"I don't want your pity!" I just want you to understand. I may have done a lot of bad things in my life but I don't want to go down having taken the blame for something I didn't do. I made a deal with the devil."

Will pulled up a chair and spun it around backward then sat down. "I'm waiting," he prompted.

Ciccone began coughing, his face red. "Get some water in here," he told the guard. Ciccone continued his coughing fit as Will waited. When the guard brought back a bottle water Will twisted off the cap and slid the bottle roughly across to Ciccone, water sloshing onto the table.

After taking a few sips Ciccone spoke slowly, his voice rough from his coughing fit. "I don't know what's on the memory card exactly, but I know it had something to do with the newspaper ads Jackson Mattice printed on the front page every week."

Ciccone's big hound-dog eyes stared into Will's for several moments as Will stared right back, his arms crossed. "Let's say, hypothetically of course, that someone paid Jackson Mattice to print innocuous advertisements on the front page of his paper every week. Let's also say, again, hypothetically, that all those advertisements were a code for something. Possibly something regarding, I don't know, say, drugs or weapons, or maybe something else."

"So you're saying that you paid Jackson Mattice to print these ads, ads that he discovered were a bit more than innocuous than he had originally thought. He broke the code and put the results on a memory card, giving the card to Julianna Brennan."

"I didn't pay Jackson Mattice. I was simply the go-between. Or rather, one of my associates was."

"Why you?"

"Because, like myself, I imagine this man, or woman, prefers delegation and knew I, or rather my associate, would do an effective job with them out of the loop. That's all I'm saying, Delaney. I've already said too much, and I have my family to protect."

"Who hired you, Ciccone?" Will asked, his voice low.

"You can stay here until the Lord comes, young agent, but I'm not saying another word," Ciccone told him, standing up. "Guard!" he yelled. "We're finished here."

"You'll leave when I say you leave, Ciccone," Will told him, waving off the guard. "Who killed those agents, and where the hell is Julianna Brennan?"

Ciccone began coughing violently again. Red-faced and gasping, he frantically grabbed the bottle of water off the table, but before he could untwist the cap he fell to the floor, clutching his chest. "Get someone in here *now!*" Will yelled at the guard, kneeling down beside Ciccone on the floor.

His meaty hand was surprisingly strong as he grabbed the front of Will's shirt and pulled him down. "Look at the crumb, Delaney," he gasped, his voice barely a whisper. "He's in your yard."

"Who is it, Ciccone?" he asked frantically, frighteningly aware that this was likely his last opportunity to get answers. Ciccone's eyes rolled back in his head and he was gone.

Chapter 31

Will was so lost in thought he nearly missed his turn on the Grand Central Parkway. He contemplated what Ciccone had told him and it suddenly started to fall into place. Some of it, anyway. Now he just had to figure who was behind it, and what, exactly, they were behind. Will hadn't heard the term "crumb" in a long time. It was old mob-speak indicating a working man, someone legitimate. It had to be someone at the FBI.

Will drove in the direction of the newspaper office, circled the block a few times looking for a parking space, and finally dove into one as a Honda Civic evacuated it.

At the information desk he was instructed to take the elevator to the seventeenth floor. The place was bustling with people, which to Will looked like utter chaos, but it was obviously a very well- run paper. He asked a woman at a desk where Jackson Mattice's office was. Her eyes widened as he held up his badge.

"It's down that hall and to the right, but... I think you need to talk Frank first," the woman directed, pointing to a middle-aged man who was seated a few desks down.

"Okay, thanks," Will said.

Frank was leaning ridiculously close to a computer monitor as he read something on the screen. "Frank?" Will asked.

"Yup?" Frank acknowledged without looking away from the monitor.

"I'm FBI Special Agent Delaney and I'm investigating the death of Jackson Mattice and the disappearance of Julianna Brennan," Will told him, once more holding up his badge for inspection. As far as the public knew, Jackson Mattice was dead instead of his brother Ray.

"Uh-huh," Frank replied, still absorbed in his work.

"Frank!" Will reached over and turned off the monitor, quickly getting Frank's attention. "I need access to the front cover of every newspaper for the past twelve months. I also want to see Jackson Mattice's office."

Frank, clearly annoyed, had finally turned to the agent and stared at him through bottle-thick lenses. "What are you looking for?" he asked, sizing Delaney up.

"That's privileged," Delaney answered. He wasn't sure exactly *what* he was looking for, but he had a feeling he'd know it when he found it.

"It's down that hall, fourth door on the right," Frank said, indicating the direction with a nod of his head. "You won't find anything, though," he informed them, finally looking up from the typewriter.

"Why is that?" Will inquired.

"Someone else already looked. Place was trashed a few nights ago. Someone broke in. I didn't bother calling NYPD though. Doesn't look like anything was taken. Computer's still there."

"I'll just take a look around. And I also need to access those newspapers."

Wordlessly Frank got up from his desk and lead the way to Mattice's office. Will noticed several boxes into which the contents of the office had been stashed, presumably after it had been ransacked.

Before beginning the search, he stood in the doorway for a few moments and visually made his way around the room. On the right was a large desk on which sat a computer. Behind the desk was a table with a printer, fax machine and more boxes piled with odds and ends. On the beige walls were framed awards that that the newspaper had won.

He did a thorough inspection of the boxes and desk but didn't find anything incriminating or suspicious, not that he expected to. If anything, Jackson Mattice had been careful.

Frank had set up the computer and shown him how to get to the next issue. Since he was just looking at the cover of each edition the work went quickly and a pattern began to emerge. Every Friday there was an ad, two inches by two inches with a black border around it, which suddenly began to show up about six month ago. They looked innocent enough – one for a furniture store, another for a wig shop, and yet another for a bar – but the wording for each was similar. There were twenty-four ads total, each with advertising a different business. Will would check it out and see if there was a common thread between each business, but he doubted there would be. He had a feeling the business wasn't the key, but rather the actual text of the ad.

He printed each of them out on the printer behind him and found an empty file folder beside the printer to stash them in. Just what did you discover, Mattice? He wondered.

Will walked back out to Frank's desk. "Where is Julianna Brennan's office?" he asked.

"She doesn't have one," Frank told him, clearly irritated at being bothered yet again by the FBI agent. "She uses a cubicle like the rest of the staffers. It's over there – second one from the end," he said using a pen to point toward a row of cubicles at the other end of the room.

Eliciting stares and whispers from those in the room, Will walked to Julianna's cubicle and sat down at her desk. The cubicle was very neat and orderly, just as he imagined it would be. Other than a few photos encased in black matte frames there were very few personal items. Will picked up one of the photos. There was a little girl of about six or seven standing in front of a man and woman, the woman's features eerily familiar. He wondered how difficult it was for Julianna to be reminded of her mother every time she looked in the mirror. The young Julianna was smiling, her wide grin revealing two missing front teeth. Her parents each had a hand on her shoulder, as if in a gesture of protection. She was clearly well-loved and Will's heart lurched as he thought of the pain and loss she had endured.

Two photos were of Bella the cat, with Julianna in one of them. Will held onto the one with Julianna holding Bella and stared at it for several long moments before finally putting it back on the desk.

The fourth photo was of Julianna with Jackson Mattice, and appeared to have been taken at some event, maybe a Christmas party or an awards banquet. Julianna, beautiful and radiant in a red dress, her hair cascading down her shoulders, was smiling at Mattice, who was wearing a tux. Will felt a small flutter in his stomach as he ran his finger across the photo.

Thumbtacked to a bulletin board were several yellow sticky notes containing reminders about various things. He read them but nothing stood out.

He opened the desk drawer and noted, among the usual desk junk, several tubes of lip gloss, some hair elastics and clips, a pack of gum and a nutrition bar. Again, nothing useful.

He was done here.

Chapter 32

It was morning and the sun was streaming into the bedroom as Julianna opened her eyes and blinked several times, adjusting to the brightness of the day. What time is it? she wondered, looking at the clock on the nightstand. She sat up on the edge of the bed and groaned when she remembered where she was. Her head still felt fuzzy, like she had a major hangover.

She needed a shower – maybe that would dislodge the fog from her brain. It seemed like she had been asleep for days, but the clock read 1:18. She vaguely remembered Ethan carrying her from the kitchen to the bedroom, but after that it was all a blur.

Looking down at the end of the bed, she saw a stack of packages and bags so she went over to investigate. She heard the door open and Ethan appeared before her, dressed in black jeans and a gray t-shirt. "You're awake," he observed, smiling. "Sleep okay?"

"Like the dead, but I suppose that was your doing," she replied accusingly.

Ethan shrugged, "You needed to sleep."

"What is all this?" Julianna asked, nodding toward the packages.

"I took the liberty of getting you a few things I thought you might need. Let me know if I missed anything."

The fact that he was treating her as if she was simply a guest in his home didn't go unnoticed, but she didn't verbalize those thoughts, instead replying, "Mind if I take a shower?"

"As a matter of fact, I insist on it. You'll feel so much better after a good hot shower. He handed one of the bags to her. "I believe this one contains all the toiletry items. Take your time."

Julianna took the bag from him and stood there, waiting for him to leave, but he didn't so she finally grabbed all of the bags and took them into the bathroom with her, closing the door behind her. Once inside she rummaged around until she found some underwear. She definitely wanted that first and foremost the second she got out of that shower. She then went to the sink to brush her teeth. As she looked up into the mirror she was startled to see that her bruises were no longer visible. They weren't merely faded, but were completely *gone*! Either she had been asleep for days or this guy had performed some magic trick on her face.

Running from the bathroom she realized that Ethan was no longer in the room, so she ran down the hall looking for him. She finally passed by another bedroom and saw him sitting in front of a laptop computer. When he realized she was there, he whirled around, firmly closing the cover of the laptop in one smooth motion. "What is it?" he inquired a bit hastily.

"How long was I asleep?" she demanded. "The bruises, they're gone."

"Rest assured, you were only asleep for about seventeen hours or so. I put something on them, something I picked up in Bali when I was there on a recent...trip. It's really quite amazing, isn't it?"

"So where did all the clothing and stuff come from? How did you manage that in such a short time?"

"The magic of modern technology," he explained, but didn't elaborate. "Now, go take a shower."

"Why won't you answer any of my questions?" she demanded. "And why am I here? What do you *want*?"

Ethan appraised her for a few seconds, contemplating what he wanted to say. "It's better if you don't ask questions."

"I'm not afraid of you."

"Yes, you are," he retorted.

She was, at least somewhat, but she didn't want to admit that to him. He hadn't hurt her yet, but there was still the entire matter of him kidnapping her and, oh by the way, killing those agents, though he maintained that he hadn't. "No, I'm not. I want answers, Ethan."

"Now isn't the time for this conversation, Julianna," he said gently.

"When? *When* is the time for this conversation?" she said, her voice rising with frustration.

His expression became even more guarded, if that was possible, and he said no more. She was clearly not going to get any answers from him so she spun on her heel and stormed back to her room, slammed the door, wishing with everything she had that she could lock it, and stepped into the huge shower. She turned the water on as hot as she could stand it and stood there in the warmth for a few minutes before washing her hair and scrubbing her body with tangerine scented body wash. There was even a girly, pink, safety razor in there, so she shaved her legs and underarms.

When she had finally had enough and felt halfway human again, she turned the water off and toweled herself dry, wrapping the towel around her body when she was finished. Finding a hair dryer under the sink, she dried her hair and then searched through the clothing until she found a pair of jeans, a bra and an off-white sweater. She didn't even want to contemplate how he knew her sizes, much less the exact brand of jeans and bra she always wore.

There was even a small bag of makeup. Again, the same brands and colors she always wore. She didn't bother with the makeup. She wasn't trying to impress anyone here, that's for sure.

Fully dressed but barefoot, Julianna walked out of the bathroom and into the bedroom where she knew Ethan would be waiting. For the longest time he just stared at her, then looked at her feet. "You need shoes," he said, handing her a box that she had somehow missed before.

He withdrew a pair of black ballet flats and she put them on, again her exact size. "How did you know what sizes to buy?" she asked, her eyes narrowed at him.

"I am the consummate observer, Julianna. It's what I do best."

"Well, good. Have you observed that I don't want to be here?" she queried sarcastically.

"Yes, of course I have, Julianna, but there's nothing I can do about that now. We'll talk about this soon, I promise. Are you hungry?"

"Starving actually," she said, deciding to let things drop. For now. She followed him down the hall and into the kitchen.

"Surprise number two," he said once they reached the kitchen. "Pizza."

"Finally, some normal food. I suppose you just happened to run by a pizza place while you were out?"

"Of course," he laughed. "It's not usually something I eat, but figured you needed something a bit more substantial. You're looking a bit too thin."

Julianna snorted. No one had ever accused her of looking too thin. She found the concept laughable. She stood at the counter and opened the box herself. Pepperoni and extra cheese, just the way she liked it. She grabbed a slice and took a bite, then, realizing what she had done immediately stopped chewing, her eyes wide with realization.

Ethan laughed and took the slice from her, taking a bite himself, chewing and swallowing. "I didn't put anything in it, I promise."

"Just like you didn't put anything in it yesterday," Julianna reminded him sarcastically.

"I didn't put anything in your food, Julianna, but I did give you something to make you sleep."

"Then why was I so dizzy?"

"I don't know – fatigue I imagine. Your mind was running a mile a minute. You were exhausted, but wouldn't let yourself fully rest. You've had a lot happen to you in the past week, so I did what I had to do to help you regain your strength." Ethan slid the box toward her, indicating that she needed to eat.

Julianna took another slice and chewed thoughtfully, contemplating what he had said. Since he wouldn't give her anything concrete she would just have to piece the conversations together to try to figure out his M.O.

Ethan watched her with interest as she ate. Most women were so dainty when they ate, but not Julianna. She hadn't even put on the makeup he had purchased for her. She truly didn't seem to care what he thought of her. It was refreshing.

"Live a little, Ethan. Have another slice," she told him, noticing he had stopped eating. "You really never eat pizza?"

"Hardly ever."

She just shrugged and grabbed another slice, leaning over the box as she ate. "Do you have anything to drink?" she asked between bites.

"Water, diet soda, juice," he told her, opening the fridge behind him.

"Water is fine. I definitely don't need any more calories after eating all this," she said, reaching for a third slice.

Ethan grabbed a bottle of water for himself, as well as another slice of the pizza.

Julianna watched Ethan out of the corner of her eye as he drank from the bottle of water. He was clearly happy that she was being so compliant, which was a good sign because she had a plan. She first had to get him to trust her and make him believe that she wasn't going to run.

She had noticed the computer in his bedroom earlier. She somehow had to get to that computer and send an email. She hadn't seen any phones in the house, just the jacks for them, which led her to believe that he either didn't have a phone or he plugged it in when he needed to use it, keeping it hidden somewhere the rest of the time. Of course he did have a cell phone, but getting that would require getting very, very close to him, and as handsome as the man was, she wasn't sure she was ready to go down that road. The laptop would have to do, but it would be trickier. She needed to come up with a plan to distract him. She didn't think the man would be easily distracted. In fact, it might be downright impossible, but she had to try. It was her only shot at getting out of here.

There was also the little problem of where she was. Even if she was able to send an email, she didn't know where she was so how would she be able to summon help? She couldn't just tell someone that she was in a place with lots of trees. Damn, there were too many complications. She would probably only get one shot so she'd better be prepared. Okay, think Julianna, *think*.

"So, what are your plans for the day?" she asked him before swigging some of her water.

"Plans? Well, I don't know. What would you like to do?"

"I'm not sure," she replied vaguely as she sauntered out of the kitchen and headed toward the living room. She had seen a stereo in there.

Ethan followed behind her, ever her shadow, and watched as she went over to the stereo and flipped the switch to turn it on.

"Care to dance?" she asked, finding a radio station. Radio stations always gave out their location every few songs, she thought. And even if the station came from out of town she could at least get an idea of where she was, and then use other methods to narrow it down.

Ethan must have realized it too, for he ran over and flipped the radio off. "How about a CD instead?" he offered.

"Sure, whatever you like," she replied, smiling sweetly through her disappointment. She looked through his CD collection, finally settling on Michael Bublé, one of her favorites. She was actually surprised since she didn't know many men who enjoyed Michael Bublé. He must have it here to woo the ladies. Or maybe one of those ladies gave it to him.

Ethan took the disc out of her hand, put it into the player and within seconds the room was filled with Michael's soothing voice perform a remake of an old Bee Gee's song.

"I seem to remember a dance invitation?" Ethan reminded her, extending his hand to her.

"Okay," Julianna said, hesitating for just a split-second before stepping toward him and taking his hand. Keeping his left hand in her much smaller right one, he put his other arm on her back, gently pulling her toward him. Julianna wrapped her left arm around his neck, her head close to his chest. Ethan pulled her closer, his hand now entwined in her hair. Julianna looked up to see that his eyes were closed. Feeling her eyes on his he opened them, and looked into her eyes with a questioning expression on his face. He leaned down as his hand came around, fingers tracing along her jaw.

Oh my God, he was going to kiss her! Julianna quickly put her head down and against his chest, breaking the spell of the kiss, but not breaking precious contact. Contact she was going to need to carry out her plan.

As they continued to dance Julianna kept her eyes on the many windows in the living room, trying to figure out where she was. There was a heavy blanket of snow on the ground and there were trees, hundreds of them, and they seemed to surround this entire side of the property. Looking over them she could see the hazy silhouettes of mountains. Mountains!

As he spun her around, she maneuvered them discreetly to the other side of the room where she could see out the other windows. "Julianna, are you okay? You're trembling."

"I'm okay, just a little cold," she replied. Nervous, anxious, scared-to-death about what it was going to take to get out of here was more like it, but of course she didn't say that.

In response Ethan pulled her closer, letting go of her hand and placing it on her back, his other hand on the back of her neck and once more buried in her hair. She swallowed the lump in her throat and blinked back tears as she placed her newly freed hand against his back.

As he turned her around, she could clearly see mountains out the window. So, they were *in* the mountains, Julianna realized. She hadn't spent much time outside of the city since moving from Tennessee, but she knew she was either in the Catskills or the Poconos. So much for that, she thought. She'd just have to pinpoint her location some other way. The pizza box had been a huge disappointment. What pizza place didn't advertise their name? The box had simply stated *Pizza* – no name, no phone number.

Julianna closed her eyes, trying to drown out the song, which was fortunately almost over. It was impossible to forget that Ethan's arms were wrapped tightly around her, so she tried to imagine that he was Will instead.

Ethan had made some pretty terrible accusations about Will the day before and Julianna was still not sure what to make of them, but for the moment she would assume that

Ethan was merely playing games with her. Even if Will *had* dated a lot of women in the past, he told her that he didn't date much anymore. Could that have been a lie? Ethan was accurate when he asked her if Will had been a little *too* helpful, *too* understanding. She had assumed it was just Will's way, but could that have been a lie as well? She had liked Will taking care of her. No man had ever treated her as kindly as Will had. If he was playing her she had fallen for it hook, line and sinker, as her daddy used to say.

She detested this feeling of doubt and mistrust, but even more she hated not knowing what was real anymore. She wanted to get her life back, whatever that meant. She doubted that life would involve Will, but so be it.

Taking a deep breath as the song ended, Julianna broke their embrace and reached down onto the coffee table for the remote control to the stereo. Turning the volume down on Bublé she took Ethan's hand and led him over to the sofa where she sat down, pulling him down beside her. He eyed her suspiciously. "What game are you playing, Julianna?" he asked, his voice low.

"No game, Ethan. I just figured if we're going to spend a lot of time together we should at least get to know each other better."

"Yesterday you were running from me and today you're suddenly dancing with me? As much as I want it to it doesn't make sense, Julianna."

"Ethan, you kidnapped me! What was I supposed to think? I was afraid of you, but today...today I see that you aren't going to hurt me. You've taken such good care of me. You bought the things I needed, even knowing my sizes. And as you said before, you saved my life there in Larchmont. I know that now."

Ethan continued to look at her, his eyes narrowed, skeptical. She was no actress, but she was going to have to put forth an Academy Award-winning performance if she wanted any chance of winning him over. He had clearly been ready to kiss her earlier. She would just have to count on him giving her a second chance.

"Ethan, please," she pleaded softly, looking directly into his eyes. Bringing a trembling hand up, she placed it tenderly on his cheek, running her index finger down across his strong jaw. "Ethan," she whispered, tears springing to her eyes. "I just need... I'm just... afraid."

He traced his finger along her lower lip, his eyes never leaving hers. She leaned into him, resting her hand on his upper thigh. Ethan leaned down to her, his lips brushing against her own, but not making full contact. He placed his hand gently on top of hers and laced his fingers into hers. "Stop playing games," he whispered softly in warning, gently removing her hand from his thigh and standing up from the sofa.

"I have some work to do. Pick something to watch," he said, indicating a cabinet full of DVDs.

"Ethan, I don't under..."

"Stop, Julianna. Just stop," he interrupted. "Choose." He opened the cabinet and waited for her decision.

She opened her mouth to argue, but decided she'd best just shut up and do what he wanted, so she walked over to randomly choose a movie from the collection. Her shoulder brushed against his chest as she reached in to grab one. "This one will be fine," she said, handing it to him.

After he started the movie for her, Ethan left the room and Julianna settled back onto the sofa, staring blankly at the television screen, planning her next move.

Chapter 33

Will had stayed away from the office, holing up in a coffee shop down the street from the newspaper. He had spent hours poring over the printouts from Jackson Mattice's office. The waitress, whose name tag revealed her name as Dot, came by to refill his coffee cup. "Hun, you sure you don't want some of that apple pie? You've been sitting here a long time. Looks like you could use a little sustenance."

Will looked up from the printouts and rubbed his tired eyes, pinching the bridge of his nose. Despite the caffeine he was getting a headache. "Okay Dot, bring it on," he smiled wearily at her.

"You got it, hun. Whipped cream?" she tempted, cocking her head.

"Sure, what the heck," he replied. She winked at him, popping her gum. "You won't regret it, hun – made it myself."

Will's phone vibrated on the table in front of him. He looked at the caller ID. "Hey mom," he answered.

"Will, is everything all right? I haven't heard from you in over a week."

"I've been really busy with a case."

"Too busy to call your own mother? What am I going to do with you?" she chided, but he could tell she was smiling.

"I'm sorry mom," Will said, feeling guilty. "So, how are you?"

"I'm fine. I finally finished painting the guest room. It would be nice to have a guest, though," she hinted.

"I'll try to get out there as soon as this case is over, I promise."

"Brian, Sarah, and the baby were here last weekend," she ventured.

Will bristled at the mention of his older brother's name. "That's nice," he answered tightly.

"Oh Will," his mother sighed. "Life is too short to keep harboring this anger toward your brother. One of these days you're going to have to forgive them. It happened a long time ago. It's time to move on."

"I know mom," he said. He didn't want to think about this right now. Sure, he was still angry at Brian and Sarah for violating his trust, but the truth was, he didn't feel the same way for Sarah that he once had, and something deep inside him wondered if his feelings for her at the time had been anywhere near as strong as the feelings of anger and resentment he harbored now. His mother was right. It was long over and he had recovered, but something inside kept him from letting it go. They had been very young and Will had spent years wondering what he could have done differently to keep Sarah true to him. Sure, he could have been more attentive, picked up his socks, made sure the toilet seat was down, but he knew none of those things would have made a difference. Sarah was meant to be with Brian. She had fallen in love with the other brother, and there wasn't a thing he could have done about it. He had to stop blaming himself, and he certainly had to stop being angry at them, because all it was doing was tearing his family further apart. But right now he couldn't focus on any of that, so he pushed it out of his mind.

"Will, are you sure everything is all right? You sound tired."

"I *am* tired," Will admitted, switching the phone to his other ear. "It's been a rough week and there's no end in sight. I'm on a pretty big case right now and it's frustrating."

"Want to talk about it?"

"As much as I wish I could, you know I can't do that. But I appreciate your concern," he added. Look mom, I've got another call coming in and I have to take it. I'll talk to you soon, okay? And mom – thanks for worrying about me."

"I'll never stop. Be careful, sweetheart," she said, hanging up.

"Delaney," Will answered, clicking over to the other call. "She's awake, Delaney. I can't get ahold of Olsen. Get over to the hospital now," Walter Simpson barked into the phone.

Will pulled out his wallet and threw some money down on the table just as Dot came down the aisle with his pie. "Sorry, Dot – gotta run. Another day," he promised, flying out the door.

Chapter 34

"Delaney," Isabel Rodriguez whispered hoarsely as he walked into the room.

Will nodded to the other man in the room, an agent named Delgado, who he knew only in passing.

"How are you?" Will asked, stepping close to the bed and grasping the rail as he leaned down to better hear her.

"They say I'm going to live," she half-joked, trying to ease Will's apparent tension. "Jankowski, is he okay?"

Will shook his head slowly.

Tears sprang to her eyes. "Oh God," she whispered. "Kilbourne and Shepherd?"

"Just you, Rodriguez," he told her softly.

She didn't say anything as she collected herself. "Julianna Brennan?" she finally spoke.

"She wasn't there when we arrived on the scene."

"She didn't do this, Delaney."

"I know," Will assured her gently. "What do you remember, Isabel?"

"Just... Jankowski and I were arriving for our shift. I remember seeing muzzle flash in the house as we pulled up. At first I couldn't believe it – thought it was the television, but it was unmistakable." She paused to collect her thoughts. "Jankowski was driving. I think I leapt out of the car before it even stopped and started to run toward the house with my weapon drawn. But I guess that's when I was hit. I just remember feeling kind of shocked. I saw him coming toward me – just a black figure – black pants, shirt. I couldn't see his face. I just remember everything being so dark. I don't remember anything else, but I'm sure I fired at least one shot. Did they test my piece?"

"Yeah, and you actually managed to get off two. You did good, Rodriguez," he assured her.

"But I missed," she said dully.

"You're lucky to be alive, Isabel."

"So what do you know, Delaney?"

"Not much, but I'm working on it,"

"When you find the son of a bitch who took out Jankowski, Shepherd and Kilbourne I want to be the first to know."

"You will be, Isabel. I promise. The doctor says you need your rest. I'm going to send your family back in," he said, turning to leave.

"Delaney," she called after him just as he reached the door. "That girl, she feels a lot for you. Don't hurt her."

Will turned and walked out of the room, closing the door quietly behind him.

Chapter 35

Julianna sat on the sofa, ignoring the movie Ethan had put into the DVD player for her to watch. She looked out the window at the falling snow and tried to think of how she was going to get Ethan out of the way long enough to get to that computer. She had an internet-based email address so she could check her email from anywhere in the world, and if she could get to the computer and the internet she could access that account and send an email to someone. Maybe the FBI could trace the email – see where it came from. Surely they could contact the email provider and find out that information. Wasn't Big Brother watching everything anyway?

The only addresses she could remember were for people at the newspaper, but she could have them get the message to the FBI or police. The only problem was getting Ethan out of the way and then getting into his room and computer, which he probably had password protected. It wasn't going to be easy, but she had to give it a shot. The only question was if she was willing to do anything to get out of there. Yes, she decided, she would do anything to get out of there. She had to.

Julianna got up from the sofa and headed down the hall to the room where the computer was located. She paused for a moment and took a deep breath before she knocked softly on the door.

Ethan came to the door and opened it slightly, his eyes questioning. "Ethan," Julianna began, looking up at him, "I...may I talk to you?" she asked softly.

Ethan opened the door wider and behind him she could see the computer monitor, which was turned on. She swallowed hard, trying successfully to hide her excitement. Ethan opened the door even wider, allowing her entry. She ducked under his arm, which held open the door, and into the room.

Julianna walked over to a sitting area on the opposite side of the room from the computer. She didn't want to even look in that direction so she deliberately chose a spot where she would be facing away from it. She primly sat down on a settee and folded her hands in her lap, the tears beginning to fall silently upon them as she hung her head, looking down.

"What is it? What has happened?" Ethan asked her, standing there awkwardly. Julianna looked up at him, her eyes meeting his. Surprisingly, he looked genuinely concerned. His brow was furrowed as he waited expectantly for her to answer.

Julianna stood up and walked to the window, staring out at the heavily falling snow. She traced her index finger along with window where the moisture had accumulated. She felt Ethan walk up behind her. "What is wrong, Julianna?" he asked her gently. "You said you wanted to talk to me," he reminded her. "I'm listening."

Julianna chose her words carefully before turning around to face Ethan. "I'm afraid, Ethan," she finally told him, looking down as she spoke. Ethan stood there silently, waiting for her to finish. "I don't know what to do, what you expect of me. I'm afraid of you, I'm afraid of this, this situation." Once she started crying, she found she couldn't stop. The tears were real and what she said was true, but her intentions were far from what she hoped Ethan thought they might be. She turned back to the frosty window. The snow was falling so heavily that it was difficult to see the trees, which surrounded the property. Julianna felt as if she were being buried under a heavy white blanket.

Ethan stepped closer to her and touched his hand to her shoulder. "I don't want you to be afraid of me, Julianna. I can't give you any answers right now. This is the way it has to be. For now."

"Why?" she asked, turning around to face him once more.

"Because, it's just the way it is." Julianna could tell he wanted to say more, but something was keeping him from doing so. She decided to press further.

"I have a right to know why you're holding me here," she pleaded. She walked over to the bed and sat down on it, looking expectantly at him as he continued to hold his ground next to the window. "Ethan, please" she called softly. Shaking his head with a combination of disbelief and defeat Ethan walked slowly over to the bed, watching her face as he did so.

"What are you doing, Julianna?" he asked quietly, looking down at her.

"I just want you to hold me," she answered, reaching out to take his hand.

Ethan took her hand, but instead of sitting down on the bed, he pulled her to her feet. "Not here, and not like this."

"Yes, exactly like this," she whispered, leaning her head against his chest. He instinctively wrapped his arms around her and held her, just as she had asked to be held.

"Damnit woman," he breathed into her hair. "You are making this very difficult."

Chapter 36

Will had fallen asleep on the sofa at around two a.m. His cell phone rang, startling him awake. He stumbled to the desk, cursing as he slammed his shin into the coffee table. Fumbling for his phone, he knocked the newspaper printouts onto the floor, eliciting yet another curse. He glanced at the time as he picked up the phone – three-thirty a.m. Damn, no wonder he was so tired. The caller ID showed the number as blocked. "Delaney," he answered groggily, eyes burning from lack of sleep as he shook his head, trying to wake himself up from the fog his brain was in.

"Meet me at the all-night diner around the corner – the one with the flashing coffee cup on the sign."

Will was instantly awake. "Give me five minutes," he said, holstering his Glock and backup piece.

Chapter 37

Julianna sat huddled in the darkness where she had been since she had run out of Ethan's room after sending the email. She should have known, she told herself over and over. Ethan had the place rigged with cameras and had seen every little thing she had done. Whatever her punishment was, it wouldn't matter as long as someone got those emails.

She had managed to convince Ethan to go back to her room and her bed where he had held her in his arms until he had fallen asleep. Ethan had demanded nothing else of her, but simply provided what she had needed – the comfort of two strong arms. She had carefully removed herself from his grasp as he slept, and slipped back into the room where the computer sat, quickly composing an email and sending to her friend Allegra at the office.

As she had left the room Ethan had grabbed her, pressing a gun to her head and pushing her forward. They had ended up downstairs in yet another level of the house, in a dark and damp wine cellar, which was devoid of any actual wine. He closed and locked the door behind him, leaving her alone in the darkness. She was freezing cold, but for some reason she felt calm. She had to believe help was on the way. Maybe Ethan had even left the house knowing that she had sent the email, and any minute the door would open and her rescuer would be standing on the other side.

She had no idea what time it was, but she knew that she had been in here for several hours. She hugged her knees to her chest and tried to concentrate on something other than how cold she was and how badly she needed to use the bathroom.

Suddenly the door flew open and Julianna squinted as the light from outside the cellar flooded the room. Ethan stood in the doorway and ordered her to stand up.

Julianna stood, her right leg numb from sitting for too long. She shook it slightly, trying to get the feeling back as she took a few steps toward Ethan. "Come on," he said, his voice flat. Together they walked out of the cellar and back up to the pool area. He motioned to the door of a bathroom. "Make it fast."

Julianna finished up in the bathroom and walked out to where Ethan was waiting for her. He motioned for her to take a seat in a poolside chair and he pulled up another, his knees almost touching hers as he sat directly in front of her. Julianna watched his face for some sign of what was to come, but his stoical expression gave nothing away. Finally he spoke. "That was a stupid thing to do, Julianna. You have no idea just how stupid. I'm trying to protect you!" he said, raising his voice.

"Protect me from what Ethan?" she yelled, jumping out of her chair. "How could I possibly know you're trying to protect me if you won't *tell* me anything? You want me to be grateful to you for saving me from this imaginary person who killed those FBI agents? *You* killed them, Ethan. *You* killed those agents! Who are you trying to protect me from? Yourself?"

"Sit down," Ethan told her calmly, remaining in his chair.

"No." Julianna stood defiantly over him, her arms crossed, her expression angry.

"Sit down," he repeated, just as calmly as before.

"I will *not* sit down, Ethan. And as a matter of fact, I will not do anything else you tell me to do. You'll have to kill me first."

He sighed and raked his hands through his hair. He looked up at her, his expression defeated. Julianna glared at him in defiance.

"Please," he said quietly, motioning for her to sit. "I'll tell you everything."

She plopped down in the chair and crossed her arms, waiting.

"I was sent to protect you. That's all I've been doing. I'm not the bad guy here, Julianna." He ran his fingers through his hair again and leaned forward, placing his hand on her knee. "I don't actually work for Victor Ciccone. I'm FBI. I've been undercover for almost two years now trying to get enough on Ciccone to put him away for a long time. We needed someone on the inside."

She waited for him to continue, her face expressionless.

"Delaney and I were in the Navy SEALS together. Ciccone wanted me to deal with the situation with Jackson Mattice. I never killed anyone for him, Julianna. Everyone he had a hit on we put into Witness Protection. We'd have agents construct a phony crime scene with a phony body and I'd take a picture. That's how Ciccone wanted proof – with a photo. It was relatively easy, that aspect of it.

"I had been watching you for a while because Ciccone wanted this memory card you supposedly had. I didn't know what was on the card. I learned not to ask too many questions or he'd become suspicious. He sent his nephew Rico Cordova to rough you up, try to get the card from you – he wasn't supposed to harm you in any way. I was sent to kill Jackson Mattice. I followed him from his apartment to Chinatown and was going to corner him and bring him in, but someone got to him first. The shot came out of nowhere. Everyone was screaming and running in different directions. I was trying to find the shooter, but he must have dispersed with the crowd. I never saw him.

"Then Delaney killed Cordova, and Ciccone called out the hit on Delaney as payback. There was never a hit on you. I'm the one who placed that anonymous call to the FBI. I said there was a hit out on both of you because I figured whoever killed Jackson Mattice would probably be coming after you next. I knew Delaney would get the message so I told him I was standing in quicksand. It's a code he and I used to use when someone was in trouble. I knew he'd understand I was trying to warn him.

"I found out who was guarding the safe house and followed them there. I was down the street watching from a distance when I saw Agents Jankowski and Rodriguez go down. I never saw the guy enter the house, so I'm not sure how he got in, but by the time I got there he was gone. I never saw him, but it had to be an inside job for him to get close enough to kill four agents. I think you know the rest," he finished.

Julianna numbly sat there, taking in all he had told her. Rodriguez and Jankowski were dead too? Isabel. Tears sprang to her eyes as she remembered the agent discussing her family. All of this over some stupid memory card! "Does Will know I'm here?" she asked Ethan.

"He knows you're safe with me. That's all he wanted to know," he admitted to her. "Are you okay?"

This changed everything. Ethan hadn't lied to her. He had only been trying to protect her. "I sent an email to a co-worker and I gave her your first name. I told her to forward it to the FBI."

"I know," he said gently. "I have a key-logger on the computer."

"Did I screw up?"

"We'll see. Let's just hope Delaney got the message before anyone else did." Delaney would have texted him by now if he had gotten the message. Ethan was getting worried that he hadn't. Anyone could have intercepted the message, and he still wasn't sure who to trust.

"I'm sorry," Julianna said. "What do we do now?"

"We wait for Delaney to text me. Let's go upstairs and get something to eat – I'm starving."

Suddenly a siren went off in the house. "What is that?" Julianna cried out above the noise. "A smoke detector?"

"Oh hell!" Ethan exclaimed. He looked at her feet. "Do not move," he told her sternly. "I'll be right back." He ran up the stairs and quickly returned with a pair of boots and a coat. "Put these on!" he commanded.

The boots were far too large for her feet. "What size do you wear? A fourteen?" Julianna complained, pulling on the boots without even untying them. The coat was much the same, but at least it was warm.

"It doesn't matter – you just need something to cover your feet through the snow. "Come on," he told her suddenly, grabbing her hand and pulling her toward the door.

"What is going on, Ethan?" she demanded.

"Someone has entered the property. We've got about ten minutes before they get here." Ethan took a remote control device out of his pocket and opened the door to the outside. A blast of arctic air took her breath away as the door swung open. Ethan began to run across the dark back yard, pulling her along with him. The snow was falling heavily and the flakes hit Julianna in the face, making it difficult for her to see, not that she could see much anyway in the dark, but Ethan seemed to know where he was going. Several times she stumbled in the too-large boots as Ethan half dragged her behind him.

They finally came to a wooded area and Ethan grabbed a roll of duct tape from his jacket pocket. "What are you doing?" Julianna demanded, out of breath and clearly panicked.

"I'll come back for you," he promised her.

"What are you doing? *What*? No, Ethan," she pleaded as he ripped off a strip of the tape.

"It's for your own good. I don't trust anyone at this point. I need to feel this out first and I don't want you running toward the first person you recognize."

"I won't!" she cried.

He looked at her dubiously and wound the tape around her ankles several times as she struggled against him. He finally knocked her down on the ground and straddled her, holding her hands together over her head with one of his own as he cut off a long strip of tape with his knife.

Once her hands were tightly bound, he was able to bind her feet more easily. "Please, Ethan. Don't do this."

"I'm sorry, Julianna. I'll promise I'll come back for you." He then reached down and picked her up, hoisting her over his shoulder and walking a few feet forward. He set her down in a standing position and held onto her with one hand so she wouldn't fall. With the other he reached down and felt around in the snow until he found what he was looking for. His hand pulled up a board and Julianna's eyes widened with terror as she saw what was under the board. It appeared to be a wood box and was just the right size for one person to fit in, like a coffin.

"No, please," she begged him, her eyes filling with tears. "I don't do well in small spaces. Just take me with you," she pleaded.

"I told you, I'll come back for you," he promised.

"Ethan, no, please, no!" she screamed, tears running down her face. "*Please*, don't do this. *Please!* I can't...don't put me in there. Please don't put me in there!"

With a grunt, he picked her up again and set her into the box. She tried to fight him, but once she was down in the box it was difficult for her to move. Ethan stared down at her.
The snow was falling onto Julianna's face, but because her hands were bound she couldn't wipe the cold flakes away. Ethan took off his hat and wiped her face, looking into her terrified eyes. He ripped off another piece of duct tape with his teeth and covered her mouth with it. She struggled to breath, her panic rising. "Breathe through your nose, Julianna," he told her. "Slow breaths. That's good, baby. It's going to be okay."

He removed his coat and placed it over her before pulling down the lid of the box and padlocking it closed. "I'm sorry," he said as he turned away from where she lay and headed deep into the woods. Their tracks were being quickly covered with heavy snowfall, and within minutes there would be no sign of life anywhere near Julianna's snowy grave.

Chapter 38

Will slid into the booth across the table from Jackson Mattice. "Where the hell have you been?" he demanded.

"I had to lie low for a while," Mattice answered defensively.

"I ought to shoot you right here." Will's jaw worked. He clenched his fists to keep from reaching across the table and jerking Mattice out of the diner by the shirt collar and giving him a piece of his mind in a dark alley. He longed for some retribution for all that Julianna had endured because of this scum, but he knew Mattice was only part of the problem. He would have plenty of time to deal with Mattice later.

"I know." Mattice at least looked somewhat ashamed.

"Do you realize the...the...complete and utter mess you've created? I don't even have words to describe... If you were just honest with me from the beginning..." Will's voice trailed off as he noticed a couple at the other end of the diner watching them with keen interest. He lowered his voice collected his emotions by taking a deep breath. "I'm listening and you're talking."

Jackson Mattice rubbed the side of his face thoughtfully, and then proceeded to tell Will the entire story, beginning with the front-page ads he had placed and the money he had taken for doing so, and ending with his brother being shot in Chinatown. "I had called Ray and told him I was in trouble and needed his help. Serious help this time – not like before when I just needed some money here and there. Clearly I was convincing. He flew out, gave me some cash, told me to never contact him again, and left my apartment. I didn't really need the cash – what I needed was to disappear for a while, with some… er… documentation. But Ray just did the thing that Ray does best – threw some money at the situation and called it a day. I guess he headed into Chinatown for the hell of it and someone mistook him for me. You have no idea how many regrets I have in all of this, Delaney."

"Don't even try to make this about you, Mattice. You're not going to get any sympathy here. Why in hell did you involve Julianna Brennan?"

"I didn't mean to. I guess that's not true – I meant to, but she's a woman, I didn't think they'd do anything to her. She doesn't know anything."

"This person, or people – they don't care whether or not she's a woman!" Will shot back. "Someone killed three agents and very near killed a fourth. Two of them were women! Are you convinced now, Mattice?" Will's voice took on a dangerous edge, and forget taking him to a dark alley, it was all he could do not to reach across the table and strangle Mattice right here and now with his bare hands. He knew he was more than capable at this point.

"Where is Julianna?" Mattice asked. He placed his hands on the table and leaned forward. For a brief moment Will thought Mattice was going to reach out and take his hand. His voice had a hint of desperation.

"Julianna is no longer your concern, Mattice."

"At least let me know she's okay, Delaney."

"You don't deserve to know anything about her – ever." Will couldn't help but see the tortured look that crossed Mattice's face. He didn't want to give this lowlife anything, but he also needed answers, and in order to do that he was fully aware that there would have to be a little give along with the take.

He paused to collect his emotions before continuing. "*However*, to put your mind at rest, not that you deserve that either, she's safe. For now. But I want some answers and I want them now. Who is behind this and what the hell is the deal with the ads? I've spent the past twelve or so hours going over them and am just now getting a picture, but it's still not fully clear. Give me your take."

"You're doing better than I did – it took me weeks to figure it out," Jackson replied. "And thanks, Delaney. I know you might find this impossible to believe, but I never meant for anything to happen to Julianna. She means a lot to me – more than you could begin to realize."

Will didn't respond as he sat stone-faced waiting for Mattice to continue. "To answer your first question, I don't know who is behind it. To answer your second question, the ads were actually quite brilliant and someone went to a lot of work to execute them. They're legit ads, but the establishment in the ad had nothing to do with placing them. Someone researched real ads placed elsewhere and then placed the same ad at the appropriate time. Take the last two digits of the phone number and you have a time. 42, for example, would be 4:20. I discovered by trial and error that there wasn't a set a.m. or p.m. Everything happened at night, so if the number was 94, then it was 9:40 p.m., but if it was 33, say, then it was 3:30 a.m.

"And the address, that's easy – switch the first number with the last, so 237 would be 732. Now, this is the tricky part. Different establishments were code for different things, so a restaurant would mean one thing, a bar another, a clothing store another, and so on."

"So what did they mean?" Will asked.

"I don't know, but every Friday night at the time scheduled two men would show up, exchange a briefcase, and be on their way. One of them was always a tall guy, white, arrived in a black Mercedes. The other was a smaller guy, Middle Eastern or something, olive-skinned. He arrived in a Jag, some green color. But part of the time there would be a different guy, same olive skin, but bigger by a lot. Muscular, I mean, not fat.

"Did you ever follow them?"

"In what?"

Will sighed. Good point, Mattice didn't own a vehicle. How could he be so close, but so far from solving this thing? "Could you give a description to a sketch artist?" It was the best he could do at this point.

"I can do better than that," Mattice told him. "I took pictures. But you already know that."

"No, I don't already know that. Where are they?"

"Julianna has them. They're on a memory card," Mattice replied. "And you should, Delaney. I told you that the day after I took them."

"You never told me about any memory card, Mattice. I'm pretty sure that's something I would have remembered," Will replied irritably.

Mattice narrowed his eyes at Will. "Then someone else intercepted the call because I told *someone* about that memory card. That's why they came after her."

Will's mind raced back to a time when he wouldn't have had his phone on him. He sometimes left it on his desk when he was working. There were a million times a day when he left his phone unattended. Everything was pointing to someone on the inside. His stomach clenched. His gut had been right – he knew something wasn't quite right about this case.

"Didn't you notice it wasn't my voice?" Will asked.

"No. I did pretty much all the talking. And frankly, I wasn't paying much attention to what you, I mean he, was saying in response. It was a brief conversation."

"So did you say where the memory card was?"

"No, just that she had it and it was safe. She doesn't even know she has it. It's a tacky thing I picked up in Chinatown – a mermaid with a USB Thumb Drive hidden inside. It's gold, heavy and extremely gaudy. I told Julianna I had picked it up in Miami when I was visiting Ray. I knew she'd never wear it – she's too classy for something like that – but I also knew that she was sentimental enough to hold onto it. I never meant for her to even know what was on it. I planned to get it back from her at some point and turn it over to the FBI, but then Ray was killed and Julianna was attacked. I wasn't sure who to trust, or if she even still had it."

Will's jaw worked as he realized the damn pictures had been under his nose the entire time. He remembered seeing that hideous necklace on the ground, along with the other contents of her purse, the night she was attacked. He had put it back in her purse himself. He leaned down, elbow on the table and hand in his hair, and pressed his palm to his forehead in weary frustration. "Why did you tell her to look at the pictures of the Mayor's Ball?"

"Because I filed some of the pictures in the Mayor's Ball files for backup, just in case something happened to the memory card."

"They weren't there. Julianna and I both studied every photo in those files."

"Then someone deleted them. How could anyone know they were there?"

"Because maybe, Mattice, someone was following you or Julianna and they overheard your conversation at the coffee shop." Will didn't attempt to conceal his annoyance at the stupidity of this man. People might feel safe in a crowded area, but they were, in fact, the worst possible place to go if you didn't want someone overhearing your conversation.

"Is that all, Mattice? Is there anything else I need to know?"

"That's all I know." Mattice looked at Will expectantly. "What are you going to do with me?" he asked, worriedly.

Will picked up his coffee cup, took a sip, and looked out the window, staring out into the night for several seconds. The door of a black Chevy Suburban, parked directly in front of the diner, opened. Mattice noticed the man exit the vehicle and walk into the restaurant. "You're taking me in?" he asked, incredulous.

"I can't let you walk, Mattice. There's still a lot you'll have to answer for. Special Agent Mathers will get your official statement."

"I'm not safe in there," Mattice argued. "You know that!"

"You'll be fine, Mattice. We'll put you in protective custody."

"At least leave the handcuffs off. I'm not going to run."

Will nodded at Agent Mathers, who put his hand on Mattice's arm and led him out of the restaurant, settling him in the back seat of the Suburban.

As Will was about to close the door Mattice spoke. "Delaney, please tell Julianna how sorry I am. And if you can find just a shred of common decency I'd like the opportunity to tell her myself."

Will shook his head in disbelief. "Mattice, if *you* had a shred of common decency you would never have gotten her involved in this in the first place. Do not attempt to contact her or I will make sure your stay in our illustrious prison system is your worst nightmare. Do we understand each other?"

Mattice swallowed hard and nodded as Will firmly closed the door.

"Are you heading out to the Catskills?" Agent Mathers asked Delaney.

"What?" Will asked, perplexed.

"Olsen's been trying to reach you. We've found Julianna Brennan. SWAT team's on the way there now."

"Olsen never called me," Will said, his mind racing. "Call Simpson and tell him not to let Olsen anywhere near Julianna Brennan and that I'm on the way!" He took off running toward his apartment and Tahoe, leaving Agent Mathers bewildered on the sidewalk.

"But you don't even know where you're going!" Mathers called after him.

Chapter 39

The house and grounds were swarming with agents when Will arrived on the scene, but somehow SAC Simpson's internal radar was right on track and he spotted Will as he walked up the hill toward the house, having parked at the bottom due to the large number of vehicles.

"There's no one here," Simpson told him. "Good work on Mattice, by the way. Where's Olsen?"

"I was just going to ask you the same thing," Will responded, his heart pounding. "Isn't he here?"

"Haven't seen him," Simpson yelled above the noise of one of the SWAT helicopters as it took off above them. "He said he was trying to reach you and that's the last I heard from him."

"He never called me," Will yelled back.

Simpson motioned for Will to follow him into the house. "I don't know, Delaney," he said once they were inside the relative quiet of the house. "This doesn't look like a kidnapping to me. There are clothes and toiletries. Doesn't look like Julianna Brennan was too uncomfortable here, or being held against her will."

"But that doesn't mean she wasn't," Will argued. "Where was she going to go in these woods, and in this weather? It took me a good ten minutes to get here from the main road."

"Maybe," Simpson responded. "But I'm not convinced."

"Olsen is in on this, Simpson, I know it. Someone intercepted a call from Jackson Mattice and found out vital information. The only other person who knew about Mattice was Olsen. And you," he added.

"You're accusing *me* now, Delaney? You can't go accusing good agents, and that includes me, of things you have no proof of. Granted, I have no reasonable explanation for why Olsen isn't here," he admitted.

"I'm not accusing anyone of anything. I'm just requesting that you entertain the possibility. Have you searched the grounds? We've got to find Julianna Brennan before Olsen does."

Simpson gave him a pointed look at the accusation against Olsen. "We've got the dogs out there. If anyone's still here we'll find them."

An agent with a cell phone pressed to his ear walked up to them. "Sir, the home belongs to an Ethan Fray. He's one of us."

"What?!" Simpson yelled.

"He's one of us, sir. He's been deep undercover with Victor Ciccone for the past year and a half."

"Give me the phone," Simpson demanded, snatching it away from the bewildered agent. Amidst a bevy of "uh-huhs" and "why wasn't I informed of this?" he must have gotten the answers he was looking for as he practically threw the phone back at the young agent.

"Find Olsen," he told Will. "Because I have a feeling Fray won't be too far away."

"You know Olsen killed those agents, don't you, sir?"

"Or Fray did," he reminded Will.

"He didn't. I know Fray. He's on our side, trust me."

"I'll trust you when this is all over, your report sitting on my desk, wrapped up in a neat little package and tied with a pretty little bow, Delaney. What I want to know is how Fray ended up with Julianna Brennan at the safe house."

"He contacted me and I asked him to keep an eye on her," Will admitted.

"And once again, I'm left totally out of the loop," Simpson said, his eyes cutting daggers into Will.

"I didn't know who to trust, Simpson. That's it – bottom line." Will refused to apologize for keeping Julianna safe.

Simpson looked like he wanted to say more, much more, but instead he repeated, "Find Olsen." And then turned to walk to the back of the house where agents were combing the bedrooms. "We're done in the house. I want everyone outside!" Will heard Simpson yell to the agents as he disappeared around the corner.

Will headed down the stairs and into the pool area. Just then he heard yelling outside. He ran out the door to the sounds of shots being fired! Agents were running into the woods toward the shots, with Will among the herd.

They stopped short as they came to a cliff with a dangerously deep ravine below them. "Don't shoot him, Paul!" Will yelled. "He knows where Julianna is."

Paul, standing a few feet from the edge of the ravine with Ethan Fray directly above him on the cliff, whipped around and met Will's gaze, his expression wild with fury. But he held his fire as the agents invaded. A look passed between Ethan Fray and Will before Fray turned to assess the agents who surrounded Olsen in support. "He's on our side, Olsen," Will warned him.

"The hell he is, Delaney. He shot at me first."

Ethan gave Will a slight shake of the head to indicate no.

"Okay, Olsen. Take it easy. I'm coming over. We need to get some answers from Fray and I don't want him to jump." Will put his arm back to indicate to the other agents to hold off, and carefully edged around the ravine until he was between Olsen and Fray. He then aimed the Glock at Olsen. "Put down the gun, Olsen," he ordered.

"You're my partner, Delaney. Don't tell me you're going to believe this scumbag. He killed three agents! I'm taking him down, just as I was ordered."

Ethan studied the ravine below as Will confronted the other agent. "Don't even think about it, Fray," Will warned him, fully expecting him to jump.

"Where is she?" Olsen demanded.

"Far away from you, Olsen! You'll never find her, so just forget it," Ethan yelled back.

"Where *is* she?" Olsen demanded again, stepping closer to him.

"Back away from him, Olsen," Will warned, clicking off the safety of his Glock.

"If either of you step any closer I will jump and you will *never* find her," Ethan added.

The other agents looked from Will to Olsen to Fray, clearly confused and unsure of what was going on, who to train their weapons on.

"Okay, okay, take it easy, Fray" Olsen said, backing up slightly.

"I'm taking it plenty easy, Olsen," Ethan told him.

Suddenly a shot rang out. "What the hell? No!" Will yelled as Paul peppered Ethan Fray with bullets. Ethan fell forward off the cliff and into the ravine. Will stumbled backward, grabbing his arm as a flash of fire shot through it. His foot hit the edge of the ravine, but he caught himself just in time and lunged forward, his knee hitting a rock as he fell onto the snowy ground. "Handcuff him *now*!" he ordered, kneeling in the snow, trying to catch his breath as the adrenaline coursed through his body.

Olsen was quickly handcuffed and dragged away by two agents. Will could hear him cursing and yelling all the way back to the house.

"Agent, let me see your arm," a medic said, leaning over and removing Will's right hand from his upper left arm. Will felt dazed, no longer feeling the coldness of the snow melting into his jeans or the pain from the gunshot wound. "There's a lot of blood, but I think it's going to be okay. It looks like the bullet just grazed your arm."

Will stood up slowly. "I'm fine," he said, waving off the medic. "Find Julianna Brennan," he yelled. "I want this entire area searched! She has to be here somewhere."

Simpson arrived slightly out of breath from running down the hill from the house. "Sit down, Delaney," he ordered. "Let medical look at the arm and get the damn thing bandaged before you get blood all over my crime scene."

Will reluctantly agreed, mumbling his displeasure at being temporarily grounded. Ten excruciating minutes later he was released as he leapt up, wincing with pain where he had hit his knee on the rock, and joined the search, and for the next three hours they searched the house and grounds, but found no sign of Julianna.

"I think it's time we faced the reality that she's not here, Delaney," Simpson told him. I'm going to pack the rest of the team up except for Search and Rescue, who are still looking for Fray's body.

"She's here, Simpson. Fray was here, along with his vehicle, so where else could she be? I'm not leaving until we find her."

"Delaney, has it occurred to you that she may not even be alive?"

Will shot Simpson an angry look. "Where are the dogs?"

"They've got one of them looking for Fray."

"Why aren't the others out there searching for Julianna?" he asked, exasperated.

"Because only one of them is an avalanche dog. The others aren't trained for snow recovery, so after they searched the house and area immediately around it, they packed them up. We're not even sure she's here, Delaney, so I told them to concentrate on the recovery of Fray. I know you care about this girl, but you've got to face reality at some point. She's either dead or she's gone. We've searched very square inch of that house, and who in their right mind would stay outside all these hours? It's freezing out here."

"People have survived worse, Simpson, and you know it. It's irresponsible to not continue the search for her. It's our *job* to find her and I'm not leaving until I do."

"And we will find her, but the weather is not cooperating, Delaney. We've only got the resources we've got. That's the best I can do."

Will and Simpson had walked into the woods where the Search and Rescue Team had set up a command post. "Just give me one hour with the avalanche dog. Fray's dead, Simpson. He can wait."

"One hour, Delaney." Simpson called to the handler, Agent Maretti, to bring in the avalanche dog.

Will returned a few minutes later with a pillowcase from the room where the women's clothing was found. He prayed that was the bed Julianna had slept in because otherwise all he had was a bunch of clothes with the tags still on them.

"He'd better have a damn good sense of smell in this snow," Will told the handler, referring to the dog. "We've only got an hour, so make it count."

"Max's sense of smell is fine with or without snow, Agent Delaney, but he's been specially trained to track in the snow." She held the pillowcase down to the large black Lab. "Max can track under snow, water, you name it – he's one of our best. Come on, boy," she called to the dog. "Where do you want to start?" she asked Will.

"Where have you been concentrating?"

"We've been concentrating on the ravine area where Agent Fray was, so we'll start in that direction," she said, pointing toward a section of the woods in the opposite direction, closer to the house.

"I'm going with you," Will told her. "But I want to start with that area first," he said, indicating a section past the ravine. He rubbed his knee, trying to ease the pain, and could feel the increased swelling through his damp jeans. He saw Agent Maretti watching him, her expression dubious.

"There's nothing out there, Agent Delaney, except snow. The woods lead to that mountain over there," she told him, pointing. "Do you really think anyone could have climbed up those mountains in weather like this? It's highly unlikely."

"Just humor me, Agent Maretti, okay?"

"Whatever you say," she sighed as they headed toward the trees with Max in the lead. "You sure you can keep up with us?" she added, nodding toward Will's leg. "Once he gets going I can't slow down."

"I'm fine," he said firmly. "Start walking."

They were about a hundred yards from the trees, with the dog tracking in a zig-zag pattern, when Max suddenly stopped and perked his ears. "What is it, boy?" Agent Maretti asked him quietly, standing still herself.

Max gave a slight whine and began to run full-force toward the trees with Will and Maretti on his heels. Max suddenly stopped and began pawing the ground and looking up at Maretti, whining, his eyes pleading with her. Will dropped to his knees and began digging at the snow. "Oh my God," he breathed when he saw the lid of a padlocked door leading into the ground. "Julianna!" he yelled, pounding on the door. His heart leapt to his throat when the only sound was that of the three agents, counting the dog, as they caught their breath. "Do you have cutters?" he asked Maretti, the panic rising in his throat.

"Not for that," she answered. "What I have won't cut through something that heavy." She got on her radio.

"Someone bring some cutters for a padlock *now*! We have something out here!"

Time seemed to stand still as they waited for someone to bring something to cut the lock with. Will pounded on the door, the deafening silence underneath it sending his adrenaline into overdrive. His insides were literally trembling, and just when he thought he couldn't take another agonizing moment Will felt the cutters being thrust into his hand. He grabbed the lock and in one swift movement snapped it in two while someone else jerked the lid up. To both his horror and relief he had found her. He wasn't sure he would be able to handle it if she was... No, he wasn't even going to think about the alternative.

With a trembling hand he reached down into the box and felt for Julianna's pulse. Her eyes were closed and her skin was very pale, her lips and purplish blue from the cold. "She's alive," he breathed. "Help me get her out of here," he directed to Agent Maretti, who knelt down beside him and took Julianna's other arm. Together they pulled her out and Will quickly cut the tape from her wrists and ankles with his pocket knife. "Get the medics out here, Maretti!" he yelled, cradling Julianna's limp body in his arms.

"They're on the way, Delaney."

"Jule? I've got you. You're going to be okay, baby." Will pulled her close against his body, trying to warm her. "Where are they?" he demanded again.

He looked back down at Julianna as she opened her eyes, a small moan escaping her lips. Her eyes didn't seem to focus and she suddenly began to struggle against Will. "Jule, it's me, Will. You're going to be okay. I've got you, Julianna. You're safe now," he told her as she continued to struggle. She appeared to be looking at him, but when he looked closer, she was looking past him over his shoulder. Will turned around and saw the group of agents standing behind them. Julianna's eyes were wide with terror. "Julianna, look at *me*," Will directed her gently, pulling her chin down slightly so that her eyes were at his level. "Look at me, Julianna. Look at my eyes. You're safe now. I've got you, Julianna, *look at me!*" She kept struggling with him, shaking her head and crying.

"I think she's in shock," Agent Maretti informed him. "Here, let me try. Maybe seeing a man right now scares her. It's pretty common in kidnapping cases for women to be afraid of any man, even the good guys."

"But she knows me," Will replied.

"Doesn't matter, Agent Delaney. You know that." Maretti leaned down to Julianna and spoke softly to her as Max stood beside them in silent support. Julianna instantly calmed down and took the hand that Agent Maretti offered to her.

Will shrugged his coat off and placed it over Julianna, who he still held in his arms. He looked down at her and tenderly brushed her hair away from her face. "You're safe, Jule," he told her, taking his knit hat off and placing it on her head.

She turned to look up at him, her eyes questioning as she mouthed his name, her voice barely discernible.

"Yes, baby, I'm here," he said, smiling down at her.

She looked up into his eyes and suddenly let go of Agent Maretti's hand and grabbed his instead, holding onto it tightly. "Will," she breathed, closing her eyes. "I knew you'd come. I knew."

Chapter 40
Three Days Later...

Julianna sat on the edge of her bed looking out at the pigeons on the fire escape. She always fed them, no matter what time of year it was, but she felt especially sorry for them in the winter. Bella lay beside her, dozing in a spot of sunshine on the quilt that covered the bed.

Julianna's wan expression hadn't changed in the three days since she had been back home, and she had barely spoken to anyone. She just wanted to be alone. Her friend Allegra had come to stay with her, but even she couldn't get through to Julianna, so she simply camped out on the sofa, waiting until Julianna was ready.

Meanwhile, Will called several times a day to check on her, but she just shook her head sadly when Allegra asked if she wanted to speak to him.

"Allegra, I don't care what she says this time. I'm downstairs and I'm coming up," Will told her on the phone as Julianna watched the pigeons from her bed. "It's been three days – enough already."

"You're right. Come on up. I can't get her to respond to me either, so I'm willing to try anything at this point. I don't think she's the best person to judge what she needs right now."

"Brush your teeth and wash your face," Allegra told her when she hung up with Will. "You've got company on the way up." She began to brush Julianna's hair. When this was all over Julianna would thank her for helping her look at least somewhat presentable for the gorgeous man who was on his way up.

Julianna just shook her head. "Do it," Allegra insisted, smearing toothpaste quickly onto the toothbrush and wetting the washcloth. She gently wiped Julianna's face as Julianna stood there with the toothbrush in her hand. "There, all done. Now brush." Miraculously, she did. It was a step in the right direction anyway. Her triumph was short-lived, however, when Julianna returned to her bed the moment she was finished brushing her teeth.

When Will arrived, he sat down on the ledge of the window across from Julianna. Allegra gave him a shrug and slow shake of the head. "Good luck," she told him sincerely as she quietly left the room.

"Hey, Jule," Will greeted her gently.

She looked over in his direction, but her eyes looked past him and out the window. "Hey," she returned, her voice soft.

"Jule, we're worried about you. I want you to talk to me. If not me, then a counselor. I can recommend a good one who deals with this kind of thing. You may have Post Traumatic Stress Disorder."

"No therapist," she whispered, absently petting Bella, who played sentry to her mistress.

"Jule, talk to me," Will pleaded gently, walking over and placing his hand on her shoulder. She flinched at his touch and pulled back slightly, so he removed his hand. Bella leapt off the bed as he sat down beside her. "It's just the two of us, Julianna, just like before. Do you remember when you were at my apartment, Julianna, when you let me hold you that night you were attacked?"

"I remember," she said softly.

"Then let me help you now, Julianna, please. Please talk to me. I know you were terrified, but you *have* to talk about it. You have to get it out. It's the only way you're going to be able to move on."

"I thought I was going to die," she finally whispered, sounding very small and childlike.

Will felt his heart break as he listened to her. "When you were in the box?" he clarified.

"Lots of times."

"I'm not going to let anything happen to you, Julianna," he promised her.

"What happened to Ethan?"

"He's gone," Will told her. "Paul Olsen killed those agents. He shot Fray too, but we haven't been able to recover his body. There's no way he survived, though. He fell into a ravine that's several hundred feet deep. Search and Rescue is having a difficult time getting in there. It's too steep and the snow is too deep right now."

She met his eyes for the first time, searching them for answers. "He was trying to protect me, Will. He told me there was someone I couldn't trust – that's why he tied me up. He didn't want me running for help to the wrong person. He was right. I trusted Agent Olsen. Those agents, *Ethan*... I don't understand any of this. How is your arm?"

"It's fine. Just a little sore, but I'll live."

"Why did he do this?"

"Who, Ethan?"

"No, Olsen."

Will told her the entire story about the memory card and the newpaper ads. "We found the memory card. The mermaid pendant actually hid a thumb drive. Mattice never intended for you to find out about it. He was going to try to get the pendant back from you at some point. He knew you'd never wear it. It was simply a hiding place, nothing more. He also hid some of the photos in the file from the Mayor's Ball, but someone broke into the files and deleted them – we think it was Olsen. He also stole the pendant from the safe house when we went inside after you were taken." Will didn't tell her that she was to be victim number five that night. She probably already knew it – he'd bet his life on it – but there was no way he was going to verbalize it.

"Why that night? Why didn't he try to get it some other time – he had many opportunities."

"I'm not sure. I don't think he knew what, exactly, he was looking for at first. One theory is that maybe he saw the pendant in Chinatown when he was investigating the murder of Ray Mattice."

Will didn't tell her that Olsen had kept his eyes on her for a long time. Along with the mermaid pendant, they had found a small notebook with detailed notes on her comings and goings, what she had worn on what day, and a bevy of other very personal and disturbing entries. To think he had been sitting next to Olsen during much of the time as they investigated Julianna boiled Will's blood, and he had spent plenty of time with a punching bag in the gym taking out his frustrations.

But not only was he furious with Olsen, he was furious with himself for having this man right under his nose the entire time. And even more, Will had trusted him. He wouldn't make the same mistake twice.

"So what was on the thumb drive?" Julianna asked.

"There were photos of Olsen with a well-known terrorist. We're still working the investigation, trying to uncover all the details, but we think it had something to do with weapons. There's another man in the photos – we're still trying to identify him. What Mattice did was illegal, but he'll probably get a deal in return for his testimony. Olsen isn't talking. He is still maintaining his innocence, but I'll break him eventually."

"But if you don't?"

"There's still plenty of evidence against him. We don't really need him to confess, but it would help unravel this thing a lot faster if he did."

"So, this is all... over?"

"It's over, Julianna," he said softly.

Something in her broke then and she began to cry, her body racked with sobs. Will laid her down on her bed and stretched out beside her, covering them both with the quilt as he held her, her face pressed against his chest, her hands clinging to his shirt as her body shook. He held her for a very long time, and finally she made small hiccupping sounds and then gave a small sigh of exhaustion, her energy spent.

But still he held her, kissing her hair, rubbing her back. She loosened her vise-like grip on the front of his shirt and tentatively trailed her fingers along his jaw, one finger caressing his lips. Will looked down at her, his eyes burning into hers. He leaned forward and gently kissed her mouth, but sensing her hesitation he pulled back to look at her. "I can't fall in love with you, Delaney," she whispered.

"Why not?" he whispered back, leaning down and using his lips to forge a soft trail down her neck.

"I can't lose you, Will" she said, sitting up on the bed and scooting a slight distance away from him.

"You're serious," he said, sitting up on the bed. "I'm not going anywhere, Jule," he told her, his expression puzzled as he reached for her hand.

"No one ever intends to, Will." She took his hand and kissed his palm, then sighed and stood up from the bed. "I can't do this. I'm sorry."

"Can't do what?" he said, his frustration rising.

"*This*. You, me. Any of it." She backed toward the door. "I don't know if any of this is real and I don't even know *you*. Not really."

"What do you want to know? I'll tell you anything. Do you want to know that the first girl I loved was named Pumpkin? She was a golden retriever and I was five. She slept at the foot of my bed every night, much to the chagrin of my mother, who is, by the way, from Greenwich, Connecticut.

"Or that the second girl I loved was named Kimberly? Cute little blonde girl, third grade, Mrs. Pinetta's class. But Kimberly loved this guy named Mike because his dad owned the local roller rink. And Mike, well, I don't remember who he loved, but I'm pretty sure it wasn't Kimberly. I went to high school with him, too. He was big into theater and had this thing for Liza Minnelli. You do the math.

"Or do you want to know that in ninth grade I had a skateboard accident which resulted in a scar right here," he said, indicating his chin.

"What else do you want to know, Julianna? For you, I'm an open book."

She stood there with her hand on the door, looking at him with a mixture of emotions. But the one he didn't want to see, the one he wanted to erase from her face, was the one that spoke the loudest. She was closing herself off to him and to *them*. She left him no choice. Yes, it was probably too soon and yes, it would probably scare the hell out of her, but he was going to say it anyway. For what it was worth, he wanted her to hear it. "I love you, Julianna. I've loved you since the moment I first saw you. You were coming out of Starbucks with your hair was blowing in the wind. Your face was flushed and you looked so beautiful and so alone. I knew then, Jule. I knew..."

"You knew you wanted to protect me," she interrupted him.

"Yes, but it was more than that. I can't explain it."

"No," she argued.

"*Yes*," he insisted. "Why are you fighting this, Julianna? Why don't you want to believe me? What makes this so difficult for you to accept?"

"You don't love me, Will. You *can't*. You just wanted to save me, protect me. What happens now? I don't need your protection anymore."

"We get to know each other better just like in every other relationship. We go out on dates. We talk to each other, we spend time together."

"I don't even know you, Will! I know what Ethan told me, and it wasn't the prettiest picture, but I don't know *you*. I need you, Will, and God knows I want you, but I don't *know* you!"

"So get to know me!" he pleaded. "Julianna, I don't know what Ethan told you, but I imagine it had something to do with drinking and women, and he'd be right. There was a time, a long time ago, when I was pretty messed up. I came home one day to find my fiancée in bed with my brother. You commented about my apartment, wondering how I afforded it, I'm sure. *She* gave it to me, or rather her rich daddy did. It was my consolation prize, I suppose. I was too embarrassed to admit that to you. And it's actually not just an apartment. I own the entire floor, but I don't even use the rest of it. Sarah and I were going to turn the entire floor into our home, but obviously that never happened. I was angry, so damn angry. I should never have accepted the apartment, but I did because some stupid part of me wanted to hold on to a piece of her.

"I lived for that woman; she was the air I thought I needed to survive. I drank and I partied and then I came to my senses and sobered up. That was a lifetime ago. I haven't been with a woman in a very long time, and believe me, it shocks the hell out of me to realize this, but I have never felt about any woman, Sarah included, the way I feel about you, Julianna. If you walk out that door it will drain the very life out of me."

He stood up and walked over to her, taking her face in his hands and looking down into her eyes. "I am so in love with you that I can't even imagine a day without you in it. I don't even have to think about it, or question it. You are all that matters to me, Julianna, and you are all that ever *will* matter."

She shook her head slowly. "I can't, Will. I'm sorry... You have no idea... I just need some time. For now, I just need you to leave."

"Don't do this, Julianna," he pleaded. But he could tell she was closing herself off to him once more and he was losing her. He followed her silently as she walked out of the bedroom and into the living room toward the front door. He watched her for a few moments as she held the door open for him and stared at the floor. She wouldn't meet his eyes.

"I just gave you a piece of my soul and you're going to turn me away?" He couldn't believe this was happening. He knew she felt the same way about him, knew it with all his heart, so he just couldn't understand what she was doing, or why. For support he looked over at Allegra, who was on the sofa watching the exchange. "Can't you talk some sense into her?" She just gave him a sad look. There was nothing she could do either.

"Goodbye, Agent Delaney," Julianna told him, finally meeting his gaze.

Will grabbed his coat from the chair beside the door. "So we're back to Agent Delaney, huh? What are you so afraid of?" he asked, searching her face, trying desperately to read her expression. It was over. She had made up her mind. *She* got to decide to end it before it had really even begun, and there was nothing he could do about it.

"Don't do this, Jule. Talk to me," he pleaded with her once more, but she just stood there with her hand on the doorknob and looked past him into the hall. Bella came up to Will and rubbed against his leg. "Bye, Bella," he said to the cat, leaning down and petting her before he stood back up and tried to make eye contact with Julianna. She still wouldn't look at him and he could see tears glistening in her eyes.

"So this is it, then? *You* get to decide. Is that it, Julianna? You're not even going to give it a chance?"

Julianna could hear the anger creeping into his voice and she lifted her chin in a small gesture of strength. Maybe it was defiance. She didn't want to deal with this now, with this beautiful man, inside and out, who she was pushing out of her life. She was being a coward, she knew, but her pride kept her from reaching out and grabbing him before he escaped out of her life forever.

"I almost forgot," Will said removing Julianna's phone from the pocket of his coat. "We found your phone, so call me if there's anything you need. I took the liberty of adding my number to your contacts," he told her, not expecting a response. "You need anything at all and I'll be right over, okay?" He handed the phone to her, deliberately holding onto her hand for just a moment as he did. He then slipped out the door and heard it click as Julianna closed it gently behind him.

As soon as the door closed, the floodgates opened and the tears began to fall down Julianna's cheeks. "You okay?" Allegra asked softly from the sofa.

She put up her hand to keep Allegra from saying what she knew Allegra wanted to say, what she *should* say. That Julianna was a fool to let that incredible man, a man who had just told her he *loves* her, walk out that door, and she'd regret it for the rest of her life. "No, but I will be." She darted back to her bedroom, threw herself across her bed and sobbed. She had turned Will away, but she knew that it was for the best. She had to do it. She couldn't risk losing him, so it was better that she end it now before she got hurt. She knew it was the right decision. It had to be, but right now her heart ached for him so badly that she couldn't breathe. She wanted nothing more than to curl up into a ball and die, or at least sleep for a very long time

– anything to make the pain go away. She wondered if it ever would.

Chapter 41
Four Months Later...

"**I** *love* them!" Isabel Rodriguez exclaimed.

"I admit – they turned out pretty great," Julianna admitted, smiling as Isabel slid a pile of pink-wrapped gifts to the side and spread the photos of her daughter Angelica out onto the kitchen table. "I had a rather adorable subject who also happens to be very photogenic."

"She's definitely pretty adorable," Isabel agreed, laughing. "This one is my favorite – I love the look on her face as she's eating the popsicle."

"I'll just add this one to the pile," Julianna said, pulling a box out of her bag. "It's the bracelet with the kitten on it that she saw in SOHO last week. The one she said looked like Bella. I had to get it for her," she said smiling.

"You didn't need to get her anything, Julianna!" Isabel argued. "The pictures are more than enough. She will love the bracelet, though. Thank you."

"I think the pictures are more for her mama," Julianna laughed. "And besides, it's the least I can do for the girl whose mom almost died trying to protect me." Her voice grew serious. "I mean it, Isabel. I don't know what I would have done if something had happened to you."

"It was my job, Julianna, and I knew what I was getting into, but I appreciate you saying that. I think I am going to enjoy being a stay-at-home mom as long as I can get rid of this wheelchair sooner rather than later!"

"But the doctors think you'll be okay?"

"That's what they say. How about you? Are you okay?"

"I'm getting there," Julianna said, looking down at the table. "It's a journey, you know?"

"I know," Isabel said, searching her face. "He misses you, you know. He comes by sometimes, always brings Angelica a brownie from Fat Witch Bakery – she's seriously enamored by both Will and the brownies, by the way. I think he just wants to hear how you're doing. He's real proud of you for quitting the paper and starting your own business."

Tears sprang to Julianna's eyes and she bit her lip to keep them at bay. She looked out the window at Angelica and her friends who were laughing and giggling as a giant bunny rabbit made balloon animals for them. The adults were congregated around a table that practically moaned from the weight of all the food it held.

"Julianna, why don't you just call him?" Isabel pleaded softly.

"I'm doing just fine without him, Isabel."

"Are you? Then what's going on here?" she asked, indicating the tears. "What are you so afraid of?"

"I'm not afraid of anything. I made a decision and I'm sticking to it, that's all."

"You're being stubborn, and stubbornness is not necessarily an admirable quality in this sort of situation," Isabel pointed out.

"Then don't admire me," Julianna retorted, continuing to look out the window. To be a kid again, she thought, and having your entire happy life ahead of you, still believing in fairy tales that didn't exist.

"Come on, Jule. He misses you. You can hear it in his voice every time he asks about you. You broke his heart."

"He'll get over it," Julianna replied defensively, but the moment she said it, she regretted it. It sounded cold and rude, and she certainly didn't mean it.

Isabel threw her hands in the air. "I give up, Julianna. Go ahead, be miserable, make Will miserable. I was only trying to help."

"I know you were. I know," Julianna sighed. "I'm sorry."

"You're afraid of losing him, aren't you?"

"Yes," Julianna admitted.

"But you've lost him now," she pointed out. "By taking a chance, at least you'd be giving it an opportunity to work out. What you're doing doesn't make any sense."

"I don't want to get hurt, Isabel. He works in a dangerous job, which pretty much quadruples his chances of getting hurt, or worse. Look at what happened to you, to the other agents."

"Yes, and look at what sometimes happens to regular people on their way to their boring *non-dangerous* jobs. Things happen, Julianna. You can't live your life afraid of taking chances because of what you're afraid will happen. But if that's really what you're afraid of, that man is fully prepared to quit his job for you if you asked him to. I know it as sure as I breathe."

"I'd never ask him to do that."

"I know you wouldn't, but that's what he is willing to do for you if it would put you in his arms. Look at you – you're miserable, he's miserable..."

"No," Julianna decided, turning from the window. "I'm not going to call him."

Isabel just shook her head in frustration. "He did a great job closing the case, didn't he?" Isabel asked her.

"Don't think I don't notice how you're dropping the subject of my contacting Will, but still keeping the conversation focused on him. Very slick, Isabel." She sighed, "But yes, he did a great job. The media loves him."

"He was able to get Paul Olsen to confess to killing the agents at the safe house. They're still digging through the mess of this thing, and of course it will drag out in the court system, but there's a mountain of evidence that Olsen had been accepting bribes from a domestic terrorist group for internal information and misappropriation of evidence. He was even stealing confiscated weapons and smuggling them to the terrorist cell."

"He's doing what he was meant to do, and he's good at it," Julianna said. "I'm really proud of him, Isabel, don't think I'm not. And I didn't mean what I said earlier about him getting over it. I might sound like a complete jerk, but I really don't want him to be unhappy."

"I know you don't, Julianna." Isabel hesitated for a moment. "He sold the floor of apartments, you know."

Julianna looked up in surprise. "Why?"

"He said he didn't want any remnants of his old life and even worked things out with Sarah and Brian. He knew he had to put that part of his life to rest if he was going to move on. Some actor bought the entire floor, so he moved to a different apartment in the same building. Sarah refused the money from the sale, saying her family has plenty. She wanted him to have it, which he feels really uncomfortable with, so I'm not sure what he's going to do with it.

Julianna's heart clenched at the thought of him moving on without *her,* even though she was the very one to push him away. You can't have your cake and eat it, too, she reminded herself. "It sounds like he talks to you a lot."

"He'd rather talk to you," Isabel pointed out.

"It's been four months, Isabel. I can't contact him now. He has probably moved on."

"He hasn't."

She heaved a sigh. "Okay, if I promise to think about contacting him will you get off my back about this?"

"It's a start," Isabel smiled.

"Good!" Julianna smiled back. "I hate to cut this visit short, especially on Angelica's birthday, and goodness knows I'd love some of that cake, but I need to get going. I've got a beach wedding to shoot in North Carolina and I need to get packed. It's going to be a long weekend, not to mention a long drive. I had to rent a car for the first time since I moved here."

"Take some cake with you."

"Nah, I'm just going to sneak out while the kids are having fun. She hasn't even cut it yet. Give her a hug and email some pictures to me," Julianna said, leaning down to hug her friend goodbye.

"I will. You have a safe trip and hang out at the beach for a while. You could use the R&R."

"Actually, I plan to. Mrs. De Luca is going to check on Bella for me, so I rented a beach house for a week and will take my laptop so I can edit the wedding photos while I watch the ocean. Who knows, I might decide never to leave," she laughed.

"I wouldn't blame you! But come back and get me before you make it permanent," Isabel joked. "I'll see you when you get back."

"Count on it," Julianna told her as she closed the door behind her.

Chapter 42

"She just left," Isabel told Will as he stepped into the house. His arms overflowed with a large white teddy bear complete with a pink bow around its neck, and a small box bearing the familiar Fat Witch Bakery logo. "You spoil her," Isabel smiled, indicating the gifts.

"She's a good kid," Will shrugged, returning the smile. "And what happened? Did the paparazzi tip Julianna off that I was on my way here?" he half-joked. "I can't seem to get rid of them. You have no idea how relieved I will be when this is all over with."

"We'll all just bide our time until the next 'big thing' happens and our fifteen minutes are up. Julianna seems to be the only one using this to her advantage by starting her own photography business."

"And I say, good for her," Will followed along behind Isabel's motorized wheelchair until they were outside amidst the laughter of at least twenty little girls and the rapid-fire conversations of Isabel's large family.

"Have a beer, Delaney," Isabel offered, pointing to a bucket overflowing with drinks.

"Thanks, but I think I'll see if there's a soda in there." He popped the top on a can and looked longingly toward the food table.

"Come on," Isabel laughed. "Mom, show Agent Delaney the good stuff."

"It's *all* good stuff," her mother huffed, piling Will's plate with arroz con pollo, mofongo, pernil al horno, and pollo guisado.

"That it is," Will moaned, taking a bite of the arroz con pollo. He came up for air a few bites later. "So, seriously – why'd she leave? I thought the party was just getting started."

"She's leaving town and had to get packed."

Will's eyebrows shot up in surprise.

"Don't worry, Delaney. It's just a trip. She's shooting a beach wedding in North Carolina."

"I could use a beach right about now," Will complained.

"You should go."

"Riiiight. In case you weren't aware, she doesn't want to see me."

"She wants to see you, Delaney. She just doesn't know it yet. Well, actually, she knows it, but she doesn't want to admit it."

"What did she say?" It was the first glimmer of hope he'd gotten from Isabel in the past four months and he was very near the point of accepting the fact that that Julianna Brennan was not going to come around.

"It's what she didn't say."

"That's cryptic," he said sarcastically.

"I know," Isabel sighed. "What can I say, Delaney? She's miserable and I'm really worried about her. I think she somehow feels responsible for the deaths of Ray Mattice,

Jankowski, Shepherd and Kilbourne, and mostly, Ethan Fray. He died trying to protect her from Olsen. I think Fray is the one she's most upset over. I believe she really cared about him, probably because she knew you had trusted him to take care of her. It must be a very difficult thing to have so many people die around you. It's really scary for her to be close to someone with that fear hanging over her head."

"Why the hell would she feel responsible? She was the victim here!" Will's anger toward Jackson Mattice and Paul Olsen was still raw and it killed him to think Julianna blamed herself for *any* of this.

"It's just the way she feels, Delaney. It doesn't have to make sense."

Will didn't say anything for a few minutes as he worked on the plate of food and watched the kids running around the yard chasing after a giant rabbit.

"That might be a bit presumptuous of me, running after her to the Outer Banks. Maybe I should try talking to her when she gets back."

"Take a chance, Delaney!" Isabel exclaimed, exasperated. "*Go* to her. What's the worst that can happen? And maybe, just maybe, the change of scenery will do the situation some good. What could be more romantic than the ocean? Julianna said it always calms her soul. Maybe you'll catch her immediately after that happens," she joked.

Will shrugged. "It can't get any worse than it already is. Hmmm, maybe I will," Will decided.

Chapter 43

Julianna sat on the deck of the beach house and watched a pod of pelicans swoop down into the ocean in search of their dinner. If she turned around and looked in the other direction she would see the sunset over the sound, but she was bone tired, and moving anything at this point seemed like a monumental task. She hadn't moved in at least two hours, but the rumbling of her stomach was reminding her that she hadn't eaten since the oatmeal she had for breakfast.

The wedding was finally over, and Julianna had recorded every kiss, every smile and every minute of the lavish three-day event. She would spend the next few weeks editing all the photos and getting them ready to present to the bride and groom. But first she was going to take the next few days off and do absolutely nothing.

She reached over to the Beach Guide and found a pizza place, thinking it was too bad Mama Kwan's didn't deliver because she could really go for some of their fish tacos right about now. She glanced down through the Pizza Stop menu. Definitely not the eggplant parmesan, she thought, remembering her meal at Will's – too many memories there. She settled on a Greek salad and a small Margherita pizza, then leaned back in the lounge chair and watched as the full moon slowly emerged over the ocean.

It was a beautiful evening and she longed for someone to share it with, even if it was only Bella. She could hear a stereo playing in the house next door and glanced quickly away at the couple she could see inside who were preparing supper while sharing a bottle of wine.

She got up from the chair and repositioned herself so that she couldn't see her neighbors. She had already been tortured plenty this weekend, not only by the bride and groom, but by every other couple at the wedding who took advantage of the atmosphere and fell in love all over again. It was all too painful a reminder of what she could have had, but so stupidly threw away, so she spent the weekend focusing solely on lighting and composition.

She heard a car door close and scrambled quickly out of the chair to run inside and grab her wallet. The thought of hot stringy cheese made her mouth water with anticipation, and she suddenly found a burst of energy to run down the stairs to her prize.

She stopped short at the bottom of the stairs and gave a small gasp of surprise.

He stood there silently, leaning against a silver Porsche, holding a pizza box and salad.

Julianna gripped the railing for support. "What... I thought... Oh my God."

"I believe you ordered a pizza?" he asked gently, walking toward her.

She took the pizza box from him and set it on the step, then stared at him for a few moments before touching his face to make sure he was real, then going into his arms. "Ethan," she breathed. "I thought you were dead."

"I'm sorry," he told her, holding her tightly. "It was better that way. I had to disappear for a while, but they've got me working another case right now. Thankfully they kept my picture out of the papers, not that there are many photos of my mug floating around," he grinned.

"It's a very good mug," Julianna smiled, releasing her hold on him so that she could look at his face to make sure he was truly standing right there in front of her. "Come upstairs – I'm starving."

Julianna grabbed a couple sodas from the fridge and they settled into the chairs on the deck and shared Julianna's pizza and salad. When they finished Julianna sat in the Adirondack chair with her knees tucked under her chin. "Why did you come here, Ethan?"

"I wanted you to know I wasn't dead. I know that's been hard for you, this whole thing has."

"Ah, you've been talking to Isabel Rodriguez."

"No, she doesn't even know I'm alive. Not many do."

Julianna nodded with understanding. "So you've been talking to Will, who's been talking to Isabel. Word gets around."

"He's concerned for you."

Julianna kept a watchful eye on the moonlit ocean as couples and individuals strolled slowly along the beach. How she wished Ethan would not pursue this conversation. She couldn't talk about Will. It was far too painful. "He doesn't need to be," she finally said.

"He loves you."

Bam. Shot right in the heart.

"I can't get involved with someone and then lose them."

"Will lost someone, too, Julianna. You seem to be forgetting that. When he found his fiancée with his brother it practically killed him. He was an emotional wreck, did some really stupid and self-destructive stuff. I can't even begin to count the number of times he told me he'd never give his heart to another woman. And he didn't. Until you. He risked his entire career for you."

"Is he... okay?"

"He's not drinking, if that's what you're asking. He learned the hard way that self-destruction doesn't solve anything. But he is hurting, although he tries to minimize it. He's changed a lot since we were in the SEALS together. He isn't the same man he once was – this Will is a lot stronger. He knows what he wants, and he wants you. But he's also fully prepared to let you go if that's what you want. Don't let it be too late, Julianna. Will might have changed in a lot of ways, but I also know he won't wait forever."

Julianna sighed and ran her hand through her hair, still staring out at the ocean. She couldn't bear the thought of Will hurting over something she had done to him. She couldn't talk about this anymore with Ethan – it hurt too much. If she got her nerve up maybe she'd call Will when she got back to New York.

"I can't have this conversation with you, Ethan."

"Then have it with him," he told her.

"I might call him when I get back to New York, but I doubt he'll want to talk to me after the way I treated him."

"He will, Julianna. It's been four months. He knows you're not the same person you were that day. It was a lot to handle and you did the best you could under the circumstances. He knows how traumatized you were. He just wanted to be there for you, but you pushed him away. You're a lot stronger now, stronger than you even realize. The question is, do you love him?"

She didn't hesitate. "Yes," she answered, her voice soft. She chewed her thumbnail and got up from the chair to lean over the railing of the deck. The full moon seemed so close, like she could almost reach out and touch it. "Yes, of course I love him," she said, turning to face Ethan.

He had gotten up and was standing directly behind her. He gently turned her back around and stepped forward, his arms around her, his chin resting against her head as he pointed to a lone man standing by the surf, hands in his pockets as he stood watching them. "Then go tell him," he said gently.

She stared back at the man she loved, tears shining in her eyes, hardly daring to believe that he had risked giving her another chance. She turned around and wrapped her arms around Ethan's neck and kissed him gently on the lips. "Thank you," she whispered.

Ethan was momentarily surprised by the kiss, but quickly regained his cool demeanor. "You're welcome, kid," he smiled at her. "Now, go!"

Chapter 44

He watched her walk down the stairs of the house and then across the beach toward him, her auburn hair whipping around behind her in the night breeze. She was the most beautiful creature he had ever laid eyes on, and he swallowed a nervous lump in his throat as she neared.

Neither of them spoke. Will studied her face, waiting expectantly for her to say something, *anything*. This was her show. He had to let her take the lead.

"Will," she said softly, giving him a small smile.

"I thought you might want this back," he told her, removing his hand from his pocket and holding up one very gold and very gaudy mermaid pendant. "We got what we needed off of the memory card, of course."

"That was an awfully long drive just to return something, Agent Delaney," she joked.

"Let's walk," Will suggested, returning the pendant to his pocket since Julianna wasn't going to come near enough to him to take the pendant from his hand.

They walked slowly but silently down the beach. He glanced down at her several times, her face racked with turmoil, her arms hugging herself. For comfort? Warmth? He wished she would say something.

She suddenly stopped and turned to face him. "I love you, Will. I've loved you from the very first time I heard your voice speaking to me in that damn alley."

Will was silent, but Julianna felt his fingertips brush against her hand, his fingers lacing through her own. He reached out his other hand and placed it behind her head, pulling her gently to him. He looked into her eyes and Julianna felt the world stop spinning as Will leaned down and kissed her slowly, tenderly. He wrapped both of his arms around her and held her tightly.

"I love you, too, Jule," he whispered, his voice ripe with emotion. "You're trembling," he said, holding her more tightly against him. "Are you cold?"

"No, I'm not cold. It's just that I've never felt this way before and I'm afraid something is going to happen to make this all come crashing down." She clung tightly to him, terrified of letting him go.

"I'm not going anywhere, Julianna, ever," he said, closing his eyes and kissing her again as his hands caressed her back. "The question is," he said a few minutes later, "Are you going to bail on *me* again?"

"I'm afraid you're stuck with me. If you'll have me, that is."

"Oh, I'll have you all right," he chuckled teasingly.

"I'm sorry I pushed you away, Will. I never meant to hurt you. I was just so afraid."

"Don't do it again," he breathed against her lips, holding her tighter. Julianna pressed herself against him and kissed him back with more passion than she had ever thought was possible. No one else had ever made her feel the way she felt when she was with Will. She knew then and there that all of those long and bumpy roads she had endured for her entire life had finally led her to where she was meant to be.

She pressed her hand to his chest so she could feel the familiar beat of his heart. "Will?" she murmured against his lips, sliding her fingertips along the back of his neck.

"Hmmm?" he answered slowly, opening his eyes just slightly to look at her.

"Do you want to come back to my place? I'm pretty sure we're giving the wildlife a show," she nodded toward the beach house balconies.

"Lead the way, sweetheart," Will whispered against her mouth, kissing her gently.

Julianna took Will's hand and together they walked back to the house. Ethan's car was gone and they were left alone.

"He's a good guy, that Ethan Fray," Julianna said as they entered the house.

"That he is," Will agreed. "That's why he was the only person I trusted to take care of the most important person in my life."

"But I worry about him. He seems so lonely."

"I'm sure he is. He does the job most of us don't want to do. Going deep undercover work like he does requires a lot of sacrifice and discipline. Not many people can do it. But are we going to talk about Ethan all night? I love the guy like a brother, but..."

"Agreed, no more talk about Ethan, but give me a sec, okay?" Julianna said as she stepped into the bathroom and quickly brushed her teeth. Will certainly didn't seem to mind the fact that she had eaten pizza prior to kissing him, but she was beginning to feel really self-conscious.

When she looked in the mirror she saw Will standing behind her, smiling.

"Well, isn't this very déjà vu. Do you remember that day in my bathroom? You were looking for a toothbrush," he reminded her, leaning against the frame of the door with his arms crossed, just like he had that night.

"Yes," she smiled shyly. "You came up behind me just like this and put your robe around my shoulders." She placed the toothbrush back onto the counter but continued to watch him in the mirror.

"You took my breath away," he sighed.

"I was a mess. I looked like a boxer who hadn't fared so well in the ring," she laughed. It was easy to laugh about it *now*. It had been months ago and she had done a lot of healing in that time, although occasionally the nightmares would creep into the darkness and she would wake up in tears.

"You were still beautiful," Will assured her.

"And *you*, you were the sexiest man I had ever laid eyes on," she told him, cocking her head slightly to the side and smiling coyly at him in the mirror.

"And now?" he asked, stepping closer to her and pulling her hair to the side. He kept those sapphire eyes locked with hers in the mirror as he leaned down and kissed her neck. She closed her eyes as his lips moved lightly across her skin, sending chills all along her shoulders and down her arms.

"Even sexier," she breathed. When she opened her eyes, Will was still watching her in the mirror with a smile playing on his lips. He took her hand and led her into the bedroom where he sat down on the bed with Julianna standing in front of him. He kept his eyes on hers as he slowly unbuttoned the front of her dress. "Your hands are shaking," Julianna said murmured, running her fingers lightly across his arm.

Will cleared his throat and gave her a small smile of embarrassment. "I think I'm a little nervous," he admitted. "I've thought about this moment for a long time and now it's here. I just want to make it perfect for you, for us."

Julianna took his hands in hers and kissed each palm. "I can't imagine it being any more perfect than it already is, Will. I love you, and I want you. More than anything."

And it was. Everything about their first night together was perfect. And when sunrise came, Julianna went to the window and stood there looking out over the pounding surf as the darkness gave way to the morning in a soft mystical glow.

"The sun's coming up, Will. It's so incredible," she said as he came to stand behind her, his arms wrapped around her. She reached up and placed her hands over his. "Have you ever noticed how things that seemed so complicated at night are so much clearer once the sun comes up?"

"Yes, but I usually attribute it to sleep and we definitely didn't get much sleep last night," he chuckled. "What are you talking about, Jule?"

"I've spent so much time trying to push people out of my life. It wasn't until Isabel Rodriguez brought it to my attention that it was ridiculous to push you away for fear of someday losing you. By pushing you away I had already lost you. It reminds me *Steel Magnolias*, I believe it was, where Shelby says that she's rather have thirty minutes of wonderful than a lifetime of nothing special. I understand that now. I want to spend as much time as we have left together loving you."

"That's a depressing thought, love," Will said, kissing the top of her head. "It sounds like you're already writing us off."

"Yeah, I guess it does, doesn't it?" she laughed softly. "I didn't mean it like that. I just meant that we should treasure each day we have together and not worry about the what-ifs."

"Why don't we live each day like it's our *first,* and tomorrow...well, we'll worry about tomorrow another day, okay?" he suggested.

"Kind of like Scarlett O'Hara?" she teased.

"This isn't the end, Jule. Is that what you're afraid of?" Will asked, turning her around to look at him.

"I don't know, maybe," she said, looking into his eyes.

"This is only the beginning, Julianna. It will only get better."

When she looked into Will's eyes, she saw more love reflected there than she could have ever dreamed was possible and her heart soared. This man, this insanely handsome and kind man, loved *her*, and wanted to be with *her*. He kissed her lips softly and breathed a sigh of contentment as her body melted against his. As she wrapped her arms tightly around him, Julianna knew with all her heart that this was where she wanted to spend the rest of her life. In Will's arms she was finally home.

Author's Notes

Arms of a Stranger is a work that took me many years to write. I would write the story, go back and read it, not be fully happy with it, tweak it. I'd put it away for a few years, only to take it out again and start the process all over. I suppose Will's and Julianna's story was not meant to be told at that time. That's my excuse anyway! ☺

Any inaccuracies are my own and I take full responsibility for them. I intended this story to be entertainment for the reader, not a manual on FBI procedure and protocol. I took many liberties to ensure the story flowed smoothly and went in the direction I wanted it to.

Ethan originally had a different name and was only to be a minor character in the book. But as the storyline grew, I fell in love with the idea of giving him a larger role, and thus Ethan was born. And by the way, you *will* be seeing Ethan again! Watch for him as the lead in my next book. I am looking forward to fully developing his complex character and giving him his own happy ending.

The mermaid pendant is real. I had been looking for a clever way to conceal a memory card when I happened across a web site with these "secret" USB drives. Yes, it is just as gaudy as I described, but my mermaid sits on my desk anyway. I am rather getting used to her gaudiness. ☺ Maybe she'll turn out to be a good luck charm for me!

And finally, YES, Mama Kwan's fish tacos really are the best! So if you're ever in the Outer Banks of North Carolina, be sure to pay them a visit in Kill Devil Hills. No, they are not compensating me for plugging them, but if they could figure out a way to magically send some to me here in Nashville, I would certainly not complain! ☺

About the Author

Anne-Marie Clark lives in the Nashville, Tennessee area with her husband and multiple dachshunds and cats.

She enjoys photography, spending time on the lake, collecting unusual jewelry, reading, watching crime shows, spending as much time as she can on the beach in the Outer Banks of NC, and riding her pink Buddy Scooter.

Anne-Marie is the owner of Bella Amore Cosmetics, a mineral makeup company.

You may visit her online at Anne-MarieClark.com

Made in the USA
Charleston, SC
24 July 2011